PRAISE FOR *THE LLANO COUNTY MERMAID CLUB*

"Kathleen M. Rodgers has outdone herself with her newest, most literary novel, *The Llano County Mermaid Club*. She brings all the mysticism of New Mexico to bear in her story about heartbreak and healing, about how novels can give us the hope to carry on and the empathy to forgive the ones we love most."—Kathryn Brown Ramsperger, author of *A Thousand Flying Things*

"Shifting lyrically between the past and the present, this story of betrayal and death shattering the idyllic joy and innocence of childhood dreams allows us to see the value of an adult perspective in making peace with the past and experiencing the healing power of forgiveness."—Sue Boggio, coauthor of *Hungry Shoes: A Novel*

"Lonely train whistles wail in the night and sunsets shimmer with unforgiving heat in Llano County, New Mexico. And yet the Mermaid Club flourishes in this arid landscape. Marigold Hubbard, her two sisters and their two best friends create the Mermaid Club under the brilliant imaginative canopy offered by Marigold's mother, the undaunted Letty. From Letty the Mermaids learn to recognize magic when it fleetingly lights up their horizons. They adhere to a code that will inform their lives, and develop a love of books that will nourish them forever. This lively novel is a love song to the power of public libraries and testimony to the undying bonds of sisterhood."—Laura Kalpakian, author of *Memory into Memoir*

"A philandering father who makes promises he doesn't keep. A wistful mother who tells her own story to Eudora Welty and Kate Chopin in letters she never mails. Five young girls who swim upstream against these currents. Tragedy looms, then strikes. A suspenseful, tender, beautifully crafted novel that throbs with memory and its lingering wounds: the very real costs of betrayal and neglect, and the tortuous road to forgiveness."—Minrose Gwin, author of *Beautiful Dreamers*

"Kathleen M. Rodgers delivers a poignant portrayal of small-town New Mexico teenagers in the 1960s grappling with a shocking revelation resulting in a tragedy reverberating into present time."—Lynn C. Miller, author of *The Unmasking: A Novel*

THE LLANO COUNTY MERMAID CLUB

LYNN AND LYNDA MILLER SOUTHWEST FICTION SERIES

Lynn C. Miller and Lynda Miller, Series Editors

This series showcases novels, novellas, and story collections that focus on the Southwestern experience. Often underrepresented in American literature, Southwestern voices provide unique and diverse perspectives to readers exploring the region's varied landscapes and communities. Works in the series range from traditional to experimental, with an emphasis on how the landscapes and cultures of this distinct region shape stories and situations and influence the ways in which they are told.

Also available in the Lynn and Lynda Miller
Southwest Fiction Series:

The Problem You Have: Stories by Robert Garner McBrearty
The Last Hanging of Ángel Martinez by Kate Niles
Nopalito, Texas: Stories by David Meischen
Hungry Shoes: A Novel by Sue Boggio and Mare Pearl
The Half-White Album by Cynthia J. Sylvester
Girl Flees Circus: A Novel by C. W. Smith

a novel

KATHLEEN M. RODGERS

UNIVERSITY OF NEW MEXICO PRESS | ALBUQUERQUE

Printed in the United States of America

Library of Congress Cataloging-in-Publication Data

Names: Rodgers, Kathleen M., 1958- author. Title: The Llano County Mermaid Club : a novel / Kathleen M. Rodgers.
Description: Albuquerque : University of New Mexico Press, 2025. |
Series: Lynn and Lynda Miller Southwest fiction series
Identifiers: LCCN 2025006771 (print) | LCCN 2025006772 (ebook) |
ISBN 9780826368263 paperback | ISBN 9780826368270 epub
Subjects: LCGFT: Bildungsromans | Novels
Classification: LCC PS3618.O3555 L53 2025 (print) | LCC PS3618.O3555 (ebook) | DDC 813/.6—dc23/eng/20250408
LC record available at https://lccn.loc.gov/2025006771
LC ebook record available at https://lccn.loc.gov/2025006772

Founded in 1889, the University of New Mexico sits on the traditional homelands of the Pueblo of Sandia. The original peoples of New Mexico—Pueblo, Navajo, and Apache—since time immemorial have deep connections to the land and have made significant contributions to the broader community statewide. We honor the land itself and those who remain stewards of this land throughout the generations and also acknowledge our committed relationship to Indigenous peoples. We gratefully recognize our history.

Cover illustration by Felicia Cedillos
Designed by Felicia Cedillos
Composed in Chapparel Pro

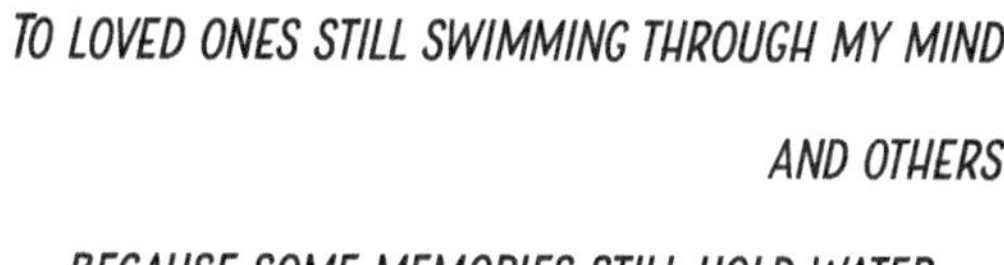

TO LOVED ONES STILL SWIMMING THROUGH MY MIND

AND OTHERS

BECAUSE SOME MEMORIES STILL HOLD WATER . . .

A book must be the axe for the frozen sea inside us.

—FRANZ KAFKA

CONTENTS

Acknowledgments

Gratitude and applause to my dedicated and hardworking agent and friend, Tracy Crow, president of Tracy Crow Literary Agency, LLC, who always tells me, "Remember, we're in this together." Tracy believed in my story from the get-go. Her professionalism, warmth, and enthusiasm for my work continues to buoy me up on this literary journey.

While working on *The Llano County Mermaid Club*, mostly set in eastern New Mexico, where I was born and raised, it hit me one day in my office here in north Texas that *I am always the daughter trying to write my way home*. What a complete joy and thrill to know that my characters and I have found a good literary home at University of New Mexico Press! A dream come true for this kid from Clovis. Clasping hands in appreciation to Elise McHugh (senior acquisitions editor), Stephen Hull (director), the two reviewers who recommended the novel be published along with their exciting suggestions for improvement, the University Press Committee for voting "Yes" on publishing my story, and the entire team at UNM Press, which includes James Ayers (assistant director and editorial, design, and production manager), Anna Pohlod (editor), Min Marcus (production assistant), Felicia Cedillos (senior designer), along with Jennie Swanson (copyeditor for UNM Press).

My deepest gratitude to Dr. Bernard Koloski, a world-renowned Kate Chopin scholar, for showing me so much kindness and answering all my questions about Kate Chopin's classic novel *The Awakening* after I sent in my initial inquiry to The Kate Chopin

International Society. Bernie was kind enough to read the manuscript once it was finished and offer his generous endorsement.

Librarian Abby Yochelson, a reference specialist in English and American Literature in the Main Reading Room at the Library of Congress, followed up with my questions about specific editions of *The Awakening*. Later, when I contacted her again with questions about Rudolfo Anaya's classic novel *Bless Me, Ultima*, Ms. Yochelson didn't hesitate to send me information that I found extremely beneficial when I worked on the chapters where the novel is mentioned.

Much love and thanks to my baby sis, Jo Rivera, for championing my work over the years. Jo isn't shy when it comes to telling others about my books and requesting her local library carry them. To my sister Laura Gulliford, a former elementary education teacher, thanks for being a good role model when it came to reading chapter books during our childhood and for helping out with the younger kids when times were tough. To my aunt Kay Lamb, thanks for gifting me with my first subscription to a writer's magazine when I was in high school, and for inviting me to come to Albuquerque in 1998 to attend the SouthWest Writers national conference.

It was at that conference where I met Sue Boggio and Mare Pearl, best friends who have now coauthored four novels published by UNM Press. Sue and I have stayed in contact all these years, and I was super elated when she offered to read my manuscript even though she had a deadline approaching. Sue not only packed up my landlocked mermaids and took them to a bona fide beach on the Gulf Coast, she wrote a moving endorsement.

Big thanks to Joyce M. Gilmour for her copyediting skills and her careful reading of my material. Joyce was the first person to read the entire story and offer me feedback.

Hugs to my longtime friends Arlene Guillen and Michelle Williams for their enthusiasm while I was writing the book and for offering to serve as first readers. Like the fictional girls in my story, both women grew up in eastern New Mexico during the decades when my story takes place.

Heartfelt thanks to literary sisters Johnnie Bernhard and Kathryn Brown Ramsperger, both award-winning novelists, for their interest and encouragement these past few years and for carving out time to read my manuscript and offer suggestions. Kathy was always up for a phone chat when I needed to discuss all things dealing with Eudora Welty. Not only did Kathy get to meet the famous author in person several times, but she's also stood in the upstairs room of the two-story Tudor in Jackson, Mississippi where Ms. Welty wrote her novels and short stories.

Friend and writer Rosa Latimer, author of several books including the popular series on Harvey Houses, took the time to chat with me about her days as the owner and operator of a charming indie bookstore in Post, Texas. Ruby Lane Books is gone now, along with Ruby the cat, the store's beloved mascot, but the memories and the magic live on and served as inspiration for the bookshop in Sandhill, New Mexico.

Thanks to retired railroader Harry Lebow of Clovis, New Mexico, a former conductor at BNSF, for answering my questions about passenger service in eastern New Mexico in the early seventies.

Hugs to Tammie Shelly, a veterinary technician, for loving my fur babies and answering my questions about microchips in cats and dogs.

Thanks to Lisa Dupuy, a friend who flies cargo planes around the world, for sharing stories about her flying career as a woman pilot in a male-dominated field. Thanks also to American Airlines captain Linda Pauwels, who was born in Argentina and came to the United States as a small child, for her insight as a young Latina with dreams to become a pilot.

I am grateful for artist Debbie Carroll's colorful painting of the abandoned church that sits off Highway 60 in Taiban, New Mexico. The church served as a model for the abandoned church in my novel. Debbie's painting graces the wall above my home altar and inspired me to keep writing.

Love to my husband, Tom, who listens closely each time I read my work out loud. He is gifted with an attentive ear and occasionally offers suggestions on how to improve a passage or find a better word choice.

To my readers: You make the long, lonely hours worthwhile.

Respect and admiration to librarians who stand on the front lines defending democracy while the battle to ban books rages on.

And finally, my deepest respect to all the writers mentioned in my novel who answered the call to become storytellers. My characters and I are indebted to each one of you for offering hope and inspiration on the journey. Most of you are no longer alive, but your stories live on.

1 SISTER FRIENDS

OCTOBER 2017

THE SOMBER STRAINS OF her flute echo through the empty window frames of the abandoned church.

Spinning around, I half expect to see her standing there, smirking at me as she plays. I rub the tops of my arms against the tingles spreading over my skin. The nubby fibers of my knee-length cardigan over a pair of boot-cut jeans can't stave off this sudden chill as the wind whistles through the graffiti-stained church, whipping my hair in every direction. Careful not to fall through missing planks in the weathered floor, I step toward the window frame void of stained glass and peek out at the cemetery.

She's buried out there beyond the dirt road, next to her Grandma Dot in a family plot not far from the foot of the low red bluffs and jagged caprock outlined on the horizon and the dry lake bed known as Red Horse Lake. Her tombstone blends in with the other upright markers lost in a sea of buffalo grass and scrub brush. I don't need to walk out there to read the inscription engraved in granite, for I know it by heart:

Melody Calloway
1960–1977
First Chair ♫

Melody Calloway and Marigold Hubbard, we were inseparable. In first grade we performed a ritual where we pricked our fingers with one of Mama's sewing needles and declared ourselves "blood sisters." We formed a secret club, which, at Mama's insistence, included my two sisters, Clover and Tansy, and Tansy's best friend, Ruthie Romero. Our club wasn't formed to shut others out. We formed it to fit in.

"Melody, is that you?" I call, my voice vibrating from deep in my chest, my teeth chattering as I try to act brave, afraid of the unknown. Afraid of what might be lurking out there in the spirit world if there is such a thing.

But the fact is, nearly forty years have passed, and I'm more afraid to face the hard truth lurking in the shadows in broad daylight.

I hold my breath, waiting. We were always holding our breath, the five of us, seeing who could hold it the longest, whether we were underwater or on dry land. I wait a little longer, but nothing. Maybe the wind is playing tricks on my head, twisting my memories round and round like her windbreaker caught on the spiky leaves of a yucca plant, fluttering like a distress signal. At least that's how I imagined it. Her windbreaker, the blue of a New Mexico sky on a day when you can see forever out here on the high plains with hardly a tree in sight.

I call again, sensing I've been summoned to this holy place where congregants like Melody's Grandma Dot once gathered to worship and find sustenance. Out here only a few antelope look up from grazing and freeze before they leap off as a car passes by on the two-lane blacktop running through the ghost town of Rosemont—population zero until someone stops by to take pictures of the decrepit church.

Until Melody came into our lives, it was just another abandoned building on the side of the road. After we formed our club when Melody and I were eight, she's the one who suggested to Daddy we drive out to Rosemont so she could show us where her Grandma Dot went to church as a child. From that day forward, Melody always referred to it as our clubhouse or mermaid castle even though we didn't go there often.

I'll never forget the last time I stepped foot in this church, or the earthshattering secret Melody told me on our drive home. A secret that changed everything. A betrayal that blew my family apart. We shunned Melody, banned her from our lives like a book that threatened our sensibilities and must be burned. We treated her as if her very existence offended us. We broke most of our club's ten commandments over it. By the time we slipped a peace offering in her locker the following week, it was too late.

The memories rush by like a speeding train, whooshing along, and I am caught up in a trip to the past.

Melody and I are sixteen, snatching leftover pumpkin pie from her grandma's kitchen. Her tiny house smells of Thanksgiving year-round, and cigarettes. Melody has lived with her Grandma Dot on Mesa Lane most of her life, sharing a bedroom with her chain-smoking mom, Edie. We drive out to Rosemont, the once bustling village where Dot grew up, Melody at the wheel of a ratty white Rambler so old it's falling apart. Even the trunk is tied down with a piece of rope.

The second we pull off the blacktop and hit a bump in the dirt road, the trunk pops open. We laugh and keep going, the Rambler lurching to a halt in front of a clapboard church with the tip of the bell tower lopped off. Dust devils swirl behind us. We slam down the trunk and retie the rope, twisting it into knots before I grab my Polaroid camera off the front seat. I had won the camera in a radio contest over the summer.

Melody sighs and gazes up at the hollow entry missing a door, torn from its hinges by vandals. "Our mermaid castle."

Pulling my hair to the side, I try to keep it from blowing in my face. "Was it always this windy here when we were kids?"

Inside the barren church we preen and take turns posing like fashion models in front of the alcove once featuring a pulpit. While we wait for the photos to develop, Melody searches the wall near the entry. "Remember when your dad wouldn't let me write my name on the wall?"

I roll my eyes, making a face. "He was so pissy that day."

"You got something to write with?" She glances back at me, impatient.

I search the pockets of my bell-bottom jeans. "Sorry, all I brought was my driver's license."

She flings her arms in the air and steps toward me, trying to hide her irritation. Placing her hands on my shoulders, she says gently, "Marigold, if you're going to be a serious writer one day, ya gotta at least carry a pencil and notepad."

"Yes, teach," I joke, but I feel like an idiot. We've outgrown our girlish pink notebooks with our club's name embellished on the covers.

Reaching into a pocket of her windbreaker, she pulls out a joint and lights up. The scent of weed fills the air like incense. "Wanna try some?" She offers me a hit.

I stiffen and back up, feeling like a prude, feeling like I'm swimming in unchartered waters she's already mastered. "When did you start smoking pot?" My voice sounds small, but my question thunders in my head as I choke on my own embarrassment because I am too uptight in my own skin.

She brushes me off and tokes away. When she's done, she saunters out to the Rambler, hips swaying in the saucy overdone way we'd practiced as preteens. She juggles the pie tin in one hand and a pumpkin-colored case in the other. Before we eat, she opens the velveteen-lined case and assembles the silver instrument that comes in three parts.

Limbering her fingers on the keys, she glances slyly my way and purrs, "When I blow into this *tiny* hole, I'm making out with the metal. That's all you have to do, Marigold. Love your instrument."

I blush at her innuendo and grumble, "Ha! Easy for you to say. You don't sit last chair."

She lifts the flute halfway to her mouth then stops. "Then *quit*! No one's forcing you to stay in band."

I blink, trying to avoid the exasperation in her huge green eyes. "It's not the band director I'm afraid of. It's Daddy."

Melody sighs, an air of hostility entering her voice. "Who cares what your dad thinks? He doesn't play anymore. Why should you?"

Once a professional flutist, Daddy abandoned his music because it didn't pay the bills. He traded his flute for a briefcase and the life of a salesman. And yet he expects me to play. Not Clover, not Tansy. Me, right there alongside Melody. Whenever she practices at our house, he's been heard to say, "Now that girl's got *talent*," right in front of me as if I don't have ears.

"Snap a picture of me for Grandma Dot."

Wanting to please her, I do what she says. Peeking through the viewfinder, I wait for the right moment to press the shutter button. After she straightens her shoulders, she lifts the lip plate to her pouty mouth and says, "Here's one of your favorites."

As she begins to play Bob Dylan's classic folksong "Blowing in the Wind," I'm struck dumb at how effortless she makes it all sound. With each controlled exhale of breath, her instrument sings. I'm envious.

The notes drift past me and seem to float out of the church through the open doorways and windows.

When she's done playing, she fluffs her frizzy mane of ginger hair and says, "This is my *ticket* out of here."

She of the straight As, big boobs on a slender frame, and a guaranteed music scholarship. And me, with my toothy grin and bone-white straight locks that can't hold a curl, applying for state and federal grants. We both understand that in our families there's no money for college after bills are paid. Her mom's single, a bookkeeper who likes to go out at night. My parents are barely scraping by. Mama longs to attend college too. Books fill the void until she can enroll.

After Melody dismantles the flute and slips it back into the fitted molds in the case, she snaps the latches shut and smiles at the Polaroid I hand her. "Mark my word, *Old Mother Hubbard*. I'm gonna get the hell outta this dry hole and be somebody."

I ignore the nickname she saddled me with in junior high and peel back the foil on the dessert. "I hear potheads get the munchies. You must be starving."

We plop down on the raised platform that once held an altar and look across the empty sanctuary and watch a freight train rumble by headed west.

Balancing wedges of pie on our fingertips, we smack our lips at the creamy filling and flaky crust.

She closes her eyes and chews, wiggling around as she makes sucking noises with her teeth and tongue. "Mmm, this is the yummiest pum'kin pie I ever tasted."

"You look like you're getting off on that pie," I grumble under my breath, my nostrils still twitching from the lingering scent of weed. I'm pissed that she's high. I'm pissed that I'm too chicken to try.

She talks with her mouth full, trying to squeeze in one more word, one more breath between bites.

A week later, her voice is silenced.

A few days before her seventeenth birthday—about a week after mine—a woman discovered Melody's Rambler on a frosty December morning while out walking her dogs at the Blue Hole, an artesian-fed pool a couple of hours west of here. I'd passed by it earlier on my way through Santa Rosa after leaving Albuquerque, but I didn't stop.

According to the story Mama told us back then, Melody's flute case and books were still on the passenger seat, along with a half-empty bottle of bourbon, most likely Grandma Dot's. The driver's door was flung open as if Melody had forgotten to shut it in her haste to get to that magical place we'd once visited as kids. "When the police found her on the shallow steps leading into the water," Mama added in the strangest whisper, "the vultures were already circling but hadn't yet swooped in. They didn't do it. It wasn't their fault."

"Whose fault was it?" I remember crying out, needing to cast blame. To reassure myself I had nothing to do with it.

Filling my lungs with cold air and courage, I lean out the window and call, "Hey, Melody! It's me, *Old Mother Hubbard*!" I end my call with our club's secret code and listen with my whole self, barely breathing.

The sound of her flute floats back to me, an energy refusing to die, moaning across the plains.

She is telling me, instructing me, what to do. She is begging across a chasm of time:

Don't forget me . . . don't forget us . . . don't . . .

From somewhere deep inside of me, I hear myself cry out, "I'm sorry, Mel. I'll tell your story. I'll tell our story. I'll write about how everything got twisted."

As I turn to leave, my gaze drifts over the walls of graffiti by the front entrance. I find myself searching the area where Melody wanted to sign her name when we were kids. A message inscribed in faded blue marker stops me cold: *I knew right then this wasn't how most moms and dads acted in our hometown . . .*

I feel like I've been sucker punched. The rest of the message is a simple plea ending in her favorite symbol (♫). It's that symbol that sends me scrambling down the rickety church steps after I snap a photo. With shaky hands, I jam the key in the ignition and spin my little SUV out of there, leaving puffs of caliche in my wake.

Before I hang a left at the blacktop and head toward Sandhill, I guzzle half a bottle of water. I drink to quench an ungodly thirst, for I feel as dry and brittle as the paint chipping away at Melody's words. As untethered as the trunk on that Rambler showing up mysteriously out of the blue weeks before she died.

I want answers. And there's only one man alive who can give them to me.

2 THE WATER BEAR

1960s

GROWING UP IN SANDHILL, New Mexico, about halfway between Albuquerque and Amarillo but farther south of Tucumcari, we were surrounded by an arid landscape dotted with windmills, stock tanks, and an occasional grove of scraggly trees. Sometimes the trees shaded a lonely house or outbuildings on land owned by ranchers and farmers.

A few miles south of town, a small oasis of cottonwood trees skirted a stagnant pond with a sign warning: DANGER: NO SWIMMING ALLOWED. Out beyond the oasis, drifts of shifting sand dunes piled up over eons. In the summers, we ran barefoot across hot dunes and tumbled down the sides one by one until we came to rest at the bottom of a hill, a pile of giggling girls spitting grit out of our teeth.

My baby sis, Tansy, born during a rare blizzard in mid-February, loved the snow. Mama always said she didn't know if the blizzard brought Tansy or if Tansy brought the blizzard, she just knew they arrived together, and both made Daddy happy. During the winters, he seemed happiest with a fresh blanket of snow on the ground. Mama said it was because it dressed up our grungy part of town like heaven had rained down pearls all around us. With Daddy in a good mood, he'd load all five of us girls in the 1960 blue Pontiac station wagon and drive out to the dunes tipped in white.

Armed with old pots and spoons—Daddy said we couldn't afford the little plastic buckets and shovels sold at TG&Y—we'd trudge up the sides of hills to find the best spot to build sandcastles while the sand was still wet. Tansy and Ruthie always skipped ahead, the first to plop down and begin digging and forming shapes. Sometimes Melody and I would roll on our backs and make sand angels, staring up at the cerulean sky, pretending the puffy clouds were sea foam as we rode on imaginary waves. Back then, the sky served as our ocean.

Clover, draped in a calico cape fashioned from an old kitchen curtain, would open a library book with a flourish and start reading to us. At nine, she had a voice that commanded us to listen as it floated up from the pages and swirled around us like the characters had come alive and joined us. Reading was her superpower, even then.

Sometimes Ruthie would jump up and take off running, her brown sinewy arms spread out like wings, her long cocoa hair flying behind her. When Daddy got antsy, he'd tug on his trouser legs and announce it was time to leave, always talking with a cigarette dangling halfway out of his mouth.

In the spring and summer on the rare days it would rain, we'd stand outside in the yard and let ourselves get soaked. Mama only called us in if she saw bolts of lightning streaking across the sky. Sometimes she'd join us. Back then, it seemed our skin was as parched as the dry, cracked lake bed west of town. Mama would throw threadbare towels at us and say, "Most little girls in Sandhill are singing for the rain to stop. But not you girls. Y'all are out there begging for more." She'd send Ruthie and Melody home in our old play clothes, their wet outfits stuffed in old bread bags.

Sometimes Tansy would sneak back out, flounce her tawny

waves of dripping hair, and start spinning, twirling around a giant fountain built as a status symbol against an arid land.

That day in 1964 when Mama brought Tansy home from the hospital, all swaddled in a blanket smelling like talcum powder, she called Clover and me over to the rocking chair in the room Mama referred to as the *parlor*.

She smiled her tired, lopsided grin with the tiny gap in her front teeth. Guess that's who I got mine from. "Be careful, girls. She's a delicate thing."

Clover, at five, leaned over Mama first. "Unwrap her, Mama. She looks like a baby burrito."

As Mama peeled back the layers of blanket, she never took her eyes off the baby. "This is Tansy. Our little Aquarius. The nurse said it means *water bearer*, not that I'm into astrology."

"Look at her toes," I gasped, touching my baby sister's tiny feet. I bent down, wanting to kiss them. "Some of her piggy toes are bunched together."

Clover's mouth gaped open. "Tansy's got duck feet."

Mama nudged us away with her elbow. "Doctor Johnson calls them webbed toes. Said unless we want to have elective surgery, which your dad says we cannot *a'ford*, she'll probably be a good swimmer." Mama tilted her head and fussed with the blanket. "'Course, I think he was razzing me about the last part."

Before Mama could push me away again, I reached down and caressed Tansy's feet, feeling the sections of flesh joining some of her toes together. Even at four, I picked up on things. I glanced at Mama's angular face, the dark circles under her tired eyes from lack of sleep, her dishwater blonde hair pulled back in a straggly ponytail. "Mama, why did the nurse call Tansy a water bear?"

Mama sighed, giving me a weary look. "Marigold, honey. That's not what the nurse said. I'll explain later. I need my rest. You girls go play." Mama snuggled the blanket around the baby and pushed back in the rocking chair, closing her eyes, and cutting me off before I could ask another question.

In my mind, Tansy and her toes were a gift. A sign of better days ahead. Secretly, I hoped her toes would bring rain. Enough rain to fill up the fountain out back that no longer sprayed water but was deep enough to go wading in. We rarely went to the public pool. Like everything else, it cost money.

Clover grabbed my elbow and we skipped outside, scooping up snow with our bare hands, licking it like ice cream and pretending it was summer. Turning around, we gazed up at the front of our dingy white two-story house thirsty for paint. Long white columns stretched forever up to the porch's roof Mama called an *awning*.

A former showplace built by a doctor in 1920, it looked parched and worn out by the time we moved in. So did the rest of our block. The house sat near the corner of Vista Boulevard and Railroad Avenue. Story goes, after the doctor died, the new owners turned it into a flophouse for railroaders and neglected the upkeep. When Daddy bought it cheap in a bank foreclosure, he said living on a *boulevard* made us look rich. He talked big about restoring the house to its former glory. That was the problem with Daddy—he was always talking big. A man with grandiose dreams but no wherewithal to follow through.

He came close a couple of times. Little girls are forgiving and wait patiently, hanging onto the promises of adults. Our imaginations filled in the cracks between Daddy's vision and reality. But later, as some of us got older and saw through Daddy's flaws, we weren't quite as forgiving . . .

That day when Tansy came home, all I could think about was her sweet face and toes. And how she went from Mama's tummy to her lap. As Clover and I licked snow from our palms, I asked her, "Did Tansy come out of Mama's hiney?"

Clover giggled. "No, silly, she came out of her pee-pee hole."

Squeezing my chubby thighs together, I clutched my privates in dread. "I'm never having a baby. Are you?"

Clover shrugged. "I dunno. Wanna color or look at books?"

Back inside, we scampered up the *L*-shaped staircase, our

secondhand saddle oxfords tapping against each wooden step as we made our way to the second floor.

Down below, we could hear our baby sister stirring with hunger, her tiny cries echoing through our drafty house. Snuggled on our long window seat facing the street, I stared at our shared box of crayons. Tansy's voice tugged at me as I tried to decide which color to choose. Part of me wanted to abandon Clover and run downstairs and ask Mama if I could hold our new baby.

That night, after Clover fell fast asleep in the big bed we shared in the room with cabbage and roses wallpaper, I pulled back the covers and tiptoed down the hall to the top of the stairs. I could hear Mama's faint footsteps below in the kitchen. But it was Daddy's deep voice, softened by the late hour, that caused me to sneak halfway down the stairs to the landing where I huddled in my thin flannel nightgown, clutching my Chatty Cathy doll. The wooden floor planks creaked beneath the oak rocking chair in the parlor.

Holding my breath, I listened as Daddy sang a lullaby I'd never heard. One he'd made up special for the new baby:

"Tansy's ship's a-sailing,
Sailing across the sea.
Tansy's ship's a-sailing,
Sailing away from me . . .
Sail, Tansy, sail, way out upon the blue.
Only don't forget to sail back home to me
Before the morning dew . . ."

The song made my heart hurt. A bittersweet hurt with longing. As I drifted back to bed, pulling the covers over my head, I pretended my top sheet was a sail and we were sailing away, far away from our little railroad town still covered in white.

The next morning, Clover and I awoke to a racket going on downstairs. Mama was yelling something fierce. "Dammit to hell, Dorian. How could you let this happen *again*?"

The baby's helpless wails ricocheted off the walls and up the stairwell and straight to our hearts. We didn't stop to slide into our robes and slippers as our bare feet hit the cold floor. Grabbing each other's hand, we descended the stairs.

At the bottom step, we almost bumped into Daddy sneaking out of the kitchen. In his overcoat, dress slacks, and tie, he shot us a sheepish wink and knuckled us playfully on the noses. "You girls be good for your mama today, and I'll take you to the dunes when the snow melts." Then he smoothed one hand over his slicked-back hair and walked toward Mama.

With her back to us, she stood in a plain cotton shift at the kitchen window and stared at a sink full of dirty dishes from the night before. Her hands and arms were all jittery as she turned the hot and cold faucets on and off. "See for yourself, *genius*. It's dry as a bone. Nothing comes out. Not even a drip."

Daddy placed one hand on Mama's shoulder. "Letty, calm down. You're scaring the baby."

Clover and I rushed over to the bassinet. Tansy's tiny fists batted the air at the clatter and harsh voices foreign to her ears. Clover and I were used to it. We never knew what might set Mama off, but it usually involved Daddy. Reaching into the bassinet, we tried to comfort our baby sister, letting her tiny fingers curl around ours. But as Tansy continued to cry, and Mama's voice raged on, Clover and I began to bawl like a couple of lost calves.

"Letty, stop! You're upsetting the girls. I said I'd take care of it."

Mama wheeled around and waved a dirty plate in Daddy's face. "Our water's been cut off again, hasn't it, Dorian? You didn't pay the water bill, did you?"

Daddy backed away, adjusting his fedora at a jaunty angle. "Letty, honey, I'm going to pay it on my way to the office." He picked up his briefcase and beelined it for the front door, stopping long enough to slip galoshes on over his dress shoes.

Before he could make his escape, Mama's sharp voice cut across the room. "While you were singing nonsense last night to the baby, you knew good and well we were behind on the water bill. If you'd trust me with the checkbook, I'd make sure the bills got paid on time."

Daddy's whole body stiffened. He rubbed his square jaw, a faint day-old beard sprouting. Without water, Daddy couldn't lather up his shaving brush and glide the silver-handled razor over his handsome face. He gritted his teeth. "I said I'd take care of it."

Without water, we couldn't brush our teeth, bathe, finger-paint, help Mama with the dishes. Without water, Mama couldn't wash Tansy's smelly diapers or bottles.

After Daddy left, Mama handed Clover the big blue jug with a little spout we took on picnics. "You and Marigold put on coats and boots and run next-door and ask Mrs. Sanchez if she can fill up the jug. Tell her our pipes froze."

At four and five, Clover and I were already learning to tell white lies. Nine times out of ten, they had to do with Daddy.

As we scrambled up the steps and knocked on Mrs. Sanchez's door, my belly did a somersault. When the door cracked open, Mrs. Sanchez greeted us with a cautious smile.

"Mama said to tell you our pipes froze," my words tumbled out as I wiggled around, afraid to look Mrs. Sanchez in the eye.

Clover dug an elbow sharply into my ribs. "Sorry to bother you again, Mrs. Sanchez." Clover thrust the jug toward our neighbor. "May we borrow some water?"

Mrs. Sanchez wiped her plump brown hands on her apron and took the jug. "Sí, señoritas. I'll be right back." The screen door slapped against the frame as she disappeared into the dark interior of her small bungalow. A few minutes later she returned, placing the jug in Clover's hand and a stack of warm tortillas wrapped in napkins in mine. "How's the new baby? You like having a new sister?"

We nodded enthusiastically and turned to leave. "Adiós, Mrs. Sanchez. Gracias," we called softly.

We were proud of ourselves. We didn't know how to speak Spanish, but we'd picked up how to say *goodbye* and *thank you* from Mrs. Sanchez.

As the snow crunched under our boots, a city work truck pulled up next to the curb. "That didn't take long," Clover said, her right shoulder drooping from the weight of the heavy jug.

I buried my face in the steamy bundle in my hands, breathing in the warm aroma of homemade flour tortillas. My belly rumbled with hunger.

Mama and Tansy greeted us as we stomped snow off our boots on the red brick porch before going inside. Some of the tiredness had lifted around Mama's hazel eyes, and the baby wasn't crying anymore. Before shutting the door, Mama eyed the city work truck at the curb. "No telling what song and dance your daddy gave the nice ladies working the front desk at the water department. Knowing him, he laid it on thick about having a new baby at home. Last time our water got cut off, it took two days for someone to come out."

She shut the door, nuzzled her face in Tansy's, then smiled in my direction. "Marigold, honey, Mrs. Sanchez's tortillas will go good with the homemade apple butter from the church bake sale."

Apple butter. My favorite. I hoped there was enough for seconds, especially since Daddy wasn't there to poke me in the side and harp about my pudgy belly.

With the baby still crooked in one arm, Mama reached down with her free hand and ran her slender fingers through Clover's honey-blonde curls. "Sis, go set that heavy jug down and run upstairs and grab a couple of picture books. You can read to us while I heat up a bottle for the baby. We'll save the water from Mrs. Sanchez for emergencies." As Clover lugged the jug toward the kitchen, Mama called after her, "In a few weeks when I get my strength back, we'll walk to the library. I'm eager to try out the new pram I bought with Green Stamps."

Before I went to set the tortillas down, I reached up on my tippy-toes to kiss the bottom of Tansy's feet, shrouded in a blanket. *Thank you, little water bear*, I wanted to say. *Mama's not mad at Daddy anymore, so we can all be happy again.*

I waited for Mama to run her fingers through my short choppy hair, or at least pat me on the top of the head. But she didn't.

Stealing a glance up at Mama when she thought no one was looking, I saw her expression change. For a second she looked like that tired-looking lady in the old photograph at the library, the one Mama always stopped by and stared at. I buried my face in Mama's side like those dirty little children in the photograph.

But then Tansy cooed, and the hollows of Mama's cheeks filled with love.

3 MIGRANT MOTHER

APRIL 1964

"GIRLS, WAIT UP." MAMA was winded by the time we reached the library a few blocks from our house.

Clover and I were already halfway up the marble steps. Mama parked the pram at the bottom and lifted the baby to her shoulder. Slowly, she made her way to the top where Clover and I proudly held the door open. The library was our favorite building in town. It was big as a mansion, with tall arched windows and a red-tiled roof.

Once inside, I breathed in the smell of books and dust and the hint of coffee percolating in some back office off-limits to the public. "Mama, I gotta go potty."

Irked, Mama took a deep breath and frowned at me. "Marigold, I told you to go before we left the house."

"I know, Mama, I'm sorry, but I didn't need to go then."

"I need to go, too," Clover said, fussing with Tansy's blanket.

Mama let out a heavy sigh as she ushered us past the counter where two librarians were busy helping people check out books. Our baby sister's blue eyes peered at us over the top of Mama's shoulder. Clover and I made goofy faces, but Tansy was too young to laugh.

Like she did every time we came to the library, Mama paused in front of a stark black-and-white photograph of a young mother holding a baby, her fingers resting against the side of her chin, a faraway look in her eyes. Two young children clung to her sides, hiding their faces. Ever since Clover learned to read, she'd stand next to Mama in front of the brass plaque at the bottom of the frame and proclaim, "*Migrant Mother*, 1936, by Dorothea Lange."

"Mama, do you think those are two little girls in the picture? Why are they so dirty, and why are they hiding their faces?"

I could tell Mama was tired of my questions because she got short with me when she answered. "I don't rightly know, Marigold."

Clover blinked up at Mama, giving her an irritated look. "They're probably sad and *ashamed* 'cause they're poor."

I glanced at Tansy, her tiny face clean and rosy, no dirt smudges on her cheeks like the baby in the photo.

My bladder was about to burst by the time we crowded into the small bathroom with a high ceiling, pedestal sink, and a single toilet with a curtainless window. The window was too high for us to look out. Clover let me go first.

When I stood up to flush, Mama hovered over me, her hair pulled back in a thin ponytail. "Marigold, you're not drinking enough water. Your urine's the color of gasoline."

Clover giggled, and together we peered into the toilet. Wriggling my nose, I pictured Daddy's gas can he kept at the top of the driveway next to the house. "It stinks, like pneumonia."

"A-mmonia," Clover corrected me. Then it was her turn.

After Clover finished, Mama glanced over and nodded her approval. "Now that's the color your urine should be, Marigold. Clear, like your sister's."

Jeez, Clover even pees better than me, I thought. "Mama, what happens if I don't drink enough water?" I stood on my tippy-toes and reached for the hot and cold faucets to wash my hands.

"You'll shrivel up and die," Clover joked, brushing up next to me and squirting pink soap into her hand.

"Girls, hurry up. Before Tansy gets fussy. It'll be time for her next bottle soon."

"Didn't you bring one?" I flitted around, gazing up at the high ceiling.

"No, I forgot. I'm plumb tuckered out, girls."

"Mama, let me hold Tansy so you can potty." Clover dried her hands on a brown paper towel and went to take the baby.

Mama's face flushed. "Thanks, honey, but I'll wait till we get home. I'm still bleeding, and I, uh, well, I forgot my supplies."

I swiveled around. "Bleeding. Where?"

Clover poked me in the side. "Down there, silly."

I snuck a glance where Mama's crotch was hidden beneath her plain cotton dress. "Her pee-pee hole?" I covered my mouth, picturing blood squirting out between Mama's legs.

Mama nudged us out the door. "Girls, clearly we need to have a talk. Guess I've been putting it off. C'mon, let's go pick out some books. Remember, stick together."

Clover grabbed my hand, and we skipped over to the children's section. The bookshelves were just our height. Two kid-size round tables sat in the middle. We were the only kids there.

Clover pulled a copy of *Madeline* off the shelf and tucked it under her arm.

"Do you see *Blueberries for Sal*?" I asked.

Clover pointed to the familiar blue-and-yellow cover and handed it to me. "Here you go."

I sat down at one of the tables and started flipping through the pages, giggling at the pictures of a little girl and her mother picking blueberries on one side of a mountain, while a mama bear and her cub ate berries on the other side. Somehow the girl and the cub got mixed up and the girl ended up with the mama bear and the cub with Sal's mama.

Clover plopped down next to me. "Look what I found. A copy of *Dick and Jane*. It's a book they teach in first grade."

"How do you know? You don't start first grade until next year."

"I dunno," Clover shrugged. "I just know." She turned the page and started reading.

As I listened to her sound out each word, I studied the colorful pictures of Dick and Jane, their little sister, Sally, and their dog, Spot. "We kinda look like them. Only our hair's not as yellow. You look like Jane, and I look like Sally, only older."

"And in a few years," Clover added. "Tansy will look like Sally." She turned the page and continued to read.

Nearby, a librarian pushed a cart along. She stopped occasionally to lift a book from the cart, study the spine, then slide it into place between other books. I found all the sounds of the library soothing. They made me feel safe.

"Father in the book reminds me of our daddy," Clover's voice brought me back to the story. "He wears a suit and tie and a hat to go to work. Just like our dad."

"And Father is handsome, too, like Daddy," I added.

"Mother wears pretty dresses and her hair's always fixed. I bet she goes to the beauty parlor. Even her aprons are clean."

"I wish Mama wore more pretty dresses. Don't you?"

"I guess, but they cost money. At least she dresses up for church."

As we stared at the pictures of the storybook family, I glanced up to see Mama shuffle past, her squishy secondhand shoes dragging on the floor like she still had on her house slippers.

Clover saw her too. "Ever since Tansy was born, Mama walks like she's still got a baby in her belly."

I turned the page in the book and pointed to the picture. "I wish we had a pedal car like Sally. We could take turns driving."

"Maybe if we had a big brother like Dick, he could help us do things."

"Daddy helps us do things sometimes," I said. "He taught you how a ride a bike without training wheels. He said he'll teach me when I'm ready, but I'm too chicken."

While Clover went back to reading, we both heard a sound that jolted us out of the story. "Did you hear that?" I whispered?

"Yea." Clover pushed out of her chair and motioned for me to follow. "It sounds like a woman crying."

I grabbed the books and nearly bumped into Clover when she stopped abruptly and froze.

With tears streaming down her sharp cheekbones, Mama swayed from side to side, rocking Tansy in her arms as she stood directly in front of the *Migrant Mother*.

Clover reached for me, and we huddled together, side by side, a few feet away, not knowing what to do. My gaze darted between Mama and the famous photograph.

Mama began to sob louder and louder.

It's like Mama forgot where she was, forgot all the rules of the library.

Miss Mavis, the kind librarian who never told us to hush, bustled out from behind the counter and came toward Mama. She always wore the same mossy pilled sweater and round horn-rimmed glasses. Her face reminded me of the front end of Daddy's Edsel. Her spectacles were big as headlights. Her nose was long like the grille, and she always sounded stuffed up when she talked. "Letty, dear, come sit down."

Mama glanced at Miss Mavis and stopped swaying. "You remember my name?"

Miss Mavis gently directed Mama to the nearest chair; the fancy one I called the Queen Chair. It was gold velvet, with a worn cushion and high back. "Oh, I hope you don't think I'm being too forward. I don't generally refer to our adult patrons by their first names, but, well . . ."

Sniffling back tears, Mama peeked up from the tiny bundle and dabbed at her eyes with Tansy's blanket. "Sorry I made a scene. I sure like being called Letty, though." She paused and gave her a tired smile. "Reminds me I'm still me."

The kindest expression spread across Miss Mavis's face. I could see her eyes light up behind her spectacles. "You and your girls are some of my favorite library patrons. You're always so respectful and you turn books in on time." She smiled at Clover and me and motioned for us to come closer.

We inched forward, moving together as one.

Mama sat up a little taller. Her voice cracked in places when she spoke. "Miss Mavis, you think that poor woman in the photograph felt trapped with no education and three little girls and nowhere to go?"

Miss Mavis bent and patted Mama's shoulder. "Maybe so, Letty. I'd say by the expression on her face, she had a hard life."

"Seeing her picture today just got to me," Mama said. "Some days I feel just like . . ." Mama stopped talking and took a deep breath.

"You're just having one of those days, Letty. My goodness, you just gave birth a few weeks ago. What has it been now, six weeks or so . . . ?"

Mama nodded. "About that." She jutted her chin toward the photograph. "Who was she? The woman in the picture? I notice her every time we come in the door. I've seen that same photograph in magazines and newspapers."

"Supposedly, she and her family were stranded at a pea-picker's camp in California. Dorothea Lange, the famous photographer who took the photograph, said she found the woman and her children living in a makeshift tent or lean-to. I suspect they were hungry and desperate. A member of our Friends of the Library donated the frame and plaque. Of course, the photograph is a reproduction of the original."

After a moment, Mama glanced around and motioned for us to join her. Gathering Clover and me in her free arm, Mama said with a look of determination in her hazel eyes, "Guess I don't have it so bad after all. Thank you for your kindness, Miss Mavis. I used to dream of being a teacher. I've never told anyone that before. Least I can do is make sure my girls can read well, don't you think?"

"You're too young to give up so fast on that dream, Letty. There's still plenty of time."

"I'm twenty-four," Mama volunteered.

"Aah, to be twenty-four again . . ." Miss Mavis closed her eyes and smiled. After a moment she continued, "Until you can attend college, the library is a good place to start. Keep reading and keep believing." She glanced over her shoulder to check on the young librarian helping two women check out books. "Before I head back, is there anything I can get you?"

Mama cleared her throat. "There is one thing, Miss Mavis, but I've been hesitant to ask. Can you recommend any classics? My school didn't have much of a library."

"Do you have an author in mind?"

"Well," Mama paused, looking around, resting her chin on top of my head. "There's this woman author I've been curious about. Her name is Willa Cather."

Miss Mavis grinned, exposing yellow teeth. "Good choice. She penned twelve novels before she died in nineteen forty-seven. She won a Pulitzer Prize in 1923 for her novel *One of Ours*. Stay put. I'll be right back."

Miss Mavis returned in a jiffy with three books. "For starters, you might try *Death Comes for the Archbishop*. It's set right here in New Mexico. I also recommend *Song of the Lark* or *My Ántonia*."

I wasn't too keen on any book with the word *death* in the title, but wouldn't you know, that's the book Mama chose and checked out.

On our way out the door, Mama paused one last time and glanced back at the *Migrant Mother*. "Girls," she chimed. "Let's head home and read."

Mama still walked slow as we took turns pushing the pram, but she chitchatted with us as we told her all about Dick and Jane and their little sister, Sally, and their dog, Spot.

The first thing I did when we walked in the door, I headed to the kitchen and glugged a tall glass of tap water.

Two weeks later when we returned to the library to drop off our books, Mama nodded respectfully to the *Migrant Mother* but kept moving. Tansy was fast asleep in her crib at home. Our kind neighbor, Mrs. Sanchez, had offered to stay and babysit when she'd dropped by unexpectantly with a plate of homemade chocolate drop cookies. Mama was learning it was okay to accept help.

While Clover and I scampered off to the kids' section, Mama stopped by the counter to chat with Miss Mavis. Mama said she wanted to discuss the book she'd just finished and what books she might read next.

Before we rounded the corner, we heard Mama say, "I learned more about New Mexico history by reading Willa Cather's *Death Comes for the Archbishop* than I ever learned in school. Imagine that, and in a *novel*."

4 BACK AT THE SANDS

OCTOBER 2017

AFTER I LEAVE THE abandoned church in Rosemont, I drive straight to the Sands, a vintage *L*-shaped motor lodge on the edge of Sandhill. The lodge sits directly across the highway from the railroad tracks where I can hear the rumble of freight cars clicking by day and night and the whistle of approaching trains. The rooms are clean and affordable and rent by the week. Although I can afford to stay at one of the newer hotels in town, I've chosen the Sands to honor a memory.

When I arrive, I discover that the kidney-shaped pool we snuck into late one night as teenagers is gone. I try not to take it personally as I breeze into the motel office to check in. A large jack-o'-lantern with a wicked grin greets me as I lean on the counter and ask the young clerk, Shilo, "What happened to the swimming pool?"

"Owners got tired of the upkeep." She shrugs and hands me a plastic key. "But we've got free Wi-Fi and complimentary breakfast." She sounds cheerful enough even though it appears I've interrupted her studying.

"You in college?" I eye the textbooks she has opened next to the computer and try not to stare at the huge holes in her earlobes from wearing gauges too long.

"Yes, ma'am. I'm taking classes online, hoping to transfer next semester."

"Where to?"

"New Mexico State."

"I remember those days. It's hard, working and going to school at the same time." I gaze up at the ceiling a moment, recalling how I carried a full load for four and a half years along with work-study to help pay tuition. But mostly I think of Mama, how she'd eventually gone to work full-time as a receptionist for Dr. Johnson and took night classes after Daddy left us. "My mama did it while raising three girls as a single parent. Took her a few years, but she eventually earned her bachelor's degree and teaching certifications."

"Caffeine and catnaps," the clerk quips.

I give her a cheerful thumbs-up. "Well, I wish you luck."

"Just one?" she inquires, looking over my shoulder as if she's expecting a husband or companion to be accompanying me.

"Yup, I'm the Lone Ranger," I joke, swallowing the catch in my throat. I don't tell her I'm a recent widow—it's been a year since my beloved Sawyer died—or that our grown daughter, Libby, is expecting her first child. That I'm a former journalist turned ghostwriter. That I'm here partly because I made a promise to Sawyer—that handsome rascal will haunt me if I don't keep it.

"Enjoy your stay," the night clerk calls as I open the door to go outside.

I wave my key and glance back at her name tag. "By the way, Shilo, I like your name. It reminds me of an old song by Neil Diamond, where he sings about his imaginary friend from childhood."

The young woman's whole face lights up. "That's who my mom named me after. She loved that song. Neil Diamond was her favorite singer."

We smile at each other, and in that long pause before I walk out the door, I realize her mama is dead too.

Lugging my tote bag with laptop and notebooks, I roll my suitcase behind me and enter the middle of the courtyard where the sparkling pool once existed. The tempting waters beaconing three restless teenagers and two preteens to trespass and break the rules has been replaced by pave stones, two tall urns with fake ivy, and refurbished metal lawn chairs.

"Well, girls," I grump, looking around as if they're with me. "Guess we won't be gliding through the water, flipping our tails, and hoping some cute boys drop by."

My mind floods with memories of that night when Clover borrowed Mama's station wagon and drove us girls to the Sands. Clover had just gotten her driver's license and told Mama we were going to get snow cones with the money she'd earned working the hotdog stand at the ballpark. We waited until dark and scaled the chain-link fence, careful not to get our flimsy thrift store bikinis caught in it as we climbed over the top. Diving into the *wet*, we felt our souls expand. No itchy swim caps or entry fees. No lifeguards blowing whistles telling us to get out. No bullies taunting us and causing a scene.

Just the five of us: Clover, Tansy, Ruthie, Melody, and me, pretending we were synchronized swimmers. We moved through the water as natural as any sea creature, although none of us had spent much time in any body of water over two feet deep. A rare dip in the Pecos River and public pool or freezing our tails off that one time at the Blue Hole had only made us thirsty for more.

Treading water, we formed a circle in the deep end and recited The Mermaids' Ten Commandments. The rules we made up as little girls, scribbling with colored pencils into our spiral notebooks, embellishing them with curlicues and mermaid tails.

I look around, alone in the courtyard except for some black crows watching me from the naked limbs of a bare tree. The sun is setting. I set my tote bag down, take a deep breath, and recite them from memory:

“Share, don’t be stingy.
Don’t be mean.
Stick together.
Don’t cheat.
Mind your manners.
Turn library books in on time.
Don’t stare at people who are different.
Don’t talk behind someone’s back.
Stand up to bullies, then flip your tail and swim away.
Once a mermaid, always a mermaid.”

My eyes flutter open as the sound of Melody’s flute echoes through my mind for the second time that day.

Don’t forget me . . . don’t forget us . . . don’t . . .

I gaze up at the crows, my only audience. Their dark silhouettes stand out against the evening sky, ablaze in blood orange. “Mel, what’s the last part? Don’t *what* . . . ?”

My heart hurts as my mind fills in the blank. “Don’t hold grudges.” I hear the words boil up out of me hoarse and raw.

A couple of black crows caw back as if in agreement.

I reread the text message Libby sent earlier: Mom, good luck in Sandhill. I hope you find what you’re looking for. Some of my favorite stories growing up were the ones you shared about your sisters and y’all’s two friends.

Breathing in the dry cold air, the pungent smell of eastern New Mexico and West Texas hits my senses full force, reminding me of my upbringing. Schooling me that I best not get all uppity in this working-class town surrounded by ranchers and farmers. I figure it’ll take me two days to get re-acclimated to the smell of cow shit.

In my room, I pull off my boots and slide my tired feet into a pair of cushy clogs. After I unpack a few things, I open a small bottle of wine and pour it into my plastic travel goblet. Swirling the golden liquid, I breathe in the heady vapors and sip. My specs on the nightstand, I stretch out on the bed and shut my eyes, occasionally opening them long enough to sip more wine, nosh on some cheese and fruit and wholegrain crackers, and reflect on my plan.

Two weeks max, hopefully less, that's how long I'm giving myself in Sandhill. Long enough to drill Daddy and settle an old score, visit Clover, and make headway on my book. After ghosting for other people, it's time I write the book I've been avoiding for forty years. A confession Sawyer had finally dragged out of me.

Sometimes it takes another writer to wave the bullshit flag, and boy did Sawyer wave it. On that cold dawn in November a year ago, days after the presidential election, Sawyer woke me with coffee in hand and led me outside to the firepit, all six-foot-two-inches of him already dressed for the day in his faded jeans and cowboy boots. Huddled around a blazing fire, we sipped our coffee and gazed at Venus, the bright morning star. I thought he'd brought me out here to cheer me up—we were both still in shock over the election—and to talk about his next book project, which came with a tight deadline and a hefty advance (rare these days, even for a writer of Sawyer's caliber), but then he said, "Quit telling other people's stories, Mari. It's time to write your own."

His words had scalded me. He'd never given me career advice, and I'd never asked for it. I didn't need a man telling me what to do, even a man as supportive as Sawyer. My eyes stung as I stared at the fire, took a swallow of coffee, and inhaled the smoky air and my wounded pride. After a moment I'd glared at him, prepared to tell him to mind his own business. Instead, I heard myself say, "But what if I get pushback?"

"Pushback from who?"

"Daddy," I shrugged. "Maybe the others."

Sawyer took a sip of coffee, his blue eyes searching mine over the rim of his mug. "Since when have you been afraid of pushback? Write the story that's been holding you hostage since I've known you. Think about that recurring dream that wakes you at night."

I gripped my mug with both hands and gazed at the morning

star. It shined like a beacon in the east, pointing me toward Sandhill as the first blush of pink woke up the horizon.

Less than an hour later Sawyer had dropped dead, moments after strapping on his helmet and rumbling down our long gravel driveway on his Harley. My tall lanky soul man leaving me to take his place as *writer in residence* at our roomy adobe on the outskirts of Moriarty—a name that became synonymous with mortuary after he left.

The dream hovers around me, like Sawyer's last words, reminding me why I've returned. Why I made myself go inside the old church today. It's my job to sift through the silt, to form and shape stories like the sandcastles we built as kids. It's my job to set the record straight about what happened and why. I owe Mel that much.

In the dream, I pull up in front of our saggy house, that former grand dame who welcomed countless boarders before our family moved in. Gripping the doorknob, I take a deep breath and slip inside, unannounced.

A white-haired little girl in a pink cotton dress sings to herself, daydreaming away in the oak rocker. When she sees me, she stops rocking and looks up all wide-eyed, clutching a Chatty Cathy doll to her chest. I hold my hand out . . . "Hey, silly, it's me. Don't be afraid. We're all grown up now."

Pushing out of the rocker, she runs into my arms like I'm her mama. We twirl together, still clumsy for we've never learned to dance. We giggle and catch our reflection in a mirror hanging over the buffet purchased at an estate sale. The gap in our rabbit teeth closes into a dazzling smile, thanks to a retainer Mama made us wear in junior high.

"I wonder how much that set Daddy back?" I chuckle, and she covers her mouth and laughs, her face blushing as pink as her dress. We both know it was Mama who paid for the retainer, so selfless she never got her own teeth fixed.

We stare at a photograph of Mama and Daddy on their wedding day, encased in a fancy frame on the buffet. Mama's nineteen, looking unsure of herself in a white bridal dress cinched at her tiny waist. A little seed named Clover is growing in Mama's belly. If Daddy feels trapped, he isn't showing it. He looks dapper in a tan suit, his bright smile lit up by a flashbulb.

"Where are the others?" I ask, gazing around the parlor. She vanishes when I hear voices calling from the backyard. Turning around, I feel myself being pulled toward the French doors leading down the brick steps to the old fountain where fairytales sprang from our imaginations.

The voices call again, the happy chatter of my sisters and friends calling me to join them. *Hurry up, Marigold. It's raining.*

I start to push open the back door as thunder rumbles and lightning crackles overhead.

Behind me I hear Mama's shrill howl echoing through the house. "Get out. Get out, you bastard."

I turn, expecting to see Daddy skipping down the stairs, his briefcase clutched in one hand and the tails of his trench coat fluttering behind him.

But it's Melody I see, standing on the dry front porch, her hair in disarray, the same pumpkin color as her flute case. Her eyes are red and puffy, accusatory as she searches my face through the open door like I've abandoned her. The faded red dictionary Melody found by a curb in sixth grade and couldn't wait to give me is splayed open at her feet, its spine broken.

My cell phone rings, startling me. Grappling for my glasses, I fumble for the phone on the nightstand.

Daddy! He doesn't know I'm in town yet. I debate whether to answer.

Back when he and Mama were still married to each other, she used to joke, "Dorian Hubbard can sell anything. He can sell life insurance to a dead person, a side of beef to a vegetarian, sheep shears to a pig farmer."

"Well, Mama," I sigh, letting it go to voicemail. "He sure sold *us* a bill of goods."

A shiver ripples through me as I recall the cryptic message left on the church wall: *I knew right then this wasn't how most moms and dads acted in our hometown . . .*

But it's those last four words followed by Melody's trademark symbol that clutch at my heart, make me want to storm over to Daddy's place and shake him. After all these years, it's still odd to call the tiny house on Mesa Lane "Daddy's place."

The last time I saw him was at Sawyer's memorial service when I called his *second* ex-wife a *skank*. By then my manners were as shot to hell as her looks as she clung to an oxygen tank while folks streamed out of the funeral home. I couldn't believe Daddy had the gall to show up with her. Seeing those two together, I thought, how is it possible to hate someone and feel sorry for them at the same time?

I wait a good solid minute before I play Daddy's message. His voice is croaky and weak from smoking two packs of cigarettes a day for decades, along with the residual effects of a stroke. A stroke that went unreported for days until the skank finally took him to the doctor.

"It's Daddy calling. Wondering how you're doing. Clover tells me you sold your house in Moriarty and moved into the city. Man, that was some kinda place y'all had." He manages a faint whistle. "I bet it's worth a million bucks, what with that acreage." Daddy goes into a coughing jag and hacks up phlegm, all recorded for my benefit as I picture him pulling a hanky from his back pocket. He clears his throat and continues. "Tansy tells me Ruthie's still flying cargo planes all over the world. Even flew a herd of elephants to the states. Said the plane stunk for weeks." Chuckling, he mumbles something I can't understand and then adds, "I have something for you. Don't imagine the others will have much use for it . . ." He sighs, coughs again, and the message goes silent.

I'm glad Tansy keeps up with Ruthie and told Daddy about the elephants. This is one time when I know Daddy's not stretching the truth. He has a habit of embellishing things. Take Tansy, for instance. He likes to brag that she's a surgeon and lives in a *beach house* on the Florida Gulf Coast. Tansy's a veterinarian and lives *five miles inland*.

When he brags about Clover, he tells everyone she owns the biggest bookshop in eastern New Mexico. The truth is, she owns the only bookshop in Sandhill. As for Daddy bragging about me, well, any bragging had more to do with me being married to Sawyer, his famous son-in-law, the author. When Daddy bragged about Sawyer, you'd think he'd *invented* the *book*.

Pushing myself up from the bed, I hold my breath, count to ten, then let out a lungful of air and decades of regret. And yes, disgust. I almost call him back out of curiosity. But I have a long night ahead of me, so it can wait. I'll text him in the morning and let him know I'm in town.

At the sink I splash my face with cool water and pat it with a rough hand towel. Its coarseness reminds me of Mama pinning our laundry to a clothesline because Daddy wouldn't spring for a dryer. Melody's Grandma Dot hung their wash on a line too.

Armed with a shot of caffeine after I make a small pot of motel coffee, I glance out the window at the courtyard where an old lamppost cast a dim glow over the metal lawn chairs. I can still see us out there, sneaking over the fence, our hearts pounding out of our chests as we try to contain our squeals when we realize we are getting away with it. Diving into the healing waters, we are setting ourselves free, washing away the stink of sweat, the constant pressure to fit in, the *sin* of being born into families without means. Water is a scarce commodity in parts of the Southwest, especially if you don't have money.

"Once a mermaid, always a mermaid," I whisper at my reflection, my breath fogging the window as I face another hard truth. Had it not been for Melody convincing me it was okay to break the rules that night, even ordering me, "Move your *butt*, Old Mother Hubbard! We're not swimming without you," I would've never made it over the fence.

Before I close the curtains, I set my coffee down and do a quick search on my cell phone for Neil Diamond's greatest hits. As I listen to him sing about Shilo, his loyal make-believe friend, I stare out at the night and see five glistening girls under the moonlight, sticking together up to their necks in deep water. With a lump in my throat, I pick up my coffee and sip, realizing the girls from my childhood live on in my memory as imaginary friends. And they always come when I call them, especially Melody.

Gathering the tools of my trade, I seat myself at the desk, limbering my fingers over the keyboard as my mind drifts across town to the city pool.

Daddy's robust voice can be heard above the screech of children, the ear-piercing whistles of lifeguards, and the *boing* of the high dive as he sails through the air . . .

5 MAKE WAVES

JUNE 1968

DADDY WHEELED MAMA'S STATION wagon into a parking spot in front of the pool house and shoved the gearshift into park. "This little jaunt's liable to set me back a week's pay."

The backs of my thighs stuck to the vinyl of the middle seat where I sat jammed between Clover and Melody, all three of us dripping with sweat. Daddy didn't believe in running the air conditioner if we were just going across town.

Mama flicked her head in our direction and hissed at Daddy, "Dorian, for once can you lay off about money?" She cut him a look and pushed open the front passenger door with her shoulder.

"Daddy, are we poor?" Tansy's voice chittered from the third seat, where she and Ruthie played with Barbie dolls dressed in tiny outfits Mama had sewed by hand.

From my vantage point, I watched Daddy's blue eyes in the rearview mirror, unblinking beneath his furrowed brow. He made a fist and covered his mouth before he cleared his throat. "Honey, we're as rich as all those fancy people sailing across the deep blue sea in ocean liners."

I thought about the song Daddy made up for Tansy when she was a baby.

He glanced over his shoulder and winked at us. "Today we happen to be riding in an eight-year-old *nine-passenger Pontiac*. Pretend it's our ocean liner on wheels." He climbed out of the car and shut the door.

"This car's as old as me and Melody," I piped up as she scratched a mosquito bite on her shin till it bled. I watched her out of the corner of my eye. She had the prettiest peaches-and-cream complexion, her face sprinkled with a few freckles.

Once she crawled out, I scooted after her, the heat from the black asphalt burning the bottom of my feet through my thin rubber flip-flops. This was our third trip to the pool since school got out, but the first time Daddy had joined us in a couple of years.

I tucked my head and sniffed my armpits. They stunk like grilled onions even though I'd bathed the night before and patted my underarms with a powder puff. Then I caught a whiff of chlorine in the air and hoped it covered my BO. That night I planned to ask Mama in private if I could start wearing deodorant. Clover should start wearing it too.

Ruthie and Tansy tumbled over the middle seat and hopped out. The electric window above the tailgate was permanently stuck—Daddy said we didn't have the funds to fix it—so anyone who rode in the third seat that faced backward had to crawl over the second seat to get out.

Craning her neck, Ruthie pointed at something in the sky. "Look! An *airplane*."

We all followed Ruthie's gaze. A silver object streaked across the blue. I pretended it was an ocean liner.

In the few months since Ruthie and her mom moved into the storybook cottage across the street, we learned quickly that Ruthie was always looking to the sky. After a few seconds, she took off running, her flip-flops slipping off the sides of her feet as she zigzagged around us.

Clover and I spun around, laughing, and watching her.

"Ruthie, what's your favorite book when we go to the library?" Clover called while Mama doled out faded beach towels and rubber swim caps she'd picked up at yard sales.

"That's easy," I smarted, picturing the book Clover, Melody, and I took turns reading to Ruthie because she and Tansy were still learning their ABCs.

Ruthie stopped long enough to collect her towel and cap from Mama. "*The Flying Sunbeam.*" She grinned and took off again.

Daddy patted his shirt pocket for his cigarettes and matches. "What's it about?" He wore dress shoes without socks, his hairy calves and athletic thighs stark white below his swim trunks.

Clover squinted. "It's about a little boy who wants to be a pilot like his dad."

"Ruthie wants to be a pilot when she grows up," I cut in, wanting to beat my big sister to the important part.

Mama's head swiveled this way and that, trying to keep track of everyone. "Tansy, come get your cap and towel." She and Ruthie were running around in circles. "Two peas in a pod. All arms and legs in constant motion."

Mama shook her head then walked toward the ticket counter, her short bathrobe flapping open, revealing her black one-piece suit with a white skirt circling her slender hips. "Girls, I have a library book due in a couple of days. We can ask the librarian if she has any books on lady pilots."

Daddy struck a match, lit the tip of his cigarette, then took a long drag. "Her best bet's to become a stewardess. I don't think women are allowed to fly airliners."

Clover frowned at Daddy. "That's a dumb rule." She crossed her arms around her towel and trudged up the steps.

Melody grabbed my hand and we skipped up the steps after Clover.

Daddy followed us. Blowing smoke out of his nose at the top of the steps, he pointed his cigarette at Clover. "I didn't make the rules, honey. I'm just stating a fact."

Clover made a pouty face. "Well, it's dumb. Girls can do anything boys can do."

Mama yelled at Tansy and Ruthie, "Girls! Y'all want to swim or not?"

Daddy stepped up to the counter and studied the swim fees painted in red on a white board. "Whew," he whistled. "You people are proud of your prices."

The young man working the counter kept a straight face. "Sir, the fees help pay for the upkeep."

Daddy pulled out his wallet and made a big show of counting out several bills. "Well, we taxpayers are getting stiffed if you ask me. It's a city pool, for cripe's sake. Not the country club."

Mama sighed and looked the other way as Tansy and Ruthie flew up the steps, out of breath, hair matted against their sweaty faces.

The young man handed Daddy a string of tickets. "Have a good time. Girls to the left, guys to the right."

After we filed through the turnstile into the girls' dressing room, Melody tugged the back of my one-piece and leaned toward me, her hot breath blowing in my ear. "Your daddy stopped by our house the other day and helped Mom change a flat tire. He wouldn't let Grandma Dot pay him."

I turned, picturing my daddy helping Melody's mom. "Daddy's good at fixin' things, especially cars."

Melody hung her head. "Grandma Dot said my daddy took off before I was born. Never bothered to marry my mom."

"Oh!" I covered my mouth. "Where did he go?"

She shrugged and made a sad face. "No idea, but Grandma Dot said it was probably for the best. She said he was as worthless as a tumbleweed." She twirled her thick ponytail through her fingers.

I didn't know what to say. I pictured a dried-up old tumbleweed blowing down the road.

We walked outside into the sunlight, greeted by the happy sounds of other kids splashing in the big blue pool. I saw Daddy coming toward us.

I had an idea. I squeezed Melody's hand. "We can share my daddy."

She hugged me tight, then we walked fast instead of running after Mama and the others because the rules said: *no running allowed*.

The tops of my stubby legs rubbed together, but when I walked beside Melody, she never teased me for being shorter. She was already two inches taller than me, almost as tall as Clover. Both of them had long legs, like Mama. Even Tansy and Ruthie had long legs, and they were only four.

Under the shade of a big sycamore tree by the kiddie pool, Mama spread out an old quilt and slathered store-brand suntan lotion on all of us. We helped each other pull on our rubber caps. Daddy finished his cigarette and ground the butt in the grass with the sole of his right dress shoe. He sat down on the quilt, unlaced each shoe, and made a big production of removing the right shoe first, then the left.

"Daddy, your feet are as white as chalk." Clover made a face and buckled her chin strap. "How come you don't wear sandals in the summer like other dads?"

He hoisted himself up and unbuttoned his short-sleeved shirt, keeping his eye on a fancy lady swaying by in a two-piece suit the color of lime sherbet. She pulled off her swim cap right in front of us and shook out her waves of sugar sand hair.

Daddy made a crude whistling sound. The woman whipped her head around and gave him a dirty look and kept walking.

My insides felt funny like all those times we'd be watching Miss America on TV and Daddy would walk into the room during the swimsuit competition. He'd whistle and carry on, right there in front of us. Mama called those sounds he made *catcalls*. He never whistled like that at her. Instead, he'd say things like, "Put some meat on your bones, Letty. Get you one of them pushup bras," when he thought no one was listening.

I peeked at Mama. She watched the lady a second then rubbed

her forehead like she had a headache coming on. "Dorian, pick your chin up off the ground and take the girls swimming."

He grinned funny at Mama. Then he clapped his hands and hollered, "Okay, girls. Last one in the pool's a rotten egg."

I looked around. Daddy was the most handsome man at the pool, even if his feet and legs were white as chalk. We all squealed and gathered around him, vying for his attention. He smelled of Aqua Velva and suntan lotion.

"Stick together," Mama called as we walked toward the shallow end. "Don't let Ruthie and Tansy out of your sight."

Hesitating, I turned and watched Mama pull a pale blue library book out of her bag. She twisted her hair up in a knot and slipped on a pair of white plastic sunglasses. After seating herself against the trunk of the shade tree, she crossed her creamy legs and propped open her book. Right then I thought she looked as fancy as the lady in the lime sherbet suit.

Mama glanced up and shooed me away. "Go on, honey. Go have fun."

"Aren't you coming in?" How could she prefer shade and a book to sun and water?

She eyed me over the top of her sunglasses. "In a minute. I'm getting to the good part."

I squinted at the familiar title in black letters: *Ethan Frome*. I started to sass that she'd read it before, at least twice that I knew of. Then I remembered all the times Clover, Melody, and I checked out *The Boxcar Children*, rereading the same chapters over and over, sometimes out loud to Tansy and Ruthie. We acted out parts of the book in the backyard, each of us taking turns playing the four Alden children: Henry, Jessie, Violet, and Benny. Tansy always played their dog, Watch, because she wanted a dog, but Daddy said, "No, we have enough mouths to feed as is."

"What's your book about?" I peeked over my shoulder to check on the others then looked back at Mama.

She barely glanced at me and turned a page. "It's about a ruined man and two women involved in a love triangle during the bitter winters up north."

"Oh, it sounds boring."

She ignored me and kept reading.

I jumped when someone thumped the back of my swim cap.

"Hurry up," Melody teased. "We can't go swimming without you." She looped her freckled arm in mine and pulled me toward the water.

We'd been playing in the shallow end with Mama after she finally stopped reading and joined us, when Norman hobbled by on metal braces. The gray in his crewcut matched the braces on his arms and legs. Drool slid down one side of his mouth. His face twitched. Mama poked me in the back. "Don't stare, Marigold. It's rude."

I spun around, stinging with shame. "I didn't mean to, Mama. I swear."

"Norman can't help himself." She touched my chin. "He had polio when he was a boy and spent time in an iron lung."

"What's an iron lung?" I looked away and watched Tansy and Ruthie turning somersaults.

Clover wiggled her fingers in the water like she was playing a piano. "A machine to help people breathe."

I squinted at her in the bright sun. "How do you know that?"

"I read about it in a book."

Melody's feet stuck out of the water. She was doing handstands.

Mama waded to the side of the pool and started doing leg lifts. I peeked over at Norman. An older boy I'd spotted at the concession stand earlier walked up behind him. I thought he was going to say hello. The boy was tall and lanky with the cutest cleft chin. He reminded me of other cute boys I'd see shooting baskets in driveways around town, at the park, on TV. He must go to a different school because I'd never seen him until today. I had a crush on him for about ten seconds, until he imitated the herky-jerky way Norman walked.

Melody came up for air and plowed past us. She pushed out of the pool and charged toward the boy. "Stop making fun of him." She wasn't intimidated by the boy's good looks or that he was at least three grades older.

Two more boys walked up. One had dreamy brown eyes, the other had a slight case of acne. All three boys looked old enough to be in fifth or sixth grade, popular boys who excelled in school and sports. Maybe the other two were going to tell their friend to cut it out, but then the boy with dreamy eyes laughed, along with the other kid. Their laughter encouraged the tall kid to keep moving his arms and legs around in spastic jerks.

Norman ignored them and kept moving. Tansy and Ruthie jumped out of the pool and rushed over to help Norman into a chair. They fussed over him like two little mamas, treating him like a giant baby as they talked softly to him even though he was old enough to be a grandpa.

I got out of the pool and stood beside Melody, holding myself and trying not to shake. The sun beat down, but I had goosebumps. My teeth chattered. I blinked up at the boy with the dimpled chin. My voice pounded in my ears. "Leave Norman alone. He's waiting for his swim coach."

The boy threw his head back and laughed. "A swim coach?" He smirked at the others. "Guess ol' Norman's training for the Olympics."

"Olympics for retards," the boy with dreamy eyes coughed.

Melody took a step toward all three. "Knock it off."

The boy with the dimpled chin elbowed the others. "She's pretty cute . . . if you like freckles."

The other boys chuckled and looked around nervously.

I tucked a loose strand of hair under my cap and grabbed Melody for support. "How come you're so mean?"

He looked at me with bugeyes. "How come you're so fat? You look like Little Lotta."

No one had ever called me that. I pictured the tubby girl with yellow hair from the comic strip. His words singed my heart. My face burned from the inside out. Ugly laughter exploded around me.

Melody took another step and thumped the tall boy's chest. "She does not. Take it back."

Ruthie rushed over and glared up at the boys, planting her hands on her narrow hips. "You mean boys go away. Leave us alone."

The boy who called me Little Lotta looked at her and spat. "Shut up, dirty Mexican. Who asked you?"

Ruthie blinked and tried not to cry. She thumbed her nose at him and stared him down, reminding me of a female David standing up to Goliath. Calling me fat was one thing, but what he called Ruthie? Well, it was worse than cruel.

Melody patted Ruthie on the back and snarled at the boys. "Sticks and stones can break our bones, but words can never hurt us."

But they did hurt, and we all knew it.

I glanced over at Tansy. She was chattering about something with Norman. *Please don't leave Norman's side*, I begged her silently. *If you come over here, they'll make fun of your toes.*

The tall boy put his hands on his hips, mimicking Ruthie. "I bet you eat refried beans every night, huh, little girl?" The other boys laughed, and one by one, they joined in singing, "Beans, beans, are good for your heart. The more you eat, the more you *fart*!"

The boys laughed and whooped and hollered. Any other time it would be funny, but not today. It was meant to hurt Ruthie, who'd done nothing wrong.

They all froze when Clover walked up with Daddy. "There a problem here, boys?" Daddy rubbed his chin and looked at them sideways.

Mama crawled out of the pool and went to check on Norman, probably to divert his attention. I could hear her saying, "Hi, Norman. I see you're wearing your favorite orange T-shirt with the school mascot."

His chin dropped to his chest as he pulled at the front of his shirt. He grinned up at Mama like she was the nicest person in the world.

"Norman loves the Sandhill Cranes football team," Tansy bragged to Mama.

I turned back and whispered hoarsely to Daddy, "That tall kid said I look like Little Lotta."

Daddy patted the top of my swim cap. Lowering his voice, he muttered out the side of his mouth, "The character from the comic strips?"

Slowly I nodded as tears leaked from my eyes.

Melody leaned over and whispered, "That kid prob'ly scratches his butt and sniffs his fingers." I wanted to laugh, but I couldn't move. My body felt on fire. I glanced at the swimming pool, wanting to disappear into the cool water.

Daddy curled his upper lip, exposing perfect white teeth like Ken, Barbie's boyfriend. He narrowed his gaze on the ringleader and cracked his knuckles. "Son, you and your buddies need to take a hike."

Out of nowhere, the fancy lady in the green two-piece sashayed up. She stood next to the tall boy. For a second I imagined she smelled nice, her voice soft and soothing like Cool Whip.

But then I noticed her frown, her big blue eyes narrowed to slits. "Mister, are you harassing my son and his friends?"

Daddy rubbed his nose, hiding a silly grin. "Pardon me, ma'am? But you've got it all wrong. Your son was making fun of Norman. Then your boy started making fun of my girls."

Her head jerked around. "Thornton Hinkle! You know better than that."

The boy she called Thornton Hinkle stood rigid as a flagpole. He placed his hand over his heart like he was about to recite the Pledge of Allegiance.

"Mother, those girls were making fun of us. I promise."

Melody got in his face. "Liar, liar, pants on fire."

The fancy lady pursed her ruby lips and pinched her son's ear to get his attention. "Thornton, you and your friends go sit down. I'll handle this."

"Yes, ma'am." He sulked a second, rubbing his ear, then gave us a snarky look before he and his buddies marched off.

She turned to Daddy. "Mister, you need to teach your daughter manners." She made a face at Melody.

Melody wriggled her nose like she'd stepped in dog poo. "Your son was making fun of Norman. Then he called Ruthie a bad name."

Daddy scratched the side of his face. "That's right, lady. My girls simply came to Norman's defense."

I don't know what surprised me more. The fact that the lady thought Melody was Daddy's daughter or that Daddy didn't bother to correct her.

Mrs. Hinkle tossed her hair over her shoulder and stormed off, her hips swaying from side to side like she thought she was the prettiest woman alive. I swear I heard her hiss, "White trash," as she left. I wanted to run after her and tell her that being pretty didn't mean everything. That being kind to others was more important than good looks. But she was an adult, and I was a little girl without a voice.

Daddy strode over to the lifeguard stand, stuck his fingers between his lips and whistled to get the guy's attention. He craned his neck and said something to the lifeguard. We were out of ear-shot.

The teenager looked down at Daddy and then glanced in our direction. He shrugged his bronze shoulders then blew his whistle at some kid for running.

Daddy crossed his arms, bit down on his bottom lip, and gazed up long and hard at the lifeguard, who said something to Daddy then turned and scanned the length of the pool.

Daddy stalked back toward us. Mama stood next to Norman and glanced over the top of her sunglasses. "Dorian, sit down and don't make a scene. It's over with. Norman will be fine. Right, Norman?"

Norman nodded and gave Mama a slobbery grin.

"Letty, it's not right." Daddy paced in front of us. We could see Mrs. Hinkle pick up her things and move to the other end of the pool. The three boys followed her. Thornton turned once and smirked in our direction. Daddy shook his fist in the air. I felt confused. How could a cute boy like Thornton turn out to be so rotten?

Moments later, the lifeguards blew their whistles for everyone to get out of the pool. It was time for the ten-minute break.

"Letty, you and the girls grab our things and meet me out front. I've had it." Before he stomped off, he turned and shook Norman's hand.

Mama stared after him a moment then whipped her head around. "You girls deaf? You heard the man. Get a move on it."

About then, Norman's swim coach showed up. We said goodbye and followed Mama to the shade tree, protesting and whining as we wrapped our towels around our shoulders, our swim caps still molded to our heads. Mama made me carry Daddy's shoes. Melody clutched his dress shirt, bending once to pick up his book of matches that fell out of the chest pocket. Clover herded Tansy and Ruthie while Mama scrambled beside us, trying not to trip over the quilt she'd gathered in one fell swoop, dragging it across the wet pool deck. "Keep moving, girls. Don't look back."

As we shuffled toward the pool house, one lifeguard was climbing down from his umbrella chair and the other had his back turned, flirting with two older girls in bikinis who were handing him a snow cone.

Mrs. Hinkle had arranged herself in a chaise lounge by the deep end when we walked by. Her face was hidden behind a magazine.

Daddy scrambled up the ladder of the high dive and walked to the end of the board. No one except the lifeguards were allowed in the pool during the ten-minute break. It was against the rules.

I bumped into the back of Mama as she stopped dead in her tracks and gazed up at Daddy. She peeked from behind her sunglasses. "Lord have mercy, he's fixin' to make waves."

We stood frozen, gathered around Mama, gawking up at Daddy on the high dive. He cupped his hands around his mouth and hollered, "Hey, lady." Then he yodeled like Tarzan and bounced off the edge of the board, gripping both knees to his chest in his world-famous cannonball. The board went *boing* and he sailed through the air.

When his body hit the water, a tidal wave sloshed over the sides of the pool, splashing the row of lounge chairs lined up by the deep end. Mrs. Hinkle got drenched. So did the three boys. The snow cones they'd purchased disappeared. All that was left were the paper cones. Mrs. Hinkle threw down her magazine, screaming at the lifeguards. She pointed at the deep end where Daddy's head surfaced. "It's that awful man."

Mama hustled us through the musty pool house. The lifeguards' sharp whistles pierced the air behind us.

Out front, a hot, dry wind blew in our faces. "Get in the car," Mama ordered. We fled down the steps, breathing hard.

"Is Daddy gonna get arrested?" My chest squeezed like it might crack open. I piled in behind Tansy and Ruthie. They climbed in the third seat, squealing as they pulled off their swim caps. Stuck between Clover and Melody, I looked around, expecting to see a flashing red light in the back window.

Mama jumped in behind the steering wheel and fired up the engine.

"Holy Toledo," Melody crowed, tapping her freckled thighs. "Where did Mr. Hubbard learn to do a cannonball like that?"

Mama shoved the gearshift into reverse. "He grew up next to an old rock quarry in Indiana. They used it as a swimming hole."

Clover propped her elbow out the window. "Daddy, the cannonball champion!"

Right before Mama backed out, he came flying out of the pool house, his white legs pumping like he was running the hundred-yard dash.

The man working the counter appeared at the top of the steps.

His head swiveled back and forth, a frantic look on his face. One of the lifeguards rushed up behind him, pointing in our direction.

Daddy flung open the passenger door and jumped in. "That's the last damn time we pay to swim here. I *gar-ron-tee* you that!" He hollered out the open window and slapped the roof of the station wagon as if it would make our getaway car go faster. "Floor it, Letty! In case they call the cops."

Mama kept both hands on the wheel and cut Daddy a look. "Speed limit's thirty. Unless you wanna pay for a speeding ticket, too."

Daddy twisted his head around, his bare shoulders covered in water droplets. "That punk and his mother had it coming. Sometimes you haveta stand up to bullies. Who's got my ciggies?"

I glanced at Melody. Daddy's pack of Marlboros nested in her palms like a treasure, his shirt wadded up on her lap. "Grandma Dot says if she ever catches me smoking one of Mom's or her cigarettes, she'll cut off my fingers."

Daddy laughed and took the cigarettes as Melody fumbled for his book of matches.

After Daddy lit a cigarette, he leaned back in his seat and puffed away. Hot air blew through the open windows, sweeping out the smell of sulfur. We rode across town in silence, passing a drive-in where carhops on roller skates swooped in and out between cars.

"Can we stop and get a soda?" Tansy broke the silence from the backseat. "Ruthie and I are thirsty."

Daddy flicked his cigarette butt out the window. "There's lemonade at home."

A mangy mutt darted between cars in the opposite lane.

"Poor puppy dog." Tansy's sad voice floated past my ears. I watched her turn and look out the back window. "I hope he doesn't get run over."

Ruthie handed her a Barbie. "Don't worry, Tansy. He's tough like us."

Tansy took the doll, and she and Ruthie started playing. I

fiddled with the chin strap on my swim cap, wishing I was back at the swimming pool. Underwater, I could hide from bullies. I could pretend my legs were long and lean, like Esther Williams in the movies. Underwater, I didn't feel like *the tubby girl with yellow hair from the comics*.

A few blocks from home, Mama stopped at a red light and banged her forehead against the steering wheel. "Oh no, I think I left my library book at the pool."

Clover tapped Mama on the shoulder and held up the blue book. "Don't worry, Mama. I've got *Ethan Frome* right here. He's not going anywhere."

Daddy glanced at Mama then back at Clover. "Good thing you grabbed that book at the last second. Replacing it would've cost me a fortune."

"Poor Ethan Frome," Mama cried out, gripping the steering wheel with both hands as she waited for the light to turn green. "You're right, Clover. That poor man's not going anywhere. He's stuck in podunk Starkfield with his awful wife, Zeena, and her sweet cousin, Mattie."

Clover leaned forward and touched Mama's shoulder again. "Can I read it when you're done?"

Mama's eyes met ours in the rearview mirror. "It's not really a book for children, but . . . Oh, I don't see why not. You might as well learn about these things in a book first."

When the light turned green, she floored it.

6 THE MAKE-DO

JULY 1968

MELODY'S MOUTH FELL OPEN at the sight of her mom in a yellow minidress and white knee-high boots, standing at the counter of Pete's Pawnshop as we shuffled in the door. Edie Calloway looked equally surprised to see all of us as she cupped something in her hand.

"Well, sakes alive, what brings y'all here?" Her voice was smoky, probably from all the cigarettes Melody said her mom smokes.

Melody broke away from our group and rushed forward. "What are *you* doing here? You're supposed to be at work. What's that in your hand?"

"I'm on lunch break." Her mom played keep away as Melody tried to pry something out of her hand.

"Afternoon, Edie. How's your day going?" Mama gripped the handles of the electric skillet Daddy gave her for their anniversary and glanced around, counting heads to make sure all five of us were present. Mama wore a knee-length white cotton shift and flip-flops. Right before we left the house to run errands, she undid her ponytail and shook out her hair, letting it fall a few inches past her shoulders.

"My day's about to get better," Edie replied in an icky sweet voice. She kept trying to shoo Melody away like she was a pesky fly. Any second I feared Edie might haul off and swat her.

"Your mom looks like Lucille Ball from the television show," I told Melody in first grade after we became friends. "They both have red curly hair and cupid's bow lips."

"I know," Melody had shrugged. "But at least *Lucy* is funny. My mom's just mean."

A big fellow in denim overalls came out of a back room. He greeted Melody's mom. "Howdy, young lady. You lookin' to buy, sell, or trade?"

Melody's mom flashed him a flirty smile. "'Scuse me a moment." She turned and yanked Melody's arm. "Quit acting like a brat. I'm trying to conduct business." She turned back to Pete. "How much you reckon you'll give me for these genuine gold cufflinks? They belonged to my pop. He's been dead a few years."

"Does Grandma Dot know you took Grandpa Don's cufflinks?" Melody cut in.

Her mom gave her a sour look. "I told you to hush your mouth."

Mama winced and motioned to Melody. "Come stand next to me, honey."

Melody twisted and huffed toward us. "Grandma Dot's gonna have a conniption." Her whisper was loud enough for everyone to hear. "My mom probably took them without asking."

I reached for Melody's hand to console her. Our palms were sweaty even though a swamp cooler blew cool air from a window unit into the shop.

While we waited, we gazed around at the items on display. "Looks like they have everything from diamond rings to musical instruments," Clover said, holding Mama's purse and acting all grown-up, like she was the one shopping.

After what seemed like forever, Pete rang up the cash register and handed Melody's mom several bills. Curious, we all looked on as she counted out each bill, opened her purse and stashed the cash. Then she gave Pete a sugary smile. "Nice doing business with you, hon."

He gave her a quick nod and waited for her to leave.

I could've sworn he glanced in Melody's direction like he was thinking, *So, this is your mom, huh? Sorry, kid.*

Finally, it was Mama's turn. We stepped up to the counter.

"Looks like you've got your hands full with all these ornery boys." Pete's broad face looked so serious, but I saw a glint in his eye.

Mama chuckled and placed the skillet on the glass countertop.

"We're not *boys*," Ruthie protested, thrusting her hands on her hips.

"Yeah," Tansy agreed, twirling around in front of the counter.

Pete chuckled and pushed a bowl of hard candy across the counter at us. "You boys help yourselves. Just don't leave any wrappers on the floor."

Clover plucked a butterscotch from the bowl and popped it in her mouth. "Thank you, sir," she said, sucking the candy and talking at the same time. She stuffed the wrapper in a front pocket of her shorts.

I brushed hair out of my eyes and selected a sourball for me and one for Melody. "How come you keep calling us boys?" I eyed him shyly.

"Well, aren't y'all?" Pete winked at me, and his eyes twinkled like Santa Claus's.

Melody's mom hovered nearby, batting her fake eyelashes at Mama's electric skillet. "You tired of cookin', Letty?"

Jeez, Melody's mom sure was nosy.

Mama flung her hair back and laughed. "I'm tired of a lot of things, Edie. Let's just leave it at that."

Edie narrowed her eyes, lined with heavy black liner. She gestured at Mama's hair. "First time I've seen you with your hair down.

You should wear it that way more often." She leaned closer, keeping her voice low, but we all heard her. "You know what they say about long hair?" She winked, making a little clicking sound with her tongue. "It drives some men wild."

"Ugh." Clover grabbed her throat like she was fixing to gag.

Melody squeezed her eyes shut and shook her head. We didn't know everything yet about the birds and the bees, but Clover, Melody, and I knew enough to know when a grown-up was talking about yucky romance stuff.

Mama's face reddened. She blinked a couple of times in Edie's direction, but she didn't say anything. Her silence said it for her. Maybe Mama was thinking, *It's not like we're best friends, Edie. We hardly know each other. The only thing we have in common is our daughters.*

Edie pulled on a pair of sunglasses. "I better scoot and get back to the office." She fluttered her fingers in a half-wave and sashayed out the door, calling over her shoulder to Melody, "You behave now, you hear."

"She's always good for me," Mama sang out loud enough for Edie to hear before the door closed behind her. Melody crunched down on the sourball rolling around in her mouth. I think she was embarrassed.

Pete rubbed the back of his neck a moment. "Sorry to keep you folks waiting. Well, now, let me guess—you're looking to unload this electric skillet." He picked it up and examined it. "I assume it still works?"

Mama gave him her best closed-lip smile. "Why, sure it does. It's perfect for cooking liver and onions, smothered steak, fried chicken. But so is my big ol' frying pan." Mama smiled again. "Actually, Pete, I was hoping I could trade it for that small black typewriter displayed in the front window." Mama bit her bottom lip, looking hopeful.

Pete set the skillet down and leaned back, cupping his chin in his hand. "Good to know your old-fashioned skillet still works," he drawled. "You had me worried there a minute. I thought you were gonna try cooking up words on paper and passing them off as food instead of feeding these boys a proper meal."

Mama played right along with him. "Sure was, Pete. Haven't you ever eaten your words before?"

Pete broke into a hearty laugh. "Follow me." He moved out from behind the counter and led the way to the window display. "Here you go. It's a Remington 5, a popular model in its day. It's lightweight, but the portable case is missing. From what I can tell, it looks to be in excellent working condition."

We all gathered around Mama as Pete lifted the typewriter and set it down on a nearby table. "Oh, it's a beauty," Mama said, clasping her hands and gazing at it like it was the prettiest thing in the world.

"And it's got the number 5 on it," Clover pointed out. She held up five fingers and counted off our names: Clover, Marigold, Tansy, Ruthie, and Melody. See, Mama. It's meant to be yours."

We all giggled, caught up in the excitement.

"Go ahead, try 'er out." Pete stepped back, giving Mama room. "Ever heard 'The Typewriter' song? Think it came out in the fifties. You can still catch it on the radio once in a blue moon."

"Yes, it's a snappy tune alright. Makes you wanna get up and dance." Mama grinned and limbered her fingers. Then placing them on the keys, she bowed her head and began to type. With each clickety-clack, a steady stream of tears rolled down Mama's cheeks.

Melody snuck up and slid her arm around Mama. "Mrs. Hubbard, what's wrong?"

Mama stopped typing and gave Melody a quick hug. "Nothing, honey. I'm just so happy."

Clover opened Mama's purse and passed her a tissue. "So, you like it, huh, Mama?"

Mama took the tissue and dabbed her cheeks. "Like it?" she laughed. "Honey, I feel like I've just struck gold."

"Then it's a deal." Pete rubbed his hands together. "Looks like you've got yourself a typewriter. I'll just need to ring it up and get you a receipt. We'll call it an even trade."

Five minutes later, we walked out of the pawnshop and helped Mama load the typewriter into the front seat of the station wagon.

Pete stood at the entrance of his shop and waved. "Pleasure doing business with you. Good luck finding a desk. Don't forget to stop by that yard sale I mentioned out by the country club."

Mama honked the horn twice as we drove away. She cranked up the air conditioner and we headed north, toward Fairway Terrace and the rich side of town.

After we left the yard sale, where Mama bought a little white kidney-shaped vanity table, she hurried inside TG&Y, leaving us girls in the car with the air conditioner running. Something Daddy would never do. Five minutes later she returned with primer and blue spray paint. "Girls, I'm going to jazz up that makeup table with a fresh coat of blue paint."

Clover peeked inside the small paper bag. "What shade of blue did you get?"

Mama backed the car up and headed out. "I don't remember the name, but the lid on the spray can reminds me of the ocean and sky."

"Can we see?" Ruthie piped up from the third seat.

Clover held up the can of paint.

"That's the color of the swimming pool," I grumbled.

"Yeah," Tansy agreed. "The one we're not allowed to go back to."

Clover twisted around in her seat and shot us a sly grin. "Some of the motels in town have swimming pools. We could pretend we're guests and get in free."

"That's illegal." Mama gave her the stink eye.

Five minutes later, we pulled into the driveway. Mama cut the engine and handed Clover her purse and keys. "Sis, I need you to go unlock the house. I'll grab the typewriter."

Clover got out of the car and went to unlock the front door.

Shoving the passenger door open, I got out first, then Melody scooted past me and waited for Ruthie and Tansy to crawl over the third seat. The white kidney-shaped vanity was wedged upside down on the passenger side where Melody usually sat.

"Mama, I liked that rolltop desk better." I followed the others around to the other side to help lift the vanity out of the car. It didn't weigh much.

"Marigold, that thing cost a fortune. It was big as a buffalo and would've swallowed up my little Remington 5." Mama headed across the yard carrying her new typewriter.

Melody laughed. "And we would've needed a pickup to haul it."

Tansy flounced around and waited while Melody and I lifted it out of the car and set it down. "Mama, can me and Ruthie carry it upstairs? We promise we won't drop it."

Ruthie flexed her muscles and grinned. "Yeah, we're strong. See?"

Before she disappeared inside, Mama called over her shoulder, "Just be careful. I don't need you two falling down the stairs."

Ruthie and Tansy lifted each end and made their way across the yard.

"Watch out for the mirror," Melody warned as they lifted the table over the threshold and went inside.

Melody and I grabbed the cans of primer and spray paint and locked up the car. We were singing "Skip to My Lou," as we pranced into the house and headed up the stairs.

"Set the vanity here in front of the window," Mama directed Ruthie and Tansy.

Mama placed the typewriter in the center and stood back to admire everything. "Oh, this is perfect," she sighed.

Natural light flooded the small nook at the top of the stairs.

"Girls, Miss Mavis once told me about a famous writer named Virginia Woolf. She grew up in a fancy part of London and was known for saying, 'A woman must have money and a room of her own if she is to write fiction.'" Mama paused and motioned for all of us to come closer. "As you girls know, I don't have much money, and I don't plan to write fiction anytime soon. But what I do have is my imagination. And let me tell you—" She looked each of us square in the eye and added with determination in her voice, "I'm gonna make do with this banged-up old makeup stand I'm fixing to paint blue. Because Lord knows I've been making do my whole life."

As we turned to leave Mama alone at the top of the stairs, rays of sunshine shimmered on the walls and floor around her. She kicked off her flip-flops and danced around. "I've got it," she shouted with glee. "I'm naming my new desk, the Make-Do!"

Two days later, after the blue paint had dried on the Make-Do and Mama had everything set up in front of the window that overlooked our backyard, I paused in front of Mama's Remington 5 and ran my fingers over the keys. I didn't press down on any of them for fear Mama would hear me and I'd get a scolding. This was her sacred place now, and we girls understood not to bother Mama's things.

But I couldn't help myself. Something about her new typewriter machine teased at my fingertips. As I studied each letter of the alphabet, a magical thing happened. I gulped when I realized the top row contained all the letters that spelled out the word *typewriter*.

Magic had entered our home, and Mama had invited it in.

7 SUGAR BEET BAKERY AND BOOKS

OCTOBER 2017

I PULL UP IN front of Clover's shop at Fourth and Main and cut the engine. Gazing up at the sign, I recall the first time Clover made the grand announcement that she was opening a combination bookstore and bakery named after an ugly taproot: "You can't always judge a book by its cover. Sometimes the sweetest stories are found inside plain wrappers. Take the humble sugar beet, for instance. There's nothing beautiful about its outward appearance. But once it's refined, it produces the sweetest flavor."

We'd gone to school with kids whose dads were sugar beet farmers. Sugar Beet Road east of town served as our dusty lover's lane for high schoolers. Once they'd crossed the railroad tracks, kids parked along the sides of irrigation ditches to smoke dope, drink beer, make out.

Tapping the keyboard on my phone, I send Clover a text: *Hey, sis, look out front.* I end it with our secret code: *Swish, swish!*

A new banner over the double doors catches my eye: WE DON'T BAN BOOKS HERE. If you can't find what you're looking for, we'll try to order it for you.

Seconds later, a door flies open in a flurry of purples and pinks and seafoam greens. I can't tell where her tinted waterfall locks end and her chiffon duster begins, but hair and fabric blend and flutter behind her like a mermaid tail.

"The Book Woman of Sandhill," I say with pride and gape at her through the windshield, admiring her courage to make a statement with her unconventional style.

"Marigold!" She moves toward me, her voice husky like mine. We Hubbard girls were born with deep, throaty voices, grown hardier over the years, as if every sound that emerges from our windpipes has come from a place of endurance. The blue-and-white-striped awning over the beveled glass doors flaps in the October breeze. "Daddy know you're in town yet? News travels fast in Sandhill." She towers over me, big boned and bossy, and envelopes me in a bear hug.

"I'll text him later." My voice is muffled in layers of fabric as I return her hug. "He called me last night when I was getting settled in my room. I let it go to voicemail. I know, I know . . . I'm a terrible daughter. He says he has something he wants to give me."

She pulls away, holding me at arm's length. "Oh?" Her green eyes are huge behind the lenses of her zebra-striped reading glasses. "I wonder what *that* could be. He hasn't said anything to *me* about it." There's the rub, ever so subtle. I'm the sister who left. She's the sister who stayed. Therefore, she should know everything going on in Daddy's life. Tansy can be forgiven for moving away; she's the baby.

"Maybe he wants to give me the Edsel," I joke, turning to retrieve my tote bag and diffuse the tension that sometimes prickles between us.

"Ah, the green hornet. I always hated that car. Nah, he finally sold it a few months ago to some collector out in West Texas." She tosses her hair back and moves for the door, a flamboyant battleship of a woman sailing into home port. A far cry from the tall gangly teenager who drove the getaway car the night we fled the motel pool after the manager caught us swimming and told us to leave.

I glance up and down Main Street. Not much has changed over the decades. The Llano Hotel with its 1930 art deco design stretches ten stories into the azure sky, and the morning sun causes the straw-colored brick to glow. The refurbished hotel is still the tallest building in town, offering affordable housing on the one hand, while renting out the glamourous ballroom on the top floor with a balcony overlooking Main Street.

Clover ushers me inside. The aroma of baked goods and new and old books awakens my senses, accompanied by the smell of freshly brewed coffee. I hesitate momentarily, glancing around, overcome by the sight of a special display of books, their covers faced out, baring the one name that still has the magnetism to pull me across a crowded room: Sawyer Allen Wallace.

I step forward and brush my fingers over a dozen hardcover titles.

Clover hovers nearby. "He's still one of my top sellers, you know. Been gone over a year. I swear his popularity keeps growing."

I swallow, nodding appreciatively. "That rascal," I blurt, half laughing, half crying as I reach for a tissue in my bag, embarrassed by the sudden avalanche of snot flowing from my nose.

My sister pats me on the arm. "I remember the first time I met him, back when he had long hair. Y'all came riding up on his Harley. I thought to myself: Here comes trouble."

Dabbing my nose, I wad the tissue and toss it in a trashcan by the front counter. Spotting a bottle of hand sanitizer Clover keeps by the register, I pump out a dollop and work it into my palms. "I'll never forget the first time I saw him. I was standing out front of the newspaper office with another reporter. I'd only been in town a week, and she was showing me the ropes. We were fixin' to jaywalk when this good-lookin' guy with a smartass grin came rumbling by on his Harley. Lord have mercy, I about fell off the curb."

"Good ol' Saw." Clover grins coyly, using his nickname. "Didn't he circle the block for a second pass and rev his engine?"

"Lord, yes. I waved like a damn fool. And then I said, 'Who in the world is that? I don't care if he just robbed a bank. I want an introduction.' My coworker laughed and said, 'Oh, honey. He's no outlaw. That's Sawyer Wallace. The new lawyer in town. I hear he's single.'"

I glance at my sister, catching a glint in those mischievous eyes, and I know what's coming.

"And a week later you were riding his hog." She elbows me and we burst out laughing like teenagers.

There are some things you can only share with a sister, and during these private moments, sibling rivalry takes a hiatus. As close as I am with my daughter, the last thing Libby wants to hear is how her daddy and I went for a ride and made love by a mountain stream in the Manzano Mountains near Moriarty less than a week after Sawyer made that first pass on his motorcycle.

That day we unwrapped each other like candy bars, physically and spiritually. He told me his dream was to become a writer. I told him about Melody. Over the years, as time began to play havoc and our bodies began to break down in all those places you take for granted in youth, our minds were supple and strong, the glue that held us together.

Clover and I are still cutting up, me doubled over with laughter when an older woman with dark bags under her eyes enters the shop and calls out good-naturedly, "Whoo-hoo. Hope I'm not interrupting anything?"

Blushing, I busy myself and pick up one of Sawyer's books. I stare at his jacket photo, the one he called his mugshot. "You criminal," I mouth at his rakish grin, cropped hair slicked straight back, his left eye squinting beneath his widow's peak as if he's sizing somebody up.

After Clover greets the newcomer, the woman says, "I'm looking for the latest novel by that handsome fella who died recently. Oh, what was his name?" She slaps her forehead. "Oh, why can't I remember? He reminds me of Sam Shepard. Poor fella, he's gone now, too."

I freeze, slowly setting down the book. Glancing sideways, I give Clover the evil eye. *Don't even think about ratting me out as Sawyer's widow.*

Clover steers the woman toward the display. "Would this be the author you're looking for?"

The woman clasps her hands together and looks heavenward before picking up a book. "That's him. Sawyer Allen Wallace."

Clover says some nicety then excuses herself and steps toward me. She flicks her head in the direction of the bakery and lowers her voice. "Why don't you grab some coffee and something to eat?"

Nodding, I try to avoid looking at the woman swooning over Sawyer's photo before she flips to the front of the book. I start to giggle and head into the bakery.

Clover catches up with me. "Let me know if you head out to Daddy's place. I'll have Juanita put together a goodie bag."

Overcome with a mixture of mirth and sorrow, I feel my sassy side emerge. "How 'bout a jug of ice water and a box of saltines, for old time's sake."

Clover scrunches her face. "Daddy's version of a picnic on those outings when Mama stayed home. At least the water was cold."

She rushes off to check on something in the children's section. I let my eyes feast on the glass cases filled with a variety of pastries, pies, cookies, cakes, and specialty breads. One whole shelf is devoted to gluten- and sugar-free versions.

I greet Juanita and introduce myself. After I learn she moved here from South Texas six months ago, I compliment her on her beautiful nails painted a brilliant turquoise.

"Gracias, Marigold." She smiles shyly, a small, pretty woman pushing seventy. "I get them done once a month. After raising a mess of kids and two husbands, it's the one thing I do for myself."

"Good for you," I say, catching her sense of humor. "Did Clover mention this side of the shop used to be the old Sutter's Bakery?"

"Sí, she sure did. She told me your friend's mom used to work here a long time ago." She smiles politely and waits for me to order.

"Ruthie's a pilot. Her mom, Carmen, made these elaborate wedding cakes. Sometimes she brought home mistakes and we pigged out on sunken cake and icing."

Juanita's smile is patient but nervous. She wrings her hands with those beautiful nails. "Are you ready to order?"

It takes me a second to realize she's not used to standing around making small talk, especially with her boss's sister.

I order quickly and glance around while Juanita preps my food. It's about nine-thirty in the morning. A handful of women are gathered around a table near the back, munching on pastries and caught up in a lively discussion. Their voices carry across the room. A book club, I assume, as one gal opens a book and begins reading a passage aloud. I can't hear what she's saying, but I'm intrigued. I love to see people discussing books, especially here in my dusty hometown where it all began.

After I pay for a banana, a coffee, and a blueberry bran muffin, I leave Juanita a generous tip and spot a bistro table by the window and park my things. Today's coffee is snickerdoodle. As I savor the rich blend of sugar, cinnamon, and smooth chocolate, I kick off my clogs and avert my eyes as the old lady who'd just purchased Sawyer's book passes by my window out on the sidewalk. Is it my imagination, or have the bags under her droopy eyes faded and is her face lifted toward the morning sunshine?

Closing my eyes, I feel Sawyer close to me, seated directly across the table, his long legs stretched out in front of him and crossed at the ankles. "Mari, honey," he says, grinning at me over his mug. "This is the life. You and me hanging out in your sister's bookstore. Just two overgrown kids sipping cookies out of a cup."

My eyes flutter open. My tote bag is stashed in the opposite chair where moments ago Sawyer appeared. I swallow against the tightness in my throat. A little over a year ago he'd been here signing books, charming readers young and old. They'd come from all over eastern New Mexico and West Texas. He had a huge fan base. His backlist never grew stale. With every new title released, the demand for his books grew.

And then he was gone in an instant, leaving his next story unwritten. But his last words to me linger. They're not going anywhere: *Write the story that's been holding you hostage as long as I've known you.*

After I polish off my muffin, I stash the banana in my bag, brush crumbs from the table, slide back into my clogs, and meander through the tables to show Clover the photograph I'd taken at the church.

When she has a free moment, I catch her before she dashes off to wait on another customer. "Sis, you got a sec?"

"You texted Daddy yet?"

Irritated by her needling, I glance around at the rows of hardcover and trade paperbacks and ignore her question. Somewhere on those shelves are several books I've ghosted. I'm proud of my work, but I'm no longer driven to write for hire.

"I stopped by the old church on my way into town yesterday. I made myself go inside. First time in forty years."

Clover flinches, her chest rising and falling. "I haven't been inside that place since I don't know when."

"Sawyer and I stopped by there once right after we got married. We were on a road trip on the Harley. He wanted to go inside and look around. I told him to go on without me. I walked over to the graveyard instead. For some reason, I found it easier to stare at her name on a headstone than face the memories inside the church."

"I've thought about stopping by whenever I head to Albuquerque or Santa Fe." Clover shrugs. "But you know, sometimes it's easier to keep driving. Better to remember the good times we had . . ."

I scratch behind my ear. "The walls are plastered in graffiti. Even more now than when we were kids. Hardly any blank space left. Remember the time Daddy had a conniption fit when Melody went to write her name on the wall?"

Clover snorts. "What a hypocrite. He said it was still a house of worship, by God, and we damn sure better respect it."

"I took this photo yesterday." I hand Clover my phone. "It's by the front entrance." I start to tell her about hearing the lonely strains of a flute but change my mind. Some things I've learned to keep private. "This is Melody's handwriting. No doubt about it."

We both stare at the image on my cell phone:

> I knew right then this wasn't how most moms and dads acted
> in our hometown . . .
> SOMEONE
> PLEASE
> HELP
> ME!!♫

Rubbing her thick upper arms, Clover leans in for a closer look. "How can you be sure these are Melody's words? You said there's graffiti everywhere."

I jut my chin at the image. "The musical notes. Dead giveaway. Half the time she signed her name using nothing but this symbol. And it's in the same spot where Daddy wouldn't let her write her name."

Clover cants her head, breathing heavier. She takes my phone, stares at it, then hands it back. "So, you're saying she stopped by the old church on her way to the Blue Hole?"

Nodding, I explain my theory. "She never showed up for band practice that day. It wasn't like her to ditch class, especially band. I'd seen her that morning at school, but of course by then we weren't speaking. Something must've set her off that day, and she went to two of the places that represented happier times. Places when we were all together, before everything fell apart."

"She probably had another fight with her mom, *Homewrecker Edie*."

"Maybe . . ." I drop my phone in my bag and glance at a shelf of books. "Or maybe something happened between her and Daddy."

I thought about the line I'd written sometime in the wee hours of the morning: "We can share my daddy." Oh, if I'd only known what I was offering back then. But I was only eight years old. And all I wanted was for my best friend to be happy.

Clover groans. "Let it go, Marigold. Why bring it up now? Daddy's so frail. What's the point?"

I breathe deeply, gaze up at the ceiling, and gather the courage to divulge why I'm in town. "So, I'm not here to pay a social visit." My voice tapers off as my throat goes dry and I swallow, trying to find my words. I'm fully expecting her complete disapproval, her resistance.

She waits, beads of sweat breaking out on her wide forehead. "What are you up to, Marigold?"

Here it comes. "I'm in town to research the book I've been meaning to write since Melody died."

Her lips part. She blinks at me a couple of times but says nothing. She doesn't have to. Her reaction is written all over her face like oversized font in a large print book: *You'll be airing the dirty laundry if you write about our family. I live in this town; you don't!*

At this moment, I'd give anything to look up and see Sawyer swagger in the door. Clover always had a soft spot for him, maybe even a secret crush. He'd sidle up next to her, drape one arm over her shoulder, and say, "Clover, honey, you're the bookseller, the champion of authors everywhere."

Then he'd turn and give me a cockeyed grin: *Since when have you been afraid of pushback?*

"I'm here to find the truth, sis. For all of us." I refuse to be intimidated even if I've put her in a bind.

For a moment the walls of books close in around me.

Removing her eyeglasses, she massages her temples and glances around, squinting as if her head hurts. "I need to get back to work." After a young employee and an older gentleman stroll by and stop in front of a section marked Southwest Books, Clover slides on her glasses and peers at something over my shoulder. "Close your eyes. I have something to show you. Don't open until I say so."

"You gonna lock me in a closet?" I joke, remembering the pranks we played as kids.

"Shut up and walk. Remember, no peeking." Her hands on my shoulders, she guides me through the shop. "Okay, open your eyes."

My scalp tingles as I stare at the kidney-shaped vanity table tucked away in a nook at the back of the shop. The vintage Remington 5 typewriter, diminutive like Mama, sits in the center.

"Mama's Make-Do!" I blurt, momentarily forgetting customers are milling about as I rush forward, giddy and fueled with joy. "Her letter-writing table. I haven't seen it since she died." I pull up a chair and sit down. My fingers brush over the familiar surface of the makeup vanity Mama converted into a desk.

Clover joins me, her hands braced on the back of my chair. "I hauled it out of the shed recently and decided to bring it to the shop. The typewriter needs to be restored, but it sure looks pretty sitting here. I thought if I pass by it every day, it might inspire me to finally sit down and write the great American novel. Fat chance of that happening."

"Mama could've written books, but she lacked the confidence," I say, eyeing my sister in the small round mirror clamped to the back of the former vanity table.

"Like *me*." Clover's voice is gruff as the secret spills between us. In high school, Clover's English teachers assumed she'd grow up to become a writer since she always had her nose in a book. Not me back then, the slow reader flipping through picture books long after Melody had caught up with Clover in devouring chapter books. Me, the girl who flunked spelling tests while Clover won spelling bees.

Our eyes lock on each other. "You're a bookseller, sis. You serve a need in this community." I look away first and run my hands up and down the spindly legs of the old vanity. The paint is chipped in places where Mama spray-painted it blue.

Clover watches me and lets out a heavy sigh that tickles the top of my head. "Didn't Mama buy it off that old boy who used to run the junk shop next to the icehouse?"

Shaking my head, I help my sister remember. Being this close in age, we are each other's memories. "Nah, remember, it came from a yard sale out by the country club. We drove straight there after we left Pete's Pawnshop where she traded the electric skillet for the typewriter."

Clover nods, tilting her head. "Some of the details are fuzzy now, but I do recall how giddy she was after she set the typewriter on the vanity and danced around. Didn't she bring up Virginia Woolf?"

"She sure did," I say. "At first, all we girls saw was a banged-up makeup stand. But not Mama. She saw possibilities."

Clover gazes at me in the mirror. "By Mama calling her desk the Make-Do, she claimed it as her own. She made it matter."

I nod and continue to study us, two middle-aged women with square faces that give the appearance of strength. Me in my plastic tortoiseshell eye frames, Clover in her black-and-white-striped frames reminding me of her first Barbie doll's one-piece swimsuit. Clover's face is puffier with age, but she disguises it with the right blend of makeup topped off by a crowning mane of righteous color. My shoulder-length hair has turned brassy—I'm overdue at the salon—and my makeup skills are lacking compared to Clover. Most days I haphazardly brush on mascara and hurriedly line my lips, often coloring outside the lines.

We stare at each other until I break the silence. "Mama didn't always feel like she mattered. Remember that time she walked up to Dorothea Lange's photograph, *Migrant Mother*, and started crying?"

Clover's coffee breath blows across the nape of my neck, but I don't mind. "She finally told us years later that she used to see herself in that image, especially right after Tansy was born. Back then Mama had three little girls and nowhere to go. Once Ruthie moved across the street and you and Melody became friends, Mama turned around and made room for two more."

I rest my chin in my palm and remember that moment. "You know what I think. I think Mama was the smartest person in the library that day. Because shortly after she had her little crying jag, Miss Mavis began to dote on her. She was always suggesting titles for Mama to read. She never got tired of answering Mama's questions about books and authors. Mama was getting her education before she ever went to college."

Clover reaches past my shoulder and touches a metal mermaid sculpture mounted on a narrow piece of driftwood painted to resemble a set of railroad tracks. "*The Rail Swimmer.*"

I stare at the crude sculpture Mama made when she went back to school. "Mama based her on the story she made up when she took us to Santa Rosa that time."

A low chuckle erupts from my sister's throat. "We were so gullible back then, wanting to believe everything Mama told us, especially Melody. Mama was always seeing things that weren't there."

I gaze at the mermaid suspended on a metal spike about six inches above the driftwood. "Mama also referred to her as *Our Lady of Hope*."

"Yup, and we weren't even Catholic." Clover's dry chuckle hangs in the air.

Swiveling around, I gaze at my sister. "Mama was always making up stories. Remember the day she dreamed up the name for our club? It hadn't rained in months. It was hotter than blue blazes and dry as a bone . . ."

Clover runs her fingers through my hair like when we were kids. "Mama was reading Eudora Welty."

I lean my head back against my sister's soft middle, both of us carried away on a cloud of memory. "And then Mama heard that train whistle . . ."

We sigh in unison, then Clover says, "Be right back. I've got something for you." She returns moments later and places a large brown envelope in my hands. It's old, velvety to the touch, but still intact. "It's been locked in my safe."

I clasp the familiar envelope against my chest and try not to blubber. "Mama's letters. I'm so glad she saved them."

"Me, too, sissy." Clover takes a deep breath then nudges me with a playful push and swishes off to work on the shop's weekly newsletter and update social media. She hasn't gone far when she stops abruptly and calls over her shoulder. "You got your laptop with you?"

I look up from peeking inside the envelope and pat the side of my tote bag propped at my feet like a loyal dog. "My trusty laptop never goes anywhere without me."

"Set up shop here. I'll let my employees know not to let anyone bother you. It's time you put Letty Hubbard's Make-Do back to work." Clover is a force as she glides across her sacred shop, surrounded by a sanctuary of books.

"Mama would've loved this place," I call softly. Turning, I slide open the shallow drawer and place the envelope inside. Then, like a priest handling the elements, I pick up Mama's sweet little Remington 5 with reverence and place it to the side, careful not to disturb Mama's artwork.

Facing the mirror, I see a gap-toothed Letty Hubbard gaze back at me. She bites her bottom lip and timidly places her quivering fingertips on her pawnshop typewriter.

Shrugging out of my cardigan, I reach for my laptop and place it on the Make-Do. "This is for you, Mama," I say, and tap myself to the backyard on Vista Boulevard.

8 CALLING OF THE MERMAIDS

AUGUST 1968

WATER SHOT OUT LIKE a geyser—a rare sight. I couldn't believe it was happening in our backyard. Daddy was still at work. Early that afternoon, right after we finished helping Mama pin clothes on the line, she had an idea. She said it was as if Eudora Welty was speaking directly to her through one of her short stories. Mama said Miss Welty had practically given her permission to break one of Daddy's biggest rules. But she needed us girls to help her carry it out. Once broken, there was no going back.

And to think, it all started with a book Mama had checked out from the public library.

Mama's long slender legs were bent at an angle, her bare calves and feet pale under the blotches of sunlight streaming through the leaves of the sycamore tree. The tree must've been a hundred years old, its shade partially covering the back steps where Mama sat reading. In her worn pedal pushers and sleeveless top, she straightened her back and placed the book on her lap.

Lifting her hands, she pressed her pointer fingers together, then her thumbs, and formed a rectangle reminding me of the picture frames we made with popsicle sticks at Vacation Bible School. Her arms bent at her elbows, she peered through the opening.

Melody and I giggled at the way Mama twisted her mouth this way and that, squeezing one eye shut then the other.

"You look like Popeye the Sailor Man," Melody laughed, swishing one end of her pigtail against her freckled face.

Slowly, Mama turned and popped both eyes open. "I'm pretending I'm a young girl in one of Eudora Welty's stories."

Clover peeked beneath the rim of her floppy sailor hat, placing her own library book face down on her chest. "Eudora Welty's that famous writer you like, right, Mama?"

Mama nodded, swiveling her head. "Yes, Miss Mavis suggested I get acquainted with Miss Welty's work."

"Miss Mavis is your favorite librarian, isn't she?" Clover added. "I like how she's always suggesting books for you to read."

Mama smiled. "Yes, and according to Miss Mavis, Eudora Welty lives in a fancy house in Jackson, Mississippi, and comes from a real good family."

I glanced at my two sisters. We wore secondhand play clothes. Nothing matched. "Do we come from a good family?" My words snuck out of me, rough and teeny.

Mama paused, her face softening behind her hands. "We're working on it. We go to church mostly. We're good people." She bit her bottom lip and squared her shoulders.

But we're not rich, I thought, wondering if you had to be rich to come from a good family.

"But what's the girl doing?" Clover asked, gesturing with her hands and imitating Mama.

"She's at a park, people watching. I guess she can get a better look by peeking through her little finger frame. She's sunbathing on a sandy beach after swimming in a lake that sparkles like diamonds."

"She got to go *swimming*?" I cut in again, the back of my shirt stuck to my sweaty body as Melody and I swayed in the green metal glider that came with the house.

Melody cupped her chin in her hand. "Did it really sparkle like diamonds?"

Mama dipped her head in Melody's direction. "It didn't exactly say that. But I can sure imagine it, can't you? A pretty little lake at a lovely park with grass and trees."

Melody and I nodded, our mouths hanging open.

Tansy and Ruthie were walking the rim of our old fountain, the basin full of nothing but brittle leaves. Ruthie, with her wiry gymnast body, and Tansy, light as a ballerina, were pretending to be tightrope walkers a hundred feet in the air. They looked over and saw Mama and came running. After a few seconds, we were all imitating Mama and making picture frames with our fingers.

When I peeked through my rectangle, I fantasized that I was looking at a lake like the one Mama read about, not the dry fountain baking under the New Mexico sun.

"What's the girl's name?" Melody squeezed her hands tight like she was peeking through a telescope.

"Doesn't say, but she's thinking about stuff."

"Like what?" Clover asked. "How old is she?"

"I don't rightly know yet." Mama dropped her hands in her lap and picked up the book. "I've only read a few lines."

I sighed, jealous of the girl in the story. "Mama, it's so hot. Why can't we go to the pool one last time before school starts?" I scooted out of the glider, the back of my damp thighs making sucking noises against the metal. I hoped Melody didn't think I tooted. Standing in front of Mama, I gripped my hands in prayer and begged with sad eyes. "It's not fair we're stuck in a backyard with ugly patches of Bermuda as yellow as hay 'cause Daddy's stingy with water. Even Mrs. Sanchez's grass is still green."

"As green as the green in my name," Clover caroled, leaning out of her chair to poke me.

I pushed her away and continued to pester Mama.

She turned a page in her book and refused to look at me. "You heard what your Daddy said, Marigold. You know the rules."

"Well, they're dumb rules." I crossed my arms and stomped off. I could smell the stink rising from my armpits. Mama still hadn't bought me or Clover any deodorant. She said she was waiting for it to go on sale. Her eyes drilled a hole straight through my heart when I turned my back on her.

"We can do a rain dance like the Indians when they need water for crops." Melody's hopeful voice clutched at my heart and stopped me midstride. "If it rains long enough, the fountain will fill up and we can splash in the water," she added.

I glared at the sky. "But there's not a cloud in sight."

About then, Mama stood up. The library book slid from her lap and hit the step with a thud. She stared at the sky. I couldn't tell if she was sniffing for rain or listening for some distant rumble of thunder way out beyond Sandhill.

Glancing first at the fountain then sideways at me, she tapped the tip of her nose with her pointer finger like she was thinking hard. After a moment she began to give orders. "Clover, run to the alley and get the trash can and set it on the patio. Marigold, you and Melody run next door and ask Mrs. Sanchez if we can borrow an extra broom and rake. Tansy and Ruthie, come help me make a pitcher of iced tea. We're going to need it."

Before any of us could ask why, Mama reached down and picked up her book. "Girls, we have Miss Eudora Welty to thank for writing her short story 'The Memory.' It's in this collection, *A Curtain of Green*." Mama held up the book, giving it a shake. "Because I was reading about a girl at a lake, which sparked an idea. But we'll have to hurry before Daddy gets home."

Clover was halfway across the yard, headed for the alley. "What's your idea?"

Mama flicked her head in the direction of the fountain. "You'll see." A wry smile lifted the corners of her mouth. "Sometimes you have to make do with what you have." With that, she turned and went inside the double French doors, Tansy and Ruthie trailing closely behind.

An hour later, I gripped the extra broom we'd borrowed from Mrs. Sanchez and swept twigs off our dark red patio missing a few bricks. "Mama says fancy people used to live here." We'd all pitched in and scooped dead leaves and trash from the basin of the backyard fountain. We were nearly done.

Clover dropped her broom on the ground, picked up her book from the metal lawn chair, and sat down in the shade. "That was a long time ago, Marigold. Back when people drove Model Ts and some still rode horses in town."

Melody hopscotched from brick to brick. Her pigtails bounced each time she jumped. "You think a horse ever drank out of y'all's fountain?" She licked the dried chocolate mustache above her lip, left over from one of Mrs. Sanchez's homemade fudgesicles.

"Maybe," I laughed, picturing a horse trotting up to get a drink. "Daddy says the man who lived here was a rich doctor. He probably drove a Model T."

Melody plopped down in the other metal lawn chair next to Clover. "Maybe he was a cowboy *and* a doctor, like you see on TV. Yup, I bet he rode a horse."

Clover blew damp bangs off her sweaty forehead and squinted at us. "He *definitely* wasn't a cowboy, and he didn't ride a horse."

Melody gave Clover a dirty look. "How do you know? Have you ever seen him?"

I leaned on my broom and stuck my hand on my hip. "Mama said he died a long time ago."

Clover made a spooky face and wiggled witchy fingers at us. "Maybe I've seen his ghost."

Invisible feet walked up my back. "Stop it, Clover." My teeth began to chatter despite the heat.

Melody nabbed Clover in the arm. "Jeez. Cut it out." She crossed her arms and stuck her nose in the air. "There's no such thing as ghosts."

Clover shrugged and went back to reading her book.

Clutching the broom handle, I tried to shake off the heebie-jeebies.

Melody motioned at something over my shoulder. I twisted around, half-expecting to see an old-timey doctor climbing down from his horse and walking toward us carrying his black medicine bag. Instead, I gazed at the fountain at the edge of our patio. Tansy and Ruthie had dragged the garden hose across the yard and were taking turns filling the basin. It was ten feet across and two feet deep.

As I watched them work, I remembered how Mama told them they had the most important job: to deliver the water. I could smell it, a clean refreshing scent washing over me. Thinking about it made me feel cooler. I didn't notice the stinging heat that radiated like the red coils in the wall heater in our upstairs bathroom.

"You guys are lucky," Melody said. "How many people in Sandhill have one of those in their backyard? Grandma Dot says we're lucky to have a roof over our heads."

Clover looked up from reading. "Yeah, but the sprayer in the middle is broken. Daddy says we don't have the money to fix it."

About then, Mama stepped outside and came down the back steps with the laundry basket. She was wearing her special apron with pockets to collect the wooden clothespins. Mama said lazy people left pins on the line. I didn't tell her I'd seen pins left on the line at Melody's house, and there was nothing lazy about Grandma Dot.

As I gazed again at Tansy and Ruthie, my mind flashed to a fountain on the other side of Sandhill. The one we drove past when we went to look at rich people's houses at Christmastime. "Our fountain's almost as nice as the one in front of the country club."

Melody picked at a scab on her knee. "Grandma Dot used to work there. One summer when I was five, she took me to work with her every day. While she waited tables, I sat in the dining room and colored and read books and stared out a window at rich kids swimming and eating snow cones all day."

A yucky feeling quivered inside me. "They didn't let you go swimming, even though your grandma worked there?" I heard my voice tremble in my chest.

"You had to be a member," Melody sniffed, thumbing her nose.

Mama stopped in front of us, plunking the empty basket at our feet. "It cost money, like everything else." Straightening, she stretched her back and gazed toward the squeals of laughter coming from the fountain. "Ruthie," Mama bellowed to get her attention, "what did you say the fountain looked like the first time you saw it?"

Ruthie raised the end of the hose in the air. "A giant wedding cake, like the ones Mommy bakes at work." She grinned at Mama as an arch of water shot out the end of the hose like a silver rainbow and splashed into the fountain.

Mama picked up the basket. "You girls should start your own club. One that doesn't cost money to join."

"You mean like a secret club, Mrs. Hubbard?" Melody sprang to her feet, making goo-goo eyes at Mama.

"What should we call it?" Clover put her book down and pushed up from the chair.

"Let me think about it. In the meantime, come help me take clothes off the line. Sometimes the best ideas come when you're not thinking too hard."

While we helped Mama, we took turns keeping an eye on the two younger girls, making sure more water went into the fountain than into the yard. I couldn't wait to get wet. We didn't change into swimsuits since Melody and Ruthie didn't bring theirs. Mama said she was proud of us for showing *solidarity*. What a big word. I counted all five syllables with my fingers. Mama said it meant sticking together.

She hummed and made small talk, her hands plucking clothes off the line like two small birds, quick and graceful. I buried my face in a clean sheet, still warm from the sun. When I looked up, Clover stood inches from my face. She had a clothespin stuck on the end of her nose. "Do I sound like Miss Mavis when I talk?"

I burst out laughing. Every time we visited the library, Miss Mavis sounded like she suffered from a permanent cold. Melody unclipped one of Mama's bras and stuffed a sock in each cup before stretching it across her flat chest. We laughed so hard my cheeks hurt. Mama laughed, too, but her cheeks turned red.

Then her head snapped up. We all turned to see Tansy shaking her hiney and waving her arms in the air, daring Ruthie to spray her.

Tansy of the webbed toes, *our little Aquarius*.

Ruthie dropped the end of the hose in the fountain and wiggled her hiney, too. She fluttered her thin brown arms in the air, and she and Tansy danced around the fountain, singing, and carrying on.

A moment later, something caught Mama's attention. She canted her head, listening hard over the happy sounds coming from the fountain. *What is it, Mama?* I thought. *Are you listening for thunder again or the sound of Daddy's green Edsel pulling in the driveway?*

Then I heard it. A train whistle far off in the distance. A passenger or freight train as it barreled down the tracks toward Sandhill. A few seconds later another whistle pierced the air. Then another.

Mama stood rigid, her hands in the pockets of her apron where she'd dropped more clothespins. "Can you hear them?" she asked softly. "They're calling to each other across Llano County. Across the whole blasted state of New Mexico."

"Who's calling, Mama?" Clover removed the clothespin from her nose.

"The other mermaids," Mama said. We'd never heard her sound so dreamy. "They whistle, like a train. Millions of years ago, this land was covered by an ocean. Now all those mermaids are trapped. New Mexico is a *landlocked* state. We don't border any large bodies of water."

"Landlocked." I repeated the word a couple of times, counting each syllable with my fingers. "Did you read that in one of your books?"

"Geography." Another whistle caught her attention. She glanced at Tansy and Ruthie then back in the direction of the last whistle.

"What are they saying?" Melody asked, dropping Mama's bra in the laundry basket.

"'Let it rain. Let it rain.' They've been taking lessons from the Indians." Mama paused and winked at Melody. "Because if it rains long enough and fills up all the dry arroyos, all those ancient mermaids can find their way to the rivers and streams and swim back to the ocean."

From the corner of my eye, I saw Melody cross her eyes and fingers like she was making a wish.

"Maybe we're all mermaids living too far from the ocean." Mama laughed and threw her head back. Her face glowed in the sunlight.

Right then, I got a glimpse of what felt like magic bubbling up out of her through the gap in her teeth. Then she thrust her arms skyward and shook her hiney. "I've got it, girls. Y'all can call yourselves 'The Llano County Mermaid Club.'"

We left the laundry basket under the empty clothesline and followed Mama to the fountain. Waving our arms in the air, we swished our imaginary tails, and chanted our club's new name.

"What's all this?" Daddy's voice thundered from the back door. Removing his fedora, he held it to his chest and came down the steps. He looked like one of those men in the Sears catalog. A cigarette dangled from the corner of his mouth, the ash growing longer by the second. His blue eyes narrowed, turning the color of water that gushed from the end of the hose propped over the edge of the fountain.

"Don't be such a sourpuss!" Mama reached into the fountain and flicked water in Daddy's direction. "The girls and I are having fun, Dorian. Don't ruin it."

I sat next to Mama on the edge of the fountain, my fingers making ripples in the water. I held my breath in case Daddy lost his temper.

Melody charged across the patio and threw herself at him. "Mr.

Hubbard. Come see our mermaid pool." The force of her thin body knocked Daddy off balance. He stumbled back as ash fell from the end of his cigarette, barely missing the top of Melody's head.

After he regained his balance, he took one final puff of his cigarette and stomped it into the ground. The scowl on his handsome face slowly disappeared. Then he slung his right arm around Melody and gave her an awkward hug.

I saw the way she beamed up at him, like Daddy was the nicest man in the world. Up to her knees in water, Clover hugged the concrete pedestal that rose from the middle where water was supposed to spray out.

Tansy skipped over, stole Daddy's hat, and plopped it on her head. She and Melody took him by the hands and led him across the patio. As they approached the fountain, Ruthie picked up the end of the garden hose and squeezed her thumb over the nozzle. A geyser shot up in the air, raining pearls of water everywhere, including on Daddy's dress shoes.

Then Tansy, our little water bear, began to twirl around him.

9 MAMA'S LETTER TO EUDORA

AUGUST 1968

THE NEXT DAY, WHILE Daddy was still at work, Mama let us play in the fountain and take turns squirting each other with the water hose. Melody and Ruthie had worn their swimsuits under their playclothes when they showed up right after lunch. Even though Mama had dabbed suntan lotion on us, we all got sunburned except Ruthie.

Hot and sweaty, and still in our damp swimsuits, we plopped down at the kitchen table and waited as Mama doled out store-brand graham crackers and filled our metal tumblers with cold chocolate milk. She acted all cheerful, as if she was some happy mom in a television commercial.

"Girls, this is the best chocolate milk you'll ever taste. I added a secret ingredient along with the Nestlé's Quik!"

"We know," Tansy sighed dramatically. "You added *love*."

"It tastes almost as good as the chocolate milk in the school cafeteria," Melody lied, licking her lips as she tried to butter up Mama.

Ruthie dipped her fingertip into her milk then pulled it out and kissed the end of it. "Yummy," she announced, twirling her finger through the air.

"Goofball," Clover laughed, pinching her nose as she lifted her tumbler to her lips.

Mama stood back with one hand on her hip, the other holding the plastic pitcher. Was she holding her breath, hoping we would like it?

None of us were fooled. We all knew it was powdered milk and there was no way to disguise it.

Mama already knew how I felt. That morning at breakfast, I'd whined as I went to pour that thin watery mess—the same grayish white as our Formica table—onto my corn flakes. Mama told me to "quit whining, you're getting to play in the water, aren't you?" I sassed that I might as well pour water over my cereal rather than taste that nasty powered milk. She told me to stop being lippy.

That's when she explained she wasn't going to the grocery store for several more days because she was pinching pennies. "Pinching pennies in other places so when the water bill comes due, we can pay it."

Mama left us to our snacks and went upstairs. When we'd finished, we took turns washing our tumblers in a pan of sudsy water then stacked them in the dishrack by the sink. Melody and I wiped crumbs off the table with Mama's worn dishrag. Then we filed into the parlor, each of us carrying a library book. Melody, Tansy, and Ruthie plopped down on the green high-back sofa with three cushions and a pleated skirt. Mama called it *Early American Colonial Revival*. Clover hung her legs over the upholstered armrest in the matching chair by the fireplace. I claimed the oak rocking chair in the corner. We weren't allowed to watch television during the day since the only thing on our one channel was soap operas.

A short time later, I finished Beverly Cleary's *The Mouse and the Motorcycle*. It was due the next day at the Sandhill Library. Clover had read it to Tansy and Ruthie a while back. Melody checked it out and finished it in two days right after school got out. I'd waited until the end of summer to read it. It took me two weeks—first, because I was slow, and second, because I wanted to savor the story. Every time I opened the book, I pretended I was Ralph, the mouse living in room 215 of the Mountain View Inn. Every time Ralph climbed on Keith's toy motorcycle and revved the engines by making motor noises, I made believe I was on that motorcycle too, zipping around the room and up and down the hallway of the hotel. Reading about a boy from Ohio and a mouse from California becoming friends made me think anything was possible . . .

At the beginning of summer, a mouse had darted in front of Mama while she was sweeping the kitchen floor. We all heard her scream and came running. I jumped up on a chair while Tansy tried to catch it. She wanted to name it Ralph and keep it for a pet. The mouse got away before Mama could smash it with her broom.

After finishing the book, I decided I wouldn't be as squeamish about mice living in our old house. The next time I found mouse turds in my underwear drawer, I'd picture Ralph riding his tiny motorcycle up and down our hallway. A little mouse on patrol, watching over us while we slept.

Over the hum of the swamp cooler blowing cool air from the window unit, I heard Mama's typewriter clacking away. My mind drifted up the *L*-shaped stairs to the nook where Mama sat at her Make-Do. I wondered what she was writing. A few seconds later I heard her mumbling. Was she talking to herself? She was the only person upstairs. She couldn't be on the phone. We only had one, and it hung on a wall in the kitchen.

Curious, I pushed up from the rocking chair. The others barely looked up. Still holding my book, I tiptoed up the stairs. A shiver skipped up my back when I thought about Clover saying, "Maybe I've seen his ghost?" I hated when she planted scary thoughts in my head.

At the landing, I stopped, waited a few seconds, then crept up and crouched at the third step from the top. Barely breathing, I was relieved to find Mama alone and not talking to some old timey doctor making a house call in his former home. Her back to me, she had no idea I was eavesdropping. Hidden at an angle on the stairs, my reflection wasn't visible to her in the round mirror at the back of the converted vanity.

Chuckling to herself, her fingers made the keys go tap-tap-tap. She stopped, cleared her throat, hit the metal carriage return handle, and typed some more. This went on another minute or two before she sighed, cranking the roller knob that clicked as she slid the paper out of the typewriter.

Scooting back in her chair—it scraped against the wood floor—she held the paper in front of her, picked up a pencil, and began to read her work out loud.

"Dear Miss Welty . . ." Mama began:

Oh, my stars, I thought, *Mama was writing a letter to the famous author.* I hung onto every word so I could blab about it later to Clover.

May I call you Eudora? My name is Letty Bishop Hubbard. I'm writing to you from Sandhill by the Sea, a dusty burg located on the Atchison, Topeka, & Santa Fe Railroad line, where the tide went out eighty million years ago and never came back!

My family lives near the train tracks and down a couple of blocks from the depot. The sound of passenger and freight trains are so common sometimes I tune them out. But yesterday when I heard a train whistle, oh, something came over me. It's like I'd been deaf my whole life, and all at once, I could hear things in that whistle that lifted me up out of my dreary backyard and set my imagination aflutter.

While I liked your title story, "A Curtain of Green," in your collection published in 1941, I must tell you that an overgrown garden of green plants could never happen here, at least not in my backyard. Except for a large sycamore tree growing near the back of our house and a giant cottonwood in the lot behind us, our yard is mostly a wasteland of dirt and weeds. Out here on the high plains of eastern New Mexico rain is a rare occurrence. Water is a precious commodity at my house. My husband, Dorian, is a tightwad, especially when it comes to the water bill. You might call him "The Water Miser Man." Sounds like a story you might write.

That's what your stories do. They pick me up and plant me smack down in the middle of somewhere else. Even though I live in the Southwest and you live in the South, you write about regular folks like me.

Miss Mavis, my favorite librarian at Sandhill Public Library, has taken an interest in selecting books for me to read. She's a big fan of yours. While I may not always understand some of your stories, I'm determined to learn from you and other writers. We don't own many books unless you count a set of encyclopedias—Dorian once worked as an encyclopedia salesman—and I pick up a few books occasionally at the thrift shop. I'd love to have a library of my own someday.

I have three daughters, plus two extras if you count a couple of their friends. Both girls' mamas are single working women; one lives with her mama and grandma, so I don't mind letting the girls stay here when they're not in school. When my youngest gets a little older, I'm getting myself a job to help pay bills and put money back for college for my girls. That's my dream too, to attend college one day and not depend on my husband.

Being married is hard some days. According to Miss Mavis, you've never been married. She's never been married either. I bet y'all would get along fine. Miss Mavis told me she wanted to be a writer when she was younger, but she's pressing fifty-five and says she's over the hill. Now that her cat died, she told me she'd be happy to sell her house and set up a cot and a hotplate in her office at the library. She said she got the idea by reading your story "Why I Live at the P.O."

Did we have fun discussing that one! Miss Mavis told me she read somewhere that you got the idea for your story when you saw an ironing board set up at the back of a country post office. To think, seeing that unexpected contraption in a place where mail is sorted sparked your idea for such an entertaining story.

Miss Mavis and I took turns reading several lines of your story out loud, of course we had to whisper. Who can forget characters like Stella-Rondo and Papa-Daddy? I felt sorry for Sister when her whole family turned against her, all because her sister, Stella-Rondo, was spoiled. I don't blame

Sister for moving her stuff to the post office where she worked as the post-mistress.

As an aside, I took in ironing once to bring in income, but Dorian came home one day from a good day at sales and said, "No wife of mine is going to be a laundress." I tried to explain I wasn't doing folks' laundry, just ironing it, but it was all the same to him.

Until I can go to college, I'm trying to educate myself by reading books, writing letters to famous authors like you, and brushing up on my typing skills. I converted an old makeup vanity into a desk. I call it the Make-Do. You should've seen the look on my husband's face when he learned I traded an electric skillet he gave me for our anniversary for a typewriter. Why do some men think the way to a woman's heart is through appliances?

Sometimes when I gaze into the mirror of my Make-Do, I pretend it's a portal to another life where I'm living in a fancy house like you do, and I'm writing novels for all my fans. Other times I see myself like a pair of scuffed dress shoes. Like I told Miss Mavis, all I need is a little polishing to make me shine. When I mentioned this to Miss Mavis, she slid her cat-eye glasses halfway down her nose and said, "You do not resemble a scuffed-up pair of shoes." But I think she was lying through her tea-stained dentures.

Your photo reminds me of Eleanor Roosevelt, another woman I greatly admire. Come to think of it, Miss Mavis looks a little like both of you. She says you're about six feet tall. What's it like to be that tall? My husband's only five foot eight. I'm a couple inches shorter than he is. I'd love to tower over him. Maybe then he would respect me.

I showed Dorian your photo. He said you weren't much to look at. I told him you're one of the most famous authors alive. What I fear is that what he meant was I'm not much to look at. He does that sometimes. Says one thing when he means another.

In another letter I'll tell you how your story "The Memory" inspired me to stand up to Dorian when it comes to letting my girls cool off with the water hose on a scorching summer day.

Your devoted fan,
Mrs. Letty Hubbard

Before I scrambled undetected down the stairs, I watched Mama insert her letter in a large brown envelope and place it in the shallow drawer of her Make-Do. I couldn't wait to tell Clover everything. I wanted her to sneak back upstairs later and read it before Mama had a chance to mail it.

10 THE WATER MISER

OCTOBER 2017

DADDY LEANS ALL CROOKED on a cane on the cracked concrete porch of the two-bedroom stucco on Mesa Lane, his scraggly beard gray and reminiscent of an old billy goat. His faded striped dress shirt, opened at the collar, hangs uneven on the wrong button, where it remains untucked over the elastic waistband of his flannel pajama bottoms. Heavy socks and lima bean Crocs have replaced his polished dress shoes.

A gray tabby curls around his ankles, rubbing its whiskers on Daddy's pantleg.

As I go to unhook my seatbelt, Mother Goose honks a favorite nursery rhyme across the plains of my mind. I join in, reciting from memory: "There was a crooked man, and he walked a crooked mile, He found a crooked sixpence against a crooked stile; He bought a crooked cat which caught a crooked mouse, And they all lived together in a little crooked house."

Dropping my keys in my tote bag, I toss my cardigan in the backseat, grab Clover's goodie bag, and climb out of the car.

Hitching up my broken-in jeans, I muster a cheerful greeting. "I remember when you hated cats." *Back in your other life when you lived on Vista Boulevard, and Tansy begged you to let her take in strays.*

"Say hell-loh to Fritz." Daddy's words come out slow, choppy. His once robust voice weakened by time and the stroke.

"Hello, Fritz," I obey, the good daughter as I bend down and massage the cat's furry head. Fritz purrs. We are instant friends.

Straightening, I lean to hug Daddy, his skeletal frame shocking to the touch. I'm not prepared for the drool swirling from his bottom lip, catching on his beard, his mouth hanging open like a haggard dog.

"I've got cold drinks in the car," I say, my resolve to rip him a new one melting into the sharp edges of his shoulder blades. A quick pat, then I release him. "And Clover, your bookselling daughter, sends goodies from the bakery." My voice strains to sound chipper.

He's gone downhill since I last saw him at the mortuary in Moriarty. Either more effects of the stroke or life now that he's living alone if you don't count the cat.

He adjusts his bifocals, the lenses coated in grime and dandruff. "What did she make me?" His words tumble out grizzled, his upper front teeth the same sallow shade of his fingernails as he bites down on his bottom lip to catch a string of drool.

"I believe ham and cheese on a croissant. Sound good?"

"Yup," he says, "those bagels she sells are too gosh darn hard to chew." His eyes scan me up and down. "You're too damn skinny."

I prop the storm door open with my hip, relieved to hear the hum of a small AC window unit keeping the interior semi-cool. The noontime sun has chased away the chill from the morning, and the day is heating up. "Funny, Daddy. I was fixin' to say the same thing about you. You drop any more weight and I'm liable to start calling you Twiggy."

He catches the joke, grumbles incoherently. His weight loss since the stroke remains a sore subject. So does getting him signed up for Meals on Wheels, according to Clover. She claims Daddy told her, "That slop's for old people."

He shuffles past me. I wince, watching him struggle. The cat dashes in after us. Setting the bag on a cluttered coffee table littered with adult sippy cups and medicine vials, I go retrieve the drinks. "Be right back."

Outside I notice two sparrows splashing around in a birdbath filled to the brim in the middle of the small front yard. The ground beneath the pedestal is bare, damp. How had I missed this? Grabbing the drinks, I spot a second birdbath in the side yard near the single carport where Edie's and Daddy's banged-up minivan is parked. Right before I open the door, I see a green garden hose coiled around a brass hook mounted low on the front of the house. Drops of water *drip, drip, drip* from its spout.

"Little fountains everywhere," I let the words roll off my tongue as I balance the second drink in the crook of my left arm and reach for the door. Had I come five minutes earlier, I would've caught the water miser of old in the act.

Back inside, I help Daddy get situated into his easy chair. Fritz jumps up and curls into Daddy's lap. Seating myself on the end of a plaid sofa—God knows what microbes are living in the worn fabric—I try not to breathe too deeply. Automatically, I sit taller. The furniture is a combination of early American and Southwest. I detect a litterbox somewhere. If I were a better daughter, I would offer to clean it. The house no longer smells of Thanksgiving year-round, but the lingering buildup of decades of cigarette smoke.

Daddy finally stopped smoking a couple of years ago. His round amber ashtray still occupies the end table, only now it's filled with more medicine vials. The dapper young dandy who swept Mama off her feet and who could sell burial plots to newlyweds has disappeared into the past.

As Daddy and I make small talk, he chomps on his food, tearing into it like a man without manners. He stops occasionally to pick up his drink. His whisker-lined mouth hunts for the straw like a baby searching for a nipple. He takes a big sip, and I fight the urge to bolt upright to help him set his drink down. Clover has already instructed me: "Don't help him unless he asks. Or unless he starts choking."

Choking . . . Another residual effect of the stroke. I would've made a lousy nurse.

I try to avoid watching him eat. I only allow my eyes to take in so much as I sit in a room where Grandma Dot once watched her soaps and read thick paperbacks on her days off. Her pug, Pugnacious, waddled around, checking on everyone's business as he waited for someone to slip him a morsel.

The last time I stepped foot in this house, Grandma Dot looked up from reading her latest grocery store find, *The Thorn Birds*, and asked in her scratchy voice, "Where you girls off to?" Melody bent to kiss her. "Our old clubhouse. It's been a while since we've been out that way." Dot reached up and touched Melody's cheek. "Don't pick up any hitchhikers," she chuckled, but new worry lines creased her saggy face. "Enjoy your novel," I said, waving as I rounded the corner into the tiny kitchen. "You mermaids be careful," Dot called as Melody grabbed her flute and we headed for the side door. "Get you some pie on your way out. And tell all my friends hello."

My friends, all those people Dot grew up with in Rosemont, most of them now lost to time.

My hand dips into my tote bag, and I feel for my cell phone. I'm trying to gauge when to spring the photo on Daddy. But something stops me. Being back in this house after decades . . . Anytime Sawyer and I came to town, we'd either visit Daddy at the bookstore or he'd stopped by Clover's house. A couple of times Edie came with him, but she stayed in the car and smoked.

Part of me wants to peek in Melody's old bedroom she shared with her mom, but what would I find there? Her stuff was probably cleared out years ago.

Ten years after Melody died and long after Pugnacious waddled somewhere over the rainbow bridge, Grandma Dot smoked her last cigarette, sipped her last highball, and checked herself into a nursing home. The last time I saw her, she was propped up in a hospital bed reading another blockbuster, *The Shell Seekers*.

I apologized for never stopping to visit. She said she understood, given the circumstances. When I asked her if she knew what happened the afternoon Melody went missing, she put her book down and sighed:

"I was out of town visiting a friend, so I don't know the specifics. But even if I'd been home, what could I do? I was caught in the middle of a horrible tug-of-war between the two people I love most in the world.

"After the funeral, I thought about kicking Edie and Dorian out, but turns out your dad was handy around the house and with the cars. After my husband was killed when Melody was five, I got a small settlement, but it barely covered funeral expenses. I've never made a lot of money, so Edie and I began to split the bills. After Melody died, I realized Edie was the only family I had left, and I didn't have the physical or emotional strength to deal with anything. On practical terms, it made sense to let them stay. Three paychecks under the same roof were better than one. Besides, by then I could care less what others said behind my back." The last thing Dot said to me on my way out: "How could I know taking out a small burial policy with your dad was inviting trouble in my front door?"

Then Dot joined Melody and Big Don next to the old church in Rosemont, and Daddy and Edie took over Dot's bedroom. After Edie divorced Daddy two years ago, she let him stay on, moving his things back into the spare bedroom Melody once shared with her mom. Clover filled me in when she started stopping by to check on Daddy a few months ago, after Edie died. And now Daddy is the sole occupant of the place, along with Fritz the cat and birdbaths brimming with water and birds.

"So, who owns the house?" I venture, figuring I have nothing to lose.

Daddy clears his throat. "It's complicated." He runs his gnarled fingers through Fritz's fur. Daddy's eyelids are getting heavy. He yawns so loud and deep I can see his tonsils.

I glance around. Part of me wants to scream: Daddy, do you know how messed up this is? Mama was right. You and Melody's mom turned *Mesa Lane* into a regular little *Peyton Place*. Didn't you and Edie Calloway—I refuse to call her Edie Hubbard—ever stop to consider the consequences?

But I'm too exhausted to confront him, especially about the photo.

"Daddy, how 'bout I come back tomorrow? We can talk more then." Tomorrow, I'll confront him tomorrow. I sound like Scarlett O'Hara in one of Grandma Dot's favorite novels, *Gone with the Wind*.

I start to get up. The force of something pushes me back into the sofa. Blinking, I swallow the tightness in my throat. My eyes come into focus, and I am staring at the image of a large seashell, the kind you can hold up to your ear and hear the ocean. Next to the seashell stands a faded photo of Daddy, Edie, and Melody at a beach. The blue of the ocean and sky contrast with the sandy beach empty of people. The photo is evidence of the time they'd snuck off to Galveston, late October 1977.

Even from across the room, I study their body language captured forever inside a rectangular picture frame up on a shelf. Edie and Dorian, a regular Barbie and Ken, completely enraptured, their arms around each other in a lovers' embrace. Edie's garish red lips are the same shade of red as her double-breasted car coat. Melody is hunkered inside her blue windbreaker; her long legs clad in her favorite bell-bottoms. Her arms hang limp at her sides, her sole pair of Dr. Scholl's sandals dangle from her fingers.

She's the only one in the photo not smiling.

Melody! I sit, stunned.

Daddy's coughing jolts me from some vortex of guilt I'm about to get sucked into. I glance over, wondering if he's caught me staring at the photo. It's not like he tried to hide it. It's not like he's ever felt an ounce of guilt for the way everything went down.

He's hunched over, hacking up more phlegm and spitting into his hanky. This time he wads it up and drops it on the end table by his chair. I should offer to spruce up the place. Ask him where his fresh stash of hankies is hidden. But I can't seem to move.

And this little piggy went wee wee wee all the way home. I'm upstairs in the big bed in the long bedroom I share with my sisters, the room where railroaders once bunked on layovers. Tansy is two. I'm six and Clover is seven. Daddy has climbed the stairs to tuck us in, calling us his three piggies in a blanket. We giggle and kiss him goodnight, any fights he or Mama had earlier, forgotten. Sometimes he sings his special song to Tansy, and we pretend we are floating away on a ship across the ocean.

"Before you leave, I have something for you. Edie wanted to get rid of it, but Dot and I stopped her."

His garbled voice intrudes on my vision. He struggles to get out of his chair. His pride, his vanity, won't let me help him. Shuffling out of the small living room, he disappears into the hallway. Fritz follows him. I think he's more dog than cat.

I hear Daddy rummaging around in one of the two bedrooms. He goes into another coughing jag. I ask if he needs help and he rallies a raspy "No."

I'm struck by the dark and twisted irony that even before Melody moved out permanently to Rosemont, Daddy had already moved in.

When he returns, I look up and catch him leaning heavily on his cane. *There was a crooked man . . .* He wobbles there in the space between the two bedrooms, the one formerly belonging to Grandma Dot, the other to Melody and her mom.

His cane probes forward, an extension of his arm. He shuffles across the living room toward me.

My eyes lock on the pumpkin-colored case tucked safely under his left arm.

I do not hear the somber strains of her flute. Or the words coming out of Daddy's mouth. All I hear is a gush of air, a sound like a hot wind. It's me, gasping for breath.

11 THE WRITING'S ON THE WALL

SEPTEMBER 1972

"WHO WANTS TO GO for a ride?" Daddy's deep voice sent us scrambling down the stairs where we found him standing by the front door, car keys in hand. After a couple of phone calls, we were on our way.

We'd already been to Sunday school and church and helped Mama clean up the kitchen after a Sunday dinner of pot roast with potatoes and carrots. We took her station wagon and left her sitting with her head in her hands at the Make-Do at the top of the stairs. She'd been grumpy after she and Daddy had another fight about money. After we picked up Ruthie, who'd already been to Mass, we drove three blocks north, crossed Grand Avenue, then hooked a left onto Mesa Lane.

Melody met us at the curb. I could tell by the look on her face she'd had another fight with her mom. Her mom's red Gremlin was parked under the carport. Grandma Dot's Ford Falcon was gone.

"What was your fight about?" I whispered when she slid in next to me.

She rolled her eyes and shook her head like she didn't want to talk about it, then tapped her fingers on her spiral notebook, pink with black musical notes and mermaid tails curling around our club's name in cursive. Besides already being good at the flute, Melody had perfect penmanship.

I studied my own notebook, the same shade of pink, but my cursive was a lot like my flute playing: shaky.

"Where do you girls want to go?" Daddy looked in the rearview mirror then over at Clover, who sat in the front seat hugging a book.

"Mr. Hubbard?" Melody leaned forward, resting her hand on the back of Clover's seat. "Can we drive out to Rosemont? It's been ages since we've been to the mermaid castle."

Daddy turned, giving her his full attention. "Okey-dokey, if you think it's okay with your mom and grandmother. It'll take us about forty-five minutes to get there. We'll be gone a while."

Melody shrugged. "It's fine. Grandma Dot's at work and, well . . . Mom won't care."

As we pulled away from the curb, her mom stepped barefoot onto the front porch. She had on a yellow halter top and cutoff shorts. And was it my imagination, or did she give a pinky wave in our direction as she took a puff from her cigarette and blew smoke out her nose?

Facing forward, I caught Daddy's reflection in the rearview mirror. I couldn't believe it. He half-smiled like an idiot and whistled through his teeth.

Cringing, I crossed my arms and groaned. I hated when Daddy acted like that in front of pretty women. But Edie Calloway? She was pretty and all, but she was my best friend's mom.

Melody pressed her back against the passenger door and faced me, ignoring her mom still standing on the porch watching us drive away. Nobody said anything as we cruised slowly down Mesa

Lane, took a left, then a right on Grand Avenue. We'd gone a block or two when Daddy cranked up the air conditioner. This meant one thing: we were going out of town.

After a while Daddy said, "Girls, enjoy this Indian summer. Fall will be here before you know it."

We settled back in our seats and gazed out the window as we picked up speed. We passed the grain elevators on our left, a trailer park on the right, then the houses faded away and the four-lane highway narrowed to two lanes as we headed west.

I smiled at Melody. She smiled back.

Clover twisted around and waved a book in the air. "Look what I brought. We have two chapters to go. It's due tomorrow, but we can finish it today." It was the book everyone gossiped about in the hallways at junior high. I gazed at the cover of Judy Blume's novel *Are You There God? It's Me, Margaret*, admiring the buttery wallpaper with diamond shapes and the drawing of Margaret Simon sitting alone on the edge of her bed with a pale blue bedspread.

We all clapped, hoping Daddy was clueless about the story.

From the backseat a few minutes later, Tansy announced, "Hey, guys, I made up a new song. Wanna hear it? It goes like this: Five little mermaids were stuck in the sand, everywhere they looked was nothing but land, they were sad as sad could be, singing, 'Daddy, Daddy, take us to the sea.'"

Daddy glanced at Tansy in the rearview mirror, his left hand on the steering wheel, the other patting his chest pocket for his cigarettes. "One day, Tansy girl."

"Yeah, Daddy, we've never been to the ocean." I leaned forward, gripping his shoulders. He felt strong, reassuring, like when we were little, and he'd lift us up and place us on his shoulders. Maybe if Tansy asked, Daddy would give in.

"Please, Daddy, will you take us?" Clover leaned toward him, pressing her hands together.

"I've never been to the ocean either," Melody piped up.

"Me neither," Ruthie joined in.

Finally, Daddy held up his hand. "Okay, okay, girls, simmer down. You've convinced me. We'll plan a trip."

"Hip, hip, hooray," we broke into song.

We were still singing when we pulled off the highway onto the dirt road leading to the old church. After we came to a stop, Daddy glanced at his watch. "Girls, you've got one hour."

We scrambled out of the car, leaving Daddy outside to smoke a cigarette. He said he had some paperwork to catch up on and was going to read the newspaper. He climbed back in the front seat and kept the driver's door propped open.

Inside, a warm wind rustled around us as we sat in a circle on the floor with our legs crisscrossed like pretzels. All five of us wore patchwork bell-bottom jeans. Grandma Dot said our colorful patches reminded her of crazy quilts. We opened our meeting the way we had opened every meeting for the past four years. We held our breath and pretended we were underwater.

We each had our own routine: Clover bit down on her thumb and stared at the second hand on her wristwatch. Melody puffed up her freckled cheeks like a blowfish and refused to blink. Ruthie squeezed her eyes shut and pressed her lips together while she made the sign of the cross. Tansy pressed her thumbs against her forefingers like the yoga lady on TV. I always kept one eye opened, pinching my nose as I watched everybody while I ticked off the seconds with my fingers.

I was usually the first to let go and gasp for air, followed shortly by Clover, then Melody.

Tansy won today, holding her breath two seconds longer than Ruthie.

Then we opened our notebooks and recited our club's ten commandments. By now, most of us could say them by heart:

Share, don't be stingy.
Don't be mean.
Stick together.

Don't cheat.
Mind your manners.
Turn library books in on time.
Don't stare at people who are different.
Don't talk behind someone's back.
Stand up to bullies, then flip your tail and swim away.
Once a mermaid, always a mermaid.

When we were done, Clover picked up her book, cleared her throat to get our attention, and began to read aloud. When she had finished, she set the book down and placed a flimsy three-ounce Dixie Cup beneath the tiny spout of the blue water jug. She tipped the cup back and drank it in two gulps.

We were all quiet for a moment, thinking about the ending. I was happy for Margaret that she got her first period, but I wasn't ready to get mine. I'd heard Mama complain about cramps, bloating, headaches, and mood swings. And I didn't quite trust that God had worked a miracle and caused Margaret's period to start just because she'd asked. I'd been praying for Daddy to build us a swimming pool after he promised, but all he did was talk about it. I also prayed he and Mama would stop bickering, but it only got worse. Sometimes talking to God was like talking to myself. I could tell myself what I wanted to hear, but that didn't mean I could make it happen.

I crunched on a saltine and talked between bites as Clover refilled her cup. "Did Mama have to sign a permission slip so you could check that book out from the school library?"

Clover took a drink then fiddled with her black cat-eye glasses. "Yes, which is kinda dumb considering we've already seen the sex education film in fifth grade."

Sex. I squirmed at the word. I couldn't figure out if it was dirty or not.

Melody crammed a cracker square in her mouth, chomped loudly, then rolled her tongue over her teeth and gums. She picked up her cup. "Grandma Dot had to sign a permission slip so I could watch the film. Remember how the boys got to hang out on the playground while they jammed all of us girls into the cafeteria and turned out the lights?" She took a sip of ice water to wash down her cracker. "They could've at least served us popcorn."

Clover and I laughed at her joke. Tansy and Ruthie were working on crossword puzzles. A cigar box filled with magic markers, colored pencils, and pens sat in the middle of our circle.

"Mommy says I'm not old enough to read *Are You There God? It's Me, Margaret.*" Ruthie looked up from her puzzle and giggled. "I haven't told her I already know the whole story."

Tansy leaned forward and exchanged a purple-colored pencil for a blue one. "You're not telling a fib, Ruthie. We haven't read it yet. Clover read it to us. That's not the same thing."

I threw my head back, feeling sassy, not the bashful girl afraid to speak up. "Are you there, God?" I yelled, my voice drowning in the wind. "It's me, Marigold. I'm twelve years old, but I'm not ready to start my period yet. Besides, Mama calls it the *curse*."

Melody chuckled, dusted cracker crumbs from her hands, and picked up Clover's book. "Are you there, God?" she sang, looking up as she thumbed through the pages of the book. "It's me, Melody. I'm twelve years old, and I'd like to order a pair of boobies, but please hold *the period*." She grinned, looking all innocent like she'd ordered a hamburger without pickles. "At least until I'm brave enough to wear tampons," she added, crossing her eyes and making a silly face.

Everybody laughed, including me. But still, I squeezed my privates. I couldn't imagine shoving one of those white cotton tubes up inside of me.

Clover nibbled another cracker. "Mama showed me where she keeps her supplies of sanitary napkins. In case Aunt Flo comes to town."

Aunt Flo. Even at our age, we knew the code words.

"That's the box with flowers on it she keeps behind the toilet paper in her bathroom," Tansy said, twirling her pencil. "One time I thought it was powdered bubble bath."

I'd thought the same thing at her age. I studied Clover. I could see bits of cracker getting stuck in her new set of braces. I wondered where I was when Mama showed her where she kept her box of Kotex. I also wondered why Clover got to get braces when I was the one with a gap in between my front teeth.

Melody slid the book across the floor to Clover. "At least in our secret club, we're not competing for who gets their period first or who gets fitted for their first bra. I felt sorry for Margaret, especially when her friend Nancy lied that she got her period when she didn't."

Tansy picked up a cracker, studied it, then glanced thoughtfully at Clover. "Aren't there little pink flowers on your new training bra?"

We all turned to stare at Clover's top with little darts sewn on the chest. She peeked inside her collar as if she needed to double-check. "Yes, but some are purple."

"Five more minutes," Daddy called, leaning against a far wall.

We all turned to stare at him. None of us had heard him come in. Had he heard us talking about bras and periods?

I lowered my head, trying to hide my face. I was burning up from the inside out. It reminded me of the time when I was in first grade and Daddy made us run an errand with him. As we crawled into the backseat of his car, I said, "Daddy, but I don't have a top on." I was barefoot, wearing nothing but shorts. Daddy was in a hurry and said it was no big deal. When we got to the store, he wouldn't let me stay in the car for fear of kidnappers. Inside the store, I crossed my arms over my flat chest and hoped people would think I was a boy, especially with my pixie haircut. At six, I felt ashamed because I wasn't covered up.

I felt half-naked sitting there inside the church.

Daddy stuffed his hands in the pockets of his slacks and studied the stained wooden ceiling beams. A couple of light fixtures missing bulbs dangled from the rafters, their wires exposed. Except for the fact that Daddy stood straight up with his feet crossed at the ankles, you'd think he was lying flat on a bed, about to take a nap.

"How long have you been standing there?" Clover pushed up from the floor, holding her book against her chest.

He pulled a pack of cigarettes from his chest pocket and tapped one out. "Not long." Stuffing the pack in his pocket, he scissored the unlit cigarette in his fingers and began to walk the length of the church, pausing to read several messages. "There's sure a lot more graffiti since the last time we were here."

Melody picked up the cigar box while I gathered the spiral notebooks. Tansy and Ruthie picked up the used paper cups and water jug, and we followed Daddy.

Near the front entrance, Melody flipped open the cigar box, grabbed a marker, and dashed forward.

"What are you doing?" I called.

"Let's write our names on the wall." Her tongue hung out the side of her mouth as she began to write her name in cursive.

Daddy stalked toward her. "Stop!"

She whirled, her mouth opened in a big *O*, her hand frozen against the wall.

In the time it took Daddy to grab the marker from her hand, he blotted out the curlicued *M* in her name like it had never been there. All that was left was a tiny blue smudge. With his unlit cigarette still dangling from the side of his mouth, he pointed with the marker at the wall. "It's still a church. A house of God. We will not *desecrate* these walls."

Clover glared at him. "But what about all those other people who wrote stuff on the walls?"

"You're not those people." Daddy handed the marker back to Melody. Then he opened his book of matches, struck a match, and the stink of sulfur filled the air. Until that second, the only thing I smelled was the fresh scent of prairie blowing through the open windows and doors of the church.

He took a long drag, turned, and blew smoke out of his nostrils as he skipped down the rickety steps.

My throat dry, I leaned my head against Melody's shoulder. "I'm sorry, Mel."

She shrugged, dropped the marker in the cigar box, and closed the lid. "Your dad's a weirdo sometimes."

"I know," I said, squinting into the sun as we followed the others outside. The whole time I kept thinking, *How can a man like my daddy who whistles at other women act so holy about God?*

12 DADDY DON'T YOU WALK SO FAST

SEPTEMBER 1972

WE STASHED OUR THINGS in the car and strolled across the dirt road to the cemetery. The last time Melody had visited her Grandpa Don's grave, she'd been with her grandma. Until today, she'd never asked us to come with her. She took the lead, walking hand in hand with Ruthie and Tansy. Cemeteries weren't high on my wish list of places to visit, especially if you had to trudge through knee-high weeds and watch out for snakes.

By the time Clover, Daddy, and I caught up with them, they were already standing over the grave with the name Don Calloway engraved in granite.

"Do you miss him?" Ruthie asked, cupping her hands on her knees as she gaped at the two-foot-high tombstone built for two.

Jamming her hands in her hip pockets, Melody shrugged and studied the grave covered in caliche with patches of prairie grass waving in the wind. "I was five when he died. But it makes me sad for Grandma."

Daddy rubbed the side of his face. "Was he from around here?"

Nodding, Melody bent and yanked a handful of weeds at the base of the tombstone. "Grandma says they grew up together. Probably rolled around as babies."

I tried to imagine Grandma Dot as a baby.

Tansy hugged herself and twisted her upper body from side to side. "So how did he die?"

Pulling up another clump of weeds, Melody examined the ends to see if she got the roots then tossed them over her shoulder. "He worked for the highway department. A gravel truck hit a patch of ice. He was able to push his crew out of the way, but the truck plowed into him."

I winced, picturing his body getting run over and smashed into the tar and asphalt.

"Your grandpa was a hero," I said at last, bending to help Melody pull weeds. I tried to avoid the name on the other side of the tombstone. The side reserved for Dorothy (Dot) Grier Calloway. Grandma Dot was the closest thing I had to a grandma since both of mine were dead.

Brushing hair out of my eyes with the heel of my hand, I ignored the sweat that trickled down the side of my neck into the collar of my T-shirt. It was so warm I could smell the heat of the day, mixed in with the scent of dry earth and my deodorant.

A few feet away, Clover kept her distance, her back to us as she surveyed the cemetery. All at once she swung her head around, squinting in our direction. "Just think, all these people used to be alive. Like us." She glanced over at the church, then back at the cemetery. "But now they're dead. Like the town itself. Even the church is nothing but a shell."

I swallowed, tugging at a stubborn weed. The root was stuck in the hard earth. Tossing the leafy section, I sniffed the wild sticky juice it left in my palm and reached for another weed.

Daddy jingled loose change in his pocket. "Nothing lasts forever, Clover. In the meantime, we have to make the most of the lives we've been given."

I studied Daddy a second. Mama said when she met him, he was the black sheep, estranged from older parents back east. *Estranged*, another word I'd jotted down in my notebook. By the time Clover and I came along, it was too late for Daddy to reconcile with his parents. Mama said they had already died.

The wind blew across the plains. Somewhere in the distance we heard the coo-OO-oo of a white-winged dove. A car swooshed by out on the highway, a horned toad scampered past and disappeared into the tall grass.

Without warning, Melody jumped up and brushed dirt off her hands. "Who wants to race me?" She laughed and took off running, getting a head start. "We're mermaids," she yelped. "Mermaids live forever." The colorful patches of her bell-bottoms perked up the barren landscape like wildflowers.

Back in the car, I stared out the window as we sailed down the blacktop toward home. I glanced over at Melody. She was leaning her head against the window, her eyes half-closed. Up ahead to our right, a freight train snaked along on the railroad tracks running through Sandhill. We were going the same direction as the train.

Nothing lasts forever, Daddy had said back at the cemetery. Guess that meant passenger trains, too. They'd stopped coming through these parts about a year ago. Air travel was replacing rail travel. I listened to Ruthie and Tansy in the backseat as they worked on another crossword puzzle. One of them yawned loudly, then the other. It must have been contagious because a few seconds later, I yawned too.

We passed the red caboose followed by boxcars, cattle cars, and cars carrying brand new cars. As we caught up with the engine, we pumped our fists, signaling for the engineer to blow his horn.

On the outskirts of Sandhill, Clover fiddled with the radio knob. The car speaker crackled to life and a disc jockey announced, "And here for all you listeners out there in radioland, Mr. Wayne Newton, singing his number one hit, 'Daddy Don't You Walk So Fast.'"

Wayne Newton began to croon about a dying love. He sang

about a daddy leaving home to catch a train, and the daughter begging him to stay, to slow down because she couldn't keep up.

All of us girls followed along, belting out, "Daddy Don't You Walk So Fast," into our fists, our imaginary microphones. Our voices competed with Wayne Newton's smooth tenor. Daddy kept both hands on the steering wheel and stared straight ahead. I wondered what he was thinking when Wayne Newton got to the sad part about leaving home for good.

We were still humming and mumbling the verses even when other songs came on. It was one of those catchy tunes that got stuck in your head and wouldn't leave for days.

When we dropped Melody off, she grabbed her pink notebook, pulled a housekey from her jean pocket, and headed toward the carport. Edie's red Gremlin and Grandma Dot's Ford Falcon were gone. Halfway up the driveway, Melody swung her head around and laughed, "Swish, swish," then wiggled her bottom.

"Swish, swish," we called, waiting until she unlocked the door and disappeared inside. A few seconds later, she appeared at the living room window. Cuddling Pugnacious, she watched us drive away.

At Ruthie's cottage built sometime in the forties, her mom, Carmen, opened the fairytale front door and stepped out onto the stoop. Still in her apron from the diner where she worked on weekends, she smiled and waved, her high cheekbones and dark beehive giving me the feeling she was a princess. After supper, she and Ruthie would count out her tips, and Ruthie would drop a few coins in her piggy bank because she was saving up for flight school.

We waved at Miss Carmen and watched Ruthie skip up the walkway. Before she went inside with her mom, she wiggled her rear and mouthed our secret code.

Back at home, Tansy burst through the front door, yelling, "Mama, Mama, Daddy's gonna take us to the ocean."

Mama was coming down the stairs. She stopped at the landing and gazed down at us. She had a book and a sheet of paper tucked in the crook of her left arm, a pencil behind her right ear. "Dorian, don't make promises you can't keep."

Daddy hustled past; his shirt cuffs unbuttoned as he rolled up his sleeves. He made a beeline to the kitchen to wash his hands and grab a beer. Tansy followed him, jabbering away about sandy beaches, swimsuits, and waves.

Wayne Newton's song played in my head as Clover and I slowly mounted the stairs. Mama stayed put, right there on the landing, as if she couldn't decide whether to go up or down. Clover paused, touching Mama on the arm. "He promised all of us. Even Melody and Ruthie."

Peeking around Clover, I spied scribbled notes in the margins of Mama's typewritten page and the name of the book in her arm, *Curtain of Green*. It was the same book Mama had checked out before. As I followed Clover up the stairs, I glanced back over my shoulder in time to see Eudora Welty's name at the top of the page. Looks like Mama was writing another letter to the famous author.

Up in our room a few minutes later, we could hear Mama banging pots and pans around as she went to heat up lunch leftovers. As I tried to focus on my homework, I kept thinking about what Clover had said about the old church. Once the town died, the church was nothing more than a shell.

I opened my pink notebook and wrote what I couldn't say out loud: *Dear Daddy and Mama, I can't remember the last time I saw y'all hug. Has your love for each other died like the town and the old church, leaving nothing but a shell? I might sit last chair in flute, but I have an ear for things that go unsaid. And Daddy, please, just this once, can you keep your promise?*

That night, I lulled myself to sleep, dreaming of ocean waves slapping against the shore, all five of us girls holding hands and running into the sea.

13 MELODY'S FLUTE

OCTOBER 2017

SIS, CAN YOU COME outside a sec? I'm at the curb.

I send the text and wait.

Seconds later, Clover comes sailing out of Sugar Beet Bakery and Books, a quizzical expression leaving plow lines on her forehead. She rips off her zebra glasses as I motion for her to go around to the passenger door where I roll down the window.

"What the hell am I supposed to do with this?" I point to the pumpkin-colored case sitting in the passenger seat. The case's brass latches are tarnished by time.

"Wait, that's not your flute. Didn't Mama hock yours when you quit band?"

"Yup. She used the money to pay for your senior class ring."

Clover wiggles her plump manicured fingers and frowns. "The ring I haven't worn in forty some years." She pokes her head in the window, her curtain of hair fanning in all directions. "Please tell me this isn't Melody's flute."

I blink at my sister, our faces inches apart in the close quarters of my small SUV. "I'm afraid to open it." I detect a hint of cashews on her breath.

Clover wriggles out of the window, sticks her glasses back on, and glides around to my side of the car.

I roll down the window. "What should I do with it?"

A memory flashes of a Father's Day when Clover, Melody, and I were vacuuming Daddy's car. We were taking turns cleaning the seats when the end of the hose partially sucked up a pair of lady's yellow bikini panties stuffed in the crack of the backseat. Clover's mouth twisted in a knot. "Those aren't Mama's." I froze, wishing the hose was a snake swallowing a baby chick instead of some woman's lacy underwear. "Maybe they were there before Daddy bought the car?" I hedged, trying to sound hopeful, afraid to touch the panties. Melody turned the vacuum off and looked like she was going to puke. Clover pinched the panties between her fingers and dropped them in the aluminum trash can we'd brought up from the alley. Then she went inside to wash her hands. Switching the vacuum back on, Melody grabbed the end of the hose, reached into the car, and began cleaning like her life depended on it.

Tapping the steering wheel, I wait, hoping my big sister will take the flute off my hands. Dispose of it without me having to deal with it. But no . . . It's not her responsibility, it's mine.

"Guess you saw the picture of them at the beach?" Clover says, glancing around. "I wanted to warn you, but . . ." Whenever Clover used to visit Daddy *before* Edie died, she would pull up in front of the house and honk. Daddy would come outside by himself, and they'd jaw about this or that. When Mama died, Edie wasn't allowed at the service.

I close my eyes, banging my forehead against the steering wheel. "Poor Melody. Did you notice how lost she looked in that photo?"

"I try to breeze in and out anytime I go over there," Clover continues. "I never sit down. I check Daddy's meds and drill him to make sure he's paying his bills. Sometimes I clean out his fridge if I'm bringing him groceries. Other than that, I try to get in and out.

I pick up my brain where I've left it in the car and insert it back in my head before I sanitize my hands and drive away."

I don't blame Clover for avoiding my question. I glance at the flute case that's missing a few stitches around the edges. Melody's nameplate is screwed onto the front of the case right above the handle where the leather is rotting away. I might as well be looking at her headstone jutting up out of the hard earth next to the headstone built for two. It mocks me the longer I stare at it. I turn back to my sister. "I could drop it off at the Salvation Army." My comment is more of a plea for advice.

Clover reaches through the open window and tousles my hair. She bites her bottom lip, reminding me of Mama. "Or you could take it back to the motel." She knuckles me on the chin. Her cell phone beeps. "Gotta run. Wanna grab a quick bite in the bakery later? Tonight's my night to close, plus we're hosting a poetry reading for a couple of local poets."

I glance at my watch. It's already four o'clock. "Can I take a raincheck? Dinner tomorrow night? My treat?"

"Sure thing, sis. Come back tomorrow and work on your book. You sure you don't want to stay with me? Now that the boys are grown, I've got three spare bedrooms and two guest baths. You can work in the sunroom. We can drink wine every night."

Mama died in your house, I want to say, but instead I mumble, "I'll think about it," as she moves for the door. Right before she goes inside, I call out, "Wouldn't it be fun to sneak down the street and put detergent in that big-ass fountain in front of the clubhouse?" *Now that you're a member of the country club set*, I want to add.

With a wink and a click of her tongue, she shakes her finger at me and disappears inside.

A few years ago, Clover walked in on her husband, Harold, in bed with another woman. She divorced his cheating ass and got to keep their sprawling Spanish-style ranch that looks out on the greens with its own private pond. After that, Daddy called her his *Lucky Clover*, and he quit trying to sell Harold more life insurance.

Heading south on Main, I hang a right at Railroad Avenue and pass the old Santa Fe Depot on the left with its crumbling stucco and red-tiled roof. The memory of diesel exhaust and creosote railroad ties saturates my mind, along with the image of a scruffy dog we found walking along the tracks. Tansy named him Hobo, but she wasn't allowed to keep him. And now Daddy has a cat.

Overcome by sudden heat—I am way past the point of having hot flashes—I crank up the AC. At Vista Boulevard, I turn right and glance briefly at Ruthie's old cottage. Someone has repainted the door canary yellow and placed a large potted fern on the stoop. I hook a U-turn at the next intersection and head back up the street, easing up next to the curb.

Mrs. Sanchez's bungalow has been bulldozed; the empty lot as flat as her homemade tortillas. "Mrs. Sanchez," I mumble, thinking of the pet cemetery at the back of the lot. "You deserve sainthood for taking in all those strays Tansy brought home but couldn't keep."

Letting the engine idle, I lean toward the passenger window as my right elbow brushes up against Melody's flute case. I gawk up at the scaffolding, grateful some new owner will finally restore this old dame to her grandeur. I wonder if Daddy has driven by here lately, regretting all the broken promises he left in his wake. The white columns need work, but they're still standing sentinel after nearly a hundred years.

A young man with a tanned face and sandy blond hair ambles out of the house. He wipes his hands on a grimy rag, his white coveralls splotched with dove blue paint. "Can I help you?" he calls, eyeing me like I'm an intruder.

"Oh, hey," I offer my brightest smile and lower the AC. "I was just admiring this old place."

"They say it's haunted." He grins, his milky white teeth too perfect for a laborer in a painter's bib. "But the only ghosts I've bumped into are a few mice."

I debate whether to tell him this is my childhood home. "Are you . . ." I hesitate.

"I'm the new owner." He beats me to my question. "My girls are gonna love this place."

I catch my breath. He can't possibly be old enough to be a daddy.

"There's a beautiful old fountain out back." He turns, waving his hand in that direction before jutting his chin at the empty lot next door. "Over yonder there, I'm going to build a diving pool, fence it in with a beautiful stone wall. My wife loves to garden, so she can plant to her heart's content."

Am I hallucinating?

He scratches behind his ear and continues. "Most of the old-timers in the railroad district have died or moved away. Me and my partner are trying to buy as many of these properties as we can and gentrify the neighborhood."

Hey, Mister Developer, I want to say, *I'm one of those old-timers.* His cell phone rings. He excuses himself to take the call.

"There's a pet cemetery in the back left corner of the empty lot," I yell, cupping my hand over my mouth.

He looks at me, startled, then gives me a thumbs-up and puts his hand over the phone. "Thank you!" he mouths, and I realize he's a good guy.

Pulling away from the curb, I glance back through the haze of time and see three worried faces peeking out the upstairs bedroom window. Clover, Tansy, and Ruthie are huddled together on the window seat where they've been waiting for me to come home. Mama steps out onto the front porch, clutching her apron that protects her buttercream pantsuit. Her face is all twisted up and streaked with tears.

Climbing out of the Rambler, I toss a photo at Melody and want to die.

Back at the motel, I stash the flute under a throw in the rear of the SUV. With my tote bag slung over one shoulder, I grab the wire handle on my box of takeout and head to my room. I don't make it five feet when I hear the voice of condemnation in my head: *How can you walk away?*

In an about-face, I sigh, head back to the SUV, retrieve the case, tuck it under my arm, and trek back to my room feeling like a two-legged pack mule hauling a burden that's more mental than physical. Setting everything down, I kick off my clogs and scurry to the restroom. The Texas-size iced tea I've been slurping all afternoon kicks in, and I barely make it in time.

Washing my hands, I gaze at myself in the mirror. For once, I'm grateful for the dim outdated lighting. Running my fingers over my face, I pause to stretch out the crevasses at the sides of my mouth. In three more years, I'll be sixty.

"Melody will never turn sixty," I remind myself, fogging the mirror as the tune from Billy Joel's song "Only the Good Die Young" plays in my head.

Switching off the light, I walk toward the table, my mouth watering at the aroma of Thai takeout. I pull up a chair in front of the window and eat chicken and veggie stir-fry in brown sauce right out of the box. A couple of work trucks with tool chests mounted in the beds pull into the courtyard and park. I watch the men file out of their cabs in work jeans and boots, some carrying hardhats as they disappear into their rooms. If Sawyer were here, he'd reminisce about the construction work that put him through college and law school.

After I dump my food containers in a trash barrel outside, I stretch out on the bed, my back supported by a pile of pillows, and then open my laptop. With my knees propped up, I stare at the screen as the room grows eerily quiet. From the corner of my eye, the pumpkin-colored case taunts me from a few feet away. It sits in the middle of the round table in front of the window where I've left it, its latches shut tight like the lid of a coffin.

I halfway expect it to start playing or a vaporous outline of Melody to hover above it.

Pushing up from the bed, I pace in my stocking feet, gnawing my knuckles instead of my nails. My laptop sits open on the bed, a bored lover snoozing until I return.

"It's a privilege to be a storyteller," Sawyer once told an eager audience of aspiring writers. "But even more so when people want to read your stories."

"Okay, Saw," I say, feeling his words prodding me to get busy. "But you try being in the same room with that thing."

Averting my eyes from the bed, I glance again at the case, tormented by the watery gaze of Daddy's blue eyes when he handed me the flute. "I thought it might mean something to you. It needs to stay in the family."

Which family, I'd wanted to snark. *The family you ditched or the other one . . . ?*

"Don't you want to keep it?" I'd whispered hoarsely, my hands shaking as I fumbled with the case on my way out.

"I don't have the lungs to play anymore." He'd begun coughing as I backed up to the door, wanting to flee from the misery he'd created.

Alone in the car, I'd started to phone Sawyer. It took a second to sink in . . . Driving away, I spotted Daddy standing in front of the living room window, cradling the cat in his feeble arms, in the same spot Melody stood decades ago, cuddling Pugnacious.

I stop pacing long enough to turn on a couple of lamps. It's starting to get dark out. I check my phone to see if I've missed a call from Tansy. I'd texted her earlier and told her to give me a call when she got off work.

Crossing my arms, I walk over to the table and stare at the object that reminds me of Melody and my own failure as a musician.

I recall the time I lifted my flute during marching season and accidently pulled out the end piece and sent it flying across the football field during halftime. Another time the band director blew his whistle during concert practice and told me, in front of the entire band, "Marigold, just sit there and look pretty." After practice, Melody put her arm around me and whispered, "At least he said you look pretty."

Wine. I need wine.

At the mini fridge, I grab a plastic Chardonnay and my travel goblet and head outside, my MacBook tucked under my arm and the room key stashed in my hip pocket.

At the phantom pool still shimmering in my mind, I ease into a metal lawn chair as strings of tiny white lights flicker like fireflies. The word *vacancy* flashes from the turquoise and pink neon sign out by the highway, a throwback to another era.

My phone beeps from the pocket of my cardigan. Balancing my laptop, I set the unopened wine on the ground and pull out my cell. It's Tansy, wanting to FaceTime. "Hey, doc," I say, holding the phone out in front of me. "You got my message."

"Yup. I take it you've been to see Daddy." At fifty-three, she's tan and fit, the outdoorsy type who likes to hike and run for the fun of it, her long tawny mane sheared off years ago and donated to charity. When she went all Dorothy Hamill, Daddy sulked for days. "Buck up, Daddy-O," she scolded. "You act like I've lost a limb."

"Who's your new fur baby?" Tansy is joined by a big slobbering mutt with long floppy ears.

"Meet Wallace," she grins, rubbing the top of his head. "He's a cross between a basset hound and a boxer. For a guy with stubby legs, he can cover ground, lickety-split."

Except for FaceTime, I haven't seen Tansy since Sawyer's memorial. "So, you know about the cat?"

"I'm good with it," she sighs, snuggling Wallace closer, but her voice has gone flat.

"Since when did he become an animal lover?"

"Since he left us," she deadpans, keeping a straight face.

Gazing at her, she's still the perfect blend of Mama's high cheekbones and Daddy's firm jawline. The girl who declared when Daddy left that she was never getting married or having children. The truth is, she's married to her veterinarian practice and her patients are like her kids.

"Where are you?" She leans closer, squinting at me through the screen.

"At the Sands Motel. I'm sitting out in the courtyard under a crescent moon, being serenaded by a chorus of crickets. Can you hear them?" I hold out the phone. "It's almost Halloween and they sound like sleigh bells."

"The *Sands*?" Tansy chuckles, her voice warm and full-bodied.

I gaze up at the night sky. "You should see the stars tonight. No light pollution like Albuquerque." I pause. "They filled in the pool."

Tansy sighs, leaning her head against Wallace. "The pool was the best part of the motel, if I remember correctly."

"I'm sitting over the deep end. They've paved it over with pretty stone, but it's not the same. Fence is gone."

"So how come you're staying there and not at one of the new hotels in town?" *She didn't have to ask why I didn't want to stay with Clover.*

I shrug, not wanting to dump too much on her. She's probably had a long day at work and is headed to bed. "Tans, I'm working on a new book, and this time I'm not ghosting."

"Okay . . ." She strokes Wallace's ears that look soft as velvet. "Is it about Melody? About us?"

"How did you guess?"

"Sawyer took me aside after Mama died and mentioned you had a book inside of you that needed to come out. He was hoping I would bug you about it. But hey, that was never my place. He meant well. He loved you so much."

I breathe in the night air, catching a whiff of the feedlots south of town. If Sawyer were alive, we'd be sitting around our firepit breathing in the intoxicating aroma of piñon and discussing each other's pages—what works or doesn't work. When Sawyer died, I lost my husband and lover, but also my trusted critique partner.

"When Daddy brought Edie here to the Emerald Coast," Tansy continues, "I felt like I was the one betraying Mama. Mama acted like she didn't care, but I know it must've hurt."

"Mama was still teaching full-time. Wasn't this shortly before she got sick?"

Nodding, Tansy stops long enough to pick up Pearl, her little white dog that likes to cuddle. "Edie thought they were staying in one of the high-rise hotels on the beach. Daddy canceled their reservations at the last minute. You know Daddy, why spring for a hotel when you can bunk for free? When they weren't at the beach, Edie parked herself out on the deck and drank coffee and smoked all day, bitching Daddy up one side and down the other. She was getting a taste of what Mama dealt with for years."

"What we all dealt with," I shoot back. "Did you ever go to the beach with them while they were there?"

"No, why would I? He didn't take us when we were kids."

"I drove by our old house today."

Pearl gazes up at Tansy, pawing at her for attention. Tansy giggles and gives her some loving, then turns back to me. "I'm surprised it's not a teardown."

"Me, too. A good-looking kid with money is revamping it. But Mrs. Sanchez's house is gone. The guy bought the lot, and he's going to put in a swimming pool for his daughters."

"Oh, no." Tansy sits up straighter, peering at me through the screen. "I hope you told him about the cemetery in the back corner. There's gotta be three or four dogs buried there. Maybe a couple of cats." Pearl and Wallace seem alert to the change in their mama's behavior.

"I did, sis. He seems like a good guy. My gut tells me he'll honor that space."

Tansy stretches her neck from side to side before she pulls Pearl and Wallace closer. "Mrs. Sanchez was more than a neighbor; she was our friend. A savior to the lost and weary travelers passing through, whether they were on four legs or two."

My sister's voice guides me like the gentle tug of a leash back to the early spring day Mrs. Sanchez stepped down from her porch, a porch surrounded by yellow jonquils, and found all five of us girls crying, huddled over a spotted beagle that followed us home.

"Señoritas, what is the problem? Are you hurt?" Mrs. Sanchez wiped her hands on a dish towel and flung it over her shoulder. She glanced sideways at our house then back at us. "Is your mother home?" Her round face crinkled up in worry.

Clover spoke first. "Yes, ma'am. She's in the kitchen getting supper ready. She just got home from running errands for a couple of shut-ins from our church. She sometimes takes them to the doctor or picks up their medicine from the pharmacy."

"I see." Mrs. Sanchez's face softened. "That's very kind of Señora Hubbard. Your mother is a good woman."

"But she won't let me keep Hobo," Tansy wailed, clutching her arms around the dog as it panted, its pink tongue hanging out.

Mrs. Sanchez came closer, her dark eyes dancing with curiosity. "And why not? Did Hobo bite you?"

Ruthie looked up from petting the dog. "No, he followed us home."

"We found him walking along the tracks," Melody added, jumping up and running over to greet Mrs. Sanchez and coax her to come closer.

"Mama says Daddy won't let us keep him because our family has too many mouths to feed," Clover explained.

"Our daddy doesn't hate dogs," I cut in, trying to cover for him. "It's that they cost money."

"I understand," Mrs. Sanchez said softly, looking toward our house. "What did Señora Hubbard say to do with this little dog you've named Hobo that followed you home?"

Wiping her nose with the heel of her hand, Tansy sniffled then brushed strands of hair out of her eyes. "She told us to drop him off at the train station."

"Oh, I see," Mrs. Sanchez whispered, lifting her chin in the direction of the depot.

"Mama says some train passenger or porter will take pity on him and at least give him food and water," I said, afraid to look Mrs. Sanchez in the eye as I kicked at a tuft of grass in our yard.

Mrs. Sanchez draped her arm around Melody. "Hobo reminds

me of a dog my husband, Albert, claimed followed him home from the railyards where he worked. He called him Smokie. My Albert and Smokie were the best of friends."

"Is your husband dead?" Melody asked, squinting up at her as she twirled a pigtail in one finger.

"Sí, señorita. He died of a heart attack years ago. After that, it was me and Smokie. He was a good little dog."

"Where's Smokie?" I asked, blinking up at her.

"He's buried out back under the peach tree. The birds used to come sit in the branches and sing to him." She smiled, clasping her hands over her heart. "He would stand under the tree and bark, and they would chirp and tweet all day. They made quite a chorus," she chuckled.

Hobo lifted his head, tilting it as if he'd been listening. He wiggled out of Tansy's grip and scampered across the yard. Mrs. Sanchez bent over laughing. She picked him up and swaddled him in her apron. "Come, we must give Hobo a bath. But first we must offer him a drink of water."

We scrambled up the steps after Mrs. Sanchez and entered her bungalow for the first time. Until that day, we'd only stood on her porch. Her house smelled of freshly baked cinnamon rolls and lemon furniture polish. Table lamps sat on crocheted doilies. Copies of *National Geographic* and *Life Magazine* were lined up on her coffee table. A large painting of a Santa Fe passenger train rounding a bend hung behind her flowered sofa.

"Mrs. Sanchez is *Catholic*," Ruthie broadcast to the whole house as she pointed out a crucifix above a tall blue statue she called The Madonna, Our Lady of Guadalupe.

"We know, that's Jesus's mama," Tansy said as she flounced through the house, following Mrs. Sanchez into her small kitchen where another crucifix hung above a white stove and oven. "The only statue we have of Mary comes out at Christmas when Mama sets up our nativity set."

Bending over, Mrs. Sanchez chuckled. "Ruthie, you're welcome to come with me to Mass anytime your mother has to work." Hobo tumbled out of her apron and shook himself off.

We all giggled, watching him wag his tail. The end of it looked like he'd dipped it in white paint. Then Ruthie and Tansy dropped to the floor and played with him while Clover asked to use the kitchen telephone so she could call Mama and let her know we were next door. At the double porcelain sink, Melody and I filled a small dish of water and set it on the floor. Hobo dipped his pink tongue into the water and lapped away.

Mrs. Sanchez took out a package of Longhorn cheese and cut off tiny strips and doled them out to each of us. "Girls, take turns feeding him. Let him take small nibbles. This will have to do. In the meantime, I'll call the dog pound to see if anyone in Sandhill has reported a missing beagle."

"He's the cutest dog ever. I love him," Tansy squealed, crawling around on all fours as she chased after Hobo.

"I know you do," said Mrs. Sanchez, a glint in her eye as she reached for the phone. "I promise you this, girls. If no one is looking for Hobo, he can stay here with me. I think he will cause the birds to sing again."

"Mrs. Sanchez kept her promise," I say at last, realizing it's getting late. "Hobo was always happy to see us, especially you and Melody."

Tansy yawns. "You know Mama kept Mrs. Sanchez supplied in dog and cat food for years. Never said a word to Daddy about it."

"In some ways it was how Mama stood up to him before everything happened." Gazing up at the stars, I whisper, "Do you ever think about Melody?"

Tansy yawns again, and I can tell she's tired after a long day. "Yes, I think about her often, especially when December rolls around."

"Me, too. What if she'd lived? Would she be playing in some famous orchestra? Or would she have walked away from music like Daddy did if she couldn't have paid the bills? Would she have kids? Would we still be friends?"

Tansy rubs her eyes, reminding me of when she was young. "Listen, sis, hate to cut this short, but I have surgery in the morning. I need to hit the sack."

"Night, Tans. Sweet dreams. It was great to catch up. Give the fur babies a kiss."

"Love you. Good luck on your book. Mama would be so proud of you."

After we hang up, I gather my things and push up from the lawn chair. "Goodnight, Moon," I say, gazing up at the lopsided smile in the night sky while the red and green pages of Libby's favorite bedtime story flip through my mind. "Goodnight, sweet baby, growing inside Libby's womb . . ."

After I place the Chardonnay in the fridge, I brush my teeth and slather on moisturizer. My laptop gapes at me from the middle of the bed.

That's all you have to do, Marigold, love your instrument.

Fluffing the pillows, I crawl under the covers and pull my laptop close. The screen glows to life. Placing my fingers on the keyboard, I begin to make music with the drumbeat of my typing.

14 DEATH OF A TRAVELING SALESMAN

SEPTEMBER 1972

CLICK-CLICK-CLACK, CLICK-CLICK-CLACK . . .

The sound echoed down the hallway into my bedroom where I sat perched on the window seat, practicing the flute. Pushing aside the rickety metal stand that held sheet music I could not comprehend, I set the flute down and reached for my pink spiral notebook and pen. I hadn't written in it since Sunday night after we got back from Rosemont. On a clean sheet of lined paper thirsty for ink, I found comfort as I jotted down words in a language I could understand:

Click-click-clack, click-click-clack . . .
The soothing rhythm of Mama's typewriter
competes against the angry squawks and screeches
that pierce the air when I blow into my flute.
Mama's music reminds me of the wheels of a train

rolling down the tracks going clickety-clack,
or the clip-clop of horses marching in a parade,
the rat-tat-tat of a woodpecker drumming away
on the lone ancient tree on the courthouse lawn.
Each time Mama strikes a letter
my heart claps to the beat
as I imagine a tiny flamenco dancer
the size of a toy soldier
tapping and twirling up and down the keys
dancing to the music only daydreamers hear . . .

Biting my pen, I studied the poem, eager to read it to Melody later over the phone. She and Ruthie had already gone home after stopping by our house after school. Clover and Tansy were downstairs at the kitchen table doing their homework. If Melody liked my poem, I'd share it with Clover and Tansy right before bed. Tansy loved to make up little ditties, but I never saw her write them down.

Gripping my notebook, I padded across the room to the doorway and gazed at Mama seated at her Make-Do. I'd give anything to trade places with her. She sat with her back straight, her arms bent at an angle, her fingers tapdancing over the keys. She was wearing a smart new turquoise pantsuit, her hair twisted and clipped in what Mama called an updo. She even had on lipstick.

"You look nice, Mama."

"I'm hoping to get a call back on a job I interviewed for. You might say I'm practicing at being a secretary." She tossed me a wink and went back to typing.

"I wish Daddy would come home early and see you sittin' all pretty at your writing desk," I said, thinking how he was getting home later and later these days. Hoping to get a rise out of Mama, I lowered my voice, pretending I was Daddy at the bottom of the stairs, bellowing, "'Letty, what's for dinner? Can't a working man get a decent meal around here?'"

Click-click-clack, click-click-clack, ding went the bell as the carriage zipped to the return position.

Mama glanced sideways at me. "Aren't you supposed to be practicing?" She obviously didn't appreciate my joke.

"I'd rather practice on your typewriter." *It has keys, too.*

Mama took a deep breath, squared her shoulders, then stared past the little mirror on her converted vanity and out the window that overlooked the backyard. She mumbled something, her forehead creased in a frown, then she began typing again.

"How did you learn to type?" I asked for the thousandth time since she'd swapped Daddy's gift for a typewriter. I knew her response by heart, but I still wanted to hear her say it.

"I took typing in high school. The teacher always said I'd make a good secretary one day. Hopefully, my typing skills will pay off. It's like riding a bike. Once you learn how to type, you never forget. It's like your fingertips have memory."

"Mama, I keep trying to learn how to play the flute and my fingertips don't have memory."

"Practice, Marigold. You'll get better."

"It's been almost a year, Mama. I'm not getting any better. And I still can't read music. It's like a foreign language to me."

"You will," was always her pat answer, especially when she was preoccupied.

"Why are you even in band?" Melody asked me one day at the end of sixth grade after we'd been in band a year. She could tell my heart wasn't in it.

All I could do was shrug and say, "I dunno. Daddy expects me to play, I guess."

"Well, look on the bright side." She swung her flute case smartly as we walked home from school that day. "At least it's another class we have together."

Resting my head on Mama's shoulder, I spied the name Eudora at the top of her paper.

Either Mama was writing *another* letter to the famous author or she was redoing the same one she'd been working on two days ago when we got back from Rosemont.

"Mama, can I use your typewriter when you're done?" My fingers were itchy to dance over the keys. We girls were not allowed to use her typewriter unless we had permission. *Peeking at her letters was another thing, though, and Clover and I kept that secret between us.*

"Maybe later," she said, gazing up at the ceiling a moment, her eyes pinched like she was in deep thought. Then she leaned in, squinted at something she'd typed, and in one swift move rolled the sheet of paper out with a flourish. About then, the phone rang downstairs in the kitchen. Mama stood abruptly, listening intently, as she placed the letter next to the typewriter.

"Mama, it's for you," came Clover's calm voice from the bottom of the stairs. "It's Dr. Johnson's office. I think it's about that receptionist job you applied for."

Mama gripped the back of her chair, took a deep breath, then held her head high and went down the stairs. Tansy met her halfway at the landing, her eyes wild with excitement. "Good luck, Mama. You sure look pretty."

I held my breath, praying Mama got the job. When I heard her proclaim, "Wonderful, thank you so much. Let me get something to write with," I turned back to her desk and began to read her letter:

Dear Eudora,

I love the sound of your name. It reminds me of a sturdy plant with deep roots . . . a plant with pink blossoms on thick green vines that can thrive in any soil. My girls are named after flowering plants. Clover is 13, Marigold, 12, and Tansy, 8. I wanted to give them roots since their daddy has been a professional vagabond for much of his career. You guessed it, a traveling salesman like the man you wrote about in your short story, "Death of a Traveling Salesman."

Nowadays, Dorian's routes are mostly confined to Llano County. His latest job title is "insurance agent," but he's a glorified salesman, going house to house to sign on policy holders. My librarian friend, Miss Mavis, says your father worked in the insurance business too.

I must confess when I originally checked out your first collection of short stories, "A Curtain of Green," and saw the title, "Death of a Traveling Salesman," in the table of contents, I was afraid to read it. At the time, I'd recently seen Arthur Miller's play "Death of a Salesman" televised on CBS, and Willy Loman's character reminded me too much of my husband. Both men suffer from defeated egos and are disillusioned when their dreams don't come true. Unlike Willy, Dorian has never been fired, to my knowledge.

So, I finally got around to reading your story when I checked out "A Curtain of Green" for the second time. Like I told Miss Mavis, your R. J. Bowman was nothing like Willy Loman in that Willy was married with two sons and poor Mr. Bowman was single with no family or friends to speak of. And yet both lived lonely lives on the road and met such sad ends. Where your Mr. Bowman longed for love and home, my husband has all these things and yet he seems restless.

Your Mr. Bowman sold shoes for fourteen years. My husband has sold everything from shoes to Fuller brushes, vacuums, used cars, Bibles, encyclopedias, farm equipment, appliances, pots and pans, car parts, burial plots, and eventually life insurance. Dorian could sell medical equipment to a mortician. What concerns me is I've seen other insurance agents who make the same amount of money as Dorian, but I don't think they live paycheck to paycheck. Sometimes I worry my husband is holding out on me.

Two days ago, he promised to take all five girls to the ocean. I'll believe it when I see it. Since the fiasco at the public pool a few summers ago, he's been promising to build the girls an in-ground swimming pool in our backyard. One Saturday a few months ago, he marked off a rectangle with wooden stakes and twine he probably pilfered from a construction site. He made a big production of all of us taking turns at the shovel in what he called our "groundbreaking ceremony." I have no idea if he has any intention of following through. Mrs. Sanchez, our kind neighbor, came over with an extra shovel. Although she smiled politely, I saw her raise her eyebrows when Dorian talked about hiring a cement truck to pour concrete. I want to believe him, but sometimes I'm as gullible as my girls.

In closing, I must ask, have you read A Tree Grows in Brooklyn *by Betty Smith? Another one of Miss Mavis's recommendations. I'm sure you would enjoy it even though it takes place up north and not in your beloved South. Imagine, an author with a plain name like Betty Smith could write something so magnificent. I've never been to New York City, much less to Brooklyn, but her story made me think. If a tree can grow and thrive among buildings and sidewalks in a big city, why can't someone like me thrive in a place like Sandhill?*

Miss Mavis has recommended I read your latest novel, Losing Battles. *She says you write about family relationships and even a big old tree that survives.*

Your devoted fan,
Letty

PS: I like how my name rhymes with Betty.

When I finished reading Mama's letter, I stared out the window past the old fountain to the place in the yard where Daddy made a big show pacing off the dimensions for a swimming pool. Daddy was a good man, but after reading Mama's letter to Miss Welty, I began to wonder why Daddy would say things to get our hopes up if all he was going to do was let us down?

Still clinging to my pink notebook, I slowly made my way down the stairs to the kitchen to congratulate Mama. I'd figured out her secret: she wasn't *brushing up* on her typing skills when she penned her letters to Miss Welty. Mama was pouring her heart out to a writer she'd never met except in the pages of her stories. I'm surprised Mama hadn't written to *Dear Abby*. Then again, maybe she had, and she'd already mailed the letter before Clover and I had a chance to snoop.

To celebrate Mama's new job, which started the following week, she made our favorite casserole: ground beef with onions, tomato sauce, kidney beans, and seashell macaroni, baked in the oven and sprinkled with grated cheddar cheese. I helped Clover make a salad and Tansy set the table. When Daddy didn't come home for dinner, Mama wrapped his food in tin foil and placed it in the oven to stay warm. Nowadays, about the only meals Daddy ate with us were on weekends.

By nine o'clock, Mama switched on the porch light and locked up the house. As we three girls lay in bed reading before lights out, we could hear Mama puttering around in her bedroom at the far end of the hall.

Tansy closed her book and laid it on top of the covers. "Marigold, my favorite part of your poem is the flamenco dancer." She tapped her book jacket with her index and middle fingers, sliding them around like a tiny dancer.

"I liked the part about the train," Clover said, not taking her eyes off her book. "And the horses. You should show it to your English teacher. Maybe she'll give you extra credit."

"That's what Melody said." I closed my notebook and slid it under my pillow.

"Can I show Ruthie tomorrow?" Tansy walked her fingers up my arm, tickling me.

"Sure. But you haveta ask me first." I didn't want anybody snooping in my journal without my permission. I felt a twinge of guilt for sneaking behind Mama's back to read her letters.

At nine-thirty a pair of headlights turned into the driveway and shut off. All three of us hopped out of bed and peeked out the window as we heard a car door shut then watched Daddy cut across the yard, his briefcase in one hand and his head bent downward under his fedora. Right before he stepped on the porch, he gazed up toward our window as if he knew we were watching. He put his finger to his mouth, making a shushing sign as if it were all a game.

"I hope he's not drunk," Clover said, turning away and crawling under the covers.

I blinked down at him, watching him fumble for his keys, feeling a mixture of love and sorrow, of relief and anger. Earlier, when Daddy hadn't returned home by eight, I pictured him dead out on some country road, his car in a ditch, nobody there to save him.

Climbing back into bed, I tried to block the murmuring noises I heard a few minutes later down in the kitchen. Mama raised her voice once, a sharp shrill that penetrated every floorboard and wall of the old house. A short time later we heard Mama's bedroom door click followed shortly by Daddy's snoring below in the parlor. Mama was making him sleep on the couch.

Tansy snuck out of bed, grabbed an extra pillow from the window seat, and tiptoed down the hallway to the stairs. A few minutes later, she returned.

"Did he say anything?" I whispered, making room as she crawled over me and snuggled into the middle.

"He wanted to sing the sailing song," she sighed, sounding older than her years. "I told him to go to sleep."

Clover punched her pillow. "Yeah, and I bet his breath stunk like the butt end of a jackass."

15 THE AWAKENING

OCTOBER 2017

TAKING MY FIRST SIP of high-octane dark roast, I stroll from the bakery toward a shelf of classics near the front of the store and wait for the caffeine to kick in. I'm still groggy from lack of sleep. I wrote until the wee hours, and I need a jolt before I sit down to work. Shifting the weight of the tote bag on my shoulder, I croon loud enough for Clover to hear: "If you want to be a *successful* writer, the *aspiring* writer has to become the *perspiring* writer."

She waves to a customer heading out the door and turns to face me. "Let me guess . . . You're stalling and haven't broken a sweat." She gestures to an empty row of folding chairs and a podium. "I remember the night Sawyer stood right over there and told a group of local writers the secret to his success was blood, sweat, and tears."

"The blood being the red ink he used to bloody his pages when he was revising," I quip. "He'd walk around the house reading his work out loud, stopping every few seconds to scratch something out, scribble something in."

"I was thinking the blood that flows from his characters." Clover glances at the special display featuring Sawyer's books. "I remember when the *New York Times* compared him to Cormac McCarthy."

"He loved and hated that compliment. On the one hand, he was flattered. On the other, he worried he could never live up to those expectations." Turning back to the classics, I bend my head this way and that, scanning the shelves packed with pocket-sized paperbacks popular on high school and college reading lists. A bright orange spine with the familiar title captures my attention. I immediately think of Mama. Without hesitation, I pull the tattered copy of Kate Chopin's *The Awakening* off a shelf and approach the front of the store. The simple drawing of a woman's profile, her creamy bare shoulders, her brown hair gathered into a knot at the nape of her neck, sends a jolt through me as powerful as any cup of coffee.

I set the book on the counter and slide it toward Clover. "Remember how Mama raved about this book?"

Clover gazes at the paperback then eyes me over the rim of her glasses. "Mama couldn't believe a book originally published in 1899 and written by a single mother with six kids could have such an impact on her, but it did."

I breathe in the rich aroma of dark brew, savor the bold flavor, and pick up where Clover left off. "Mama and Miss Mavis carried on about the novel for weeks. We were too young to understand the content back then, although this quote by Edmund Wilson"—I tap the top of the front cover—"is a *dead giveaway*. Don't know how we missed *that*."

Clover picks up the book and turns it over in her hands. "Quite uninhibited and beautifully written . . . anticipates D. H. Lawrence, in its treatment of *infidelity*." She pauses a moment after emphasizing the last word in the blurb. Pushing up her glasses, she continues. "The story deals with so much more than sexual desire. It's about a woman's search for her own autonomy." She looks up and shrugs. "I'm no scholar of course, just a fan. This is the 1964 edition from Capricorn Books, an imprint of G. P. Putnam's Sons. When I saw it at an estate sale north of here, I couldn't resist. It's only been in the shop a few weeks."

"You're not gonna keep it for yourself?"

"Nah, it's in pretty bad shape, but it'll be fun to see if someone buys it."

I gaze at the cover, the title's large white font standing out against the orange background. "It looks like the same edition Mama checked out from the library when we were kids. I've never forgotten that cover. Or the way Miss Mavis whispered to Mama that the novel was *scandalous* when it was first published."

Clover thumbs through the pages, brownish yellow at the edges. "I remember Mama telling Miss Mavis how she marveled at Kate Chopin's courage to create a protagonist who wanted more in life than being a wife and mother."

I tap the sides of my disposable coffee cup, my memory bank filling up with bits and pieces of the past. "But it was only after we were old enough to read the novel for ourselves that we could appreciate why Mama empathized with the lead character, Edna Pontellier."

"And Kate Chopin never wrote another book," Clover sighs, scratching behind her ear.

Out of the corner of my eye, a flash of brilliant white draws my attention away from my sister to a man standing with his back to us on the corner of Fourth and Main, near where my car is parked. He has an open book in his hands and appears to be reading like he doesn't have a care in the world. I can't see his face or the cover of the book he's reading, but the pages are stark white, illuminated by the morning sun.

My hair stands on end as I stare out the window. Is the man a figment of my imagination? He wasn't there a few minutes ago when I pulled in and headed to the bakery side for coffee. He looks like Sawyer from behind, tall, rangy, back when Sawyer had long hair.

My hand jittery, I set my coffee down. "Clover, do you see him?" But the store's phone is ringing, and she turns to answer it, obviously unaware of Sawyer's look-alike out on the sidewalk.

When I glance again, he's gone. I chuck my tote bag on the counter and dash toward the door. Through the shop's front window, I see he's halfway down the block by now, his long legs strutting along in cowboy boots and jeans. My eyes home in on the orange paperback gripped in his left hand. Sawyer was left-handed.

"Watch my things," I yell over my shoulder and brush past a woman coming into the store. A gush of cold air hits me in the face. I follow him, thankful I'm wearing my cushy clogs as I pull my cardigan close and keep my eyes trained on him. Leaves scuttle the sidewalk, scraping past me in a frenzy.

"Sawyer," I call, forcing my voice to punch through my throat as it grows tighter by the second. "Is it really *you*?" Blurry eyed, I quicken my pace and see him do an about-face and start walking backward, grinning at me like the old days when he'd attempt to tease something out of me, usually when I was in a foul mood.

I'm practically jogging, trying to catch up. *Am I losing my mind, chasing after a ghost?* It's not the first time I think I've seen Sawyer since he died.

The first time was the day Libby called with the news she was expecting. I was driving home from the grocery store when a guy on a Harley roared up out of nowhere and whipped around me the second Libby announced, "Mom, you're going to be a grand*maw*." The guy revved his engine, and I swore I heard him yell, "*Yeehaw!*"

Today it's chilly, and Sawyer doesn't seem bothered by the cold, his crisp white dress shirt opened at the collar, his long sleeves rolled halfway up his strong forearms.

An old man in a buffalo plaid jacket approaches me on the sidewalk; his black Doberman trots beside him, tethered by a leash. The man tips the bill of his hunter's cap as they brush past, his shoulders hunched against the cold.

"Good morning." I glance over my shoulder long enough to see the Doberman pause and look back at me. The man and his dog are as real as the delivery truck pulling up next to the curb in front of the cleaners, the cars and pickups driving up and down Main Street, a horn honking in the distance.

Up ahead, the light turns red at the next intersection. Sawyer is walking faster, his back to me as I watch him cross the street and head north.

"Wait up," I call, feeling foolish as I enter the crosswalk and hurry to the other side before the light changes. My achy knee joints don't slow me down in my quest to keep up. He cuts left at the next intersection. I round the corner moments later as he jaywalks across Sixth Street. There's no traffic, only a few cars parked horizontally on both sides of the road. I follow, stepping down from the curb, and cut across the asphalt on a diagonal.

Bracing for my right knee to rebel, I step up from the curb, swipe tears from my cheeks, and clamp my mouth shut to stop my teeth from chattering. Looming before me, I stand at the base of the majestic marble steps leading up to the old Sandhill Public Library, a grand brick structure boasting tall arched windows and a red-tiled roof. Now a Bible church, the current tenants might be the first to ban books if allowed.

Sawyer is nowhere in sight.

My knees be damned, I look around, then scramble to the top and slide down one of the thick marble slabs that frames each side of the steps. In my mind's eye, Melody is waiting at the bottom in her crocheted poncho. She grabs my hand and pulls me back up the steps, squealing, "Let's do it again," as her pigtails fly behind her in the wind.

Clover peers at me over the top of her glasses as I pull open the door a few minutes later and step inside her shop. My own glasses fog up as the smell of books and baked goods greets me for the second time that morning, along with my sister's curious expression as she sits on a stool behind the counter working on something. "Where'd you go in such a hurry?"

"A wild-goose chase down memory lane." I breeze past her on my way to the back of the shop. I don't mention anything about Sawyer. Knowing Clover, she might spoil the moment and say, "You're just like Mama, seeing things that aren't there."

"Daddy called. He wants to know if you're bringing him lunch again?"

Daddy! I whirl. "I was planning on dropping by later this afternoon, but . . ." I make a face and glance at my watch. It's already ten a.m.

"His royal highness has requested another ham and cheese on a croissant and a vanilla milkshake." Clover reaches under the counter and hands me my tote bag from where she stashed it when I dashed out the door. "Aren't you forgetting something?"

"Thanks." I sling the tote bag over my shoulder and pick up the copy of *The Awakening* to reshelve it on my way to the back of the shop. "And don't worry. I'll leave here around noon to deliver the *Earl of Sandwich* his free meal."

Clover doesn't look up, but I see her smirk.

I go to put the book back on the shelf then change my mind. After I text Tansy the photo I took at the abandoned church, I walk back up to the counter and tell Clover to ring me up.

She looks up and grins. "I have to warn you, there might be some pages missing."

"I'm not buying it to read. I'm buying it to remember."

After I fork over five bucks in exchange for the worn paperback, I grab a fresh cup of coffee and sit down to work. Gazing at the woman on the orange cover, I wonder if she represents Kate Chopin, the author baring her soul to the world through the guise of fiction, or her protagonist, Edna Pontellier, right before she strips naked and walks into the ocean. Perhaps she represents every woman who yearns to be free of society's constraints and the shackles of expectations. And, God help me, but even a woman like Edie Calloway. Why do I find it easier to dismiss a fictional character's infidelity over that of a woman in real life who I never accepted as my stepmother?

Then I think about seeing Sawyer out on the sidewalk, and once again I question my own sanity. But whether he was real or not, I know in my heart he led me to the steps of the old library.

I remember the time shortly after we got married when he found me outside in the middle of the night, fuming at the stars. "What's wrong?" he asked, and I flailed my arms in the air and lashed out, "Leave me alone."

He took a few steps back, raised his hands in the air, and said, "Okay, let me know if you wanna talk about it. Is it something I did?"

That's all it took, an invitation to spew.

"I never knew the cruelty my daddy was capable of until he left us," I railed, spinning around to face Sawyer as he stood solid under the moonlight. "What kind of a man dumps his devoted wife and three daughters to take up with another woman and her daughter? A daughter who happens to be his middle daughter's best friend?"

That night, as I walked into Sawyer's outstretched arms and leaned into his strength, he said, "Mari, when's the first time you detected something was going on between your dad and Melody's mom? Think hard, honey. It might help to write about it."

As much as we were dedicated to each other, we were dedicated to our craft. But did I write about it then? No. I pushed it far away, keeping it at bay until now. Sawyer's question from decades ago swirls around me, along with the whiff of fresh donuts wafting from the bakery.

Setting *The Awakening* next to my laptop, I breathe in the smells of the bookshop and meander down memory lane to the day Mama walked with purpose down Main Street, between the library and the bank, the little orange book tucked safely in the palm of her hand.

16 THE FIRST CLUE

NOVEMBER 24, 1972

"MISS MAVIS, DID YOU see us go down the slide?" Melody scrambled up the steps, the fringe of her poncho fluttering in the breeze.

I was right behind her, trying to keep up.

Miss Mavis stood at the entrance to the library, keeping the door propped open with one hip. According to Mama, Miss Mavis will turn sixty next year. She might be old, but there's something about her that feels young, despite the cat-eye glasses she wears now and the old-fashioned sweaters.

She smiled and said, "You mermaids are certainly innovative, turning those marble side supports into playground equipment. If I were younger and I wasn't wearing a skirt, I'd join you. Have fun, and I'll see you next time. Happy reading."

"Thanks for all your help." Mama waved the little orange book in the air while she waited for us to stop horsing around. She guarded our wagonload of books parked on the sidewalk.

"Anytime, dear." Miss Mavis turned to go inside. "Oh, Letty, where did you say you bought your pantsuit? I might get brave and try one on."

Mama glanced down at her slacks then up at Miss Mavis. She looked pleased that her favorite librarian considered her suggestion. "Sears. They're on sale all this weekend."

"Aw. Got it." Miss Mavis gave a quick nod and flicked her index finger straight up like an exclamation point. Then she cupped a hand to the side of her mouth and chuckled, "Maybe I can finally ditch this girdle." She patted her ample hip and lumbered inside, her quiet laughter cascading down the steps.

Mama's voice rippled through the air. "Okay, girls. Time to head out. Ruthie and Tansy, grab your jackets." The two youngest were taking turns sliding down the slab at the far end. Mama looked around. "Where's Clover?"

"I'm right here, Mama." Huddled over a book, Clover looked up and squinted. I knew the look: one second she's lost in a book, and the next reality intrudes.

"Girls, I need to stop by the bank to deposit my paycheck before we head home."

With her head held high and her purse dangling in the crook of her left arm, Mama walked two feet in front of us, the orange library book gripped in her right hand. We girls trailed closely behind, Clover bringing up the rear. The wheels squeaked on the rusty wagon as Ruthie and Tansy took turns pulling the handle. Melody and I held hands, swinging our arms, and jumping over cracks *to keep from breaking our mothers' backs*.

It was the day after Thanksgiving. Mama had worked half a day, and we didn't have school until Monday. In her smart belted jacket and pantsuit with low-heeled spectator pumps from Payless, Mama walked like she owned the sidewalk. She outshined the fancy ladies in town who wore mink and pearls. Before Mama started working for Dr. Johnson, she mostly wore cotton shifts and soft squishy shoes she found at the thrift store. Mama still shopped for bargains and put clothes on layaway, only now she had a reason to fix herself up.

Inside the bank, Mama breezed toward the tall dark wooden counter lined in brass, leaving us girls to mill around *The Princess of Time*, a tall bronze statue at least ten feet in height, her face looking up at a large clock in her left hand that reached skyward. Her nipples poked out like pencil erasers. She reminded me of a female version of Atlas holding up the world.

One time when Melody was nine, she jumped up on the base of the statue and bragged she could touch the clock. We burst out laughing, watching her scale the statue's body. When Mama saw what was happening, she scurried over, angry and mortified. But instead of yanking Melody down, Mama sweet-talked her like she was a baby bird. "Now, Melody, honey, you need to come down right this sec. That statue cost more than your mama will ever make in her lifetime. And if you break it . . ."

That's all it took. Melody let go and sailed through the air, landing on the polished wood floor with a thud.

Mama treated Melody better than her own mother did.

From across the lobby, we heard Mama's favorite teller, Linda, exclaim, "Well, look at you, Letty Hubbard. Don't you look sophisticated now that you're a working woman."

Mama swiveled her head from side to side, showing off her French twist. "Glad you like it."

We ran over to the counter and crowded around Mama, proud of her new look.

Linda, the teller, wore green eyeshadow and long glossy hair parted straight down the middle. She pushed up her oval-rimmed granny glasses and nodded toward the book in Mama's hand. "Are you still reading that same novel?"

Mama leaned closer. "Miss Mavis let me check it out for a *third* time. You wanna read it when I'm done?"

Linda's frosty pink lips parted in a sly grin. She reached under the counter and pulled out a magazine and slid it toward Mama. "Already one step ahead of you, Letty." She tapped the lower left corner of the magazine. "See what's in the November issue of *Redbook*?"

Melody pushed past us. "Look, it's *That Girl* from TV."

We huddled around Mama to gawk at the actress Marlo Thomas on the cover of *Redbook*, a magazine Mama never bought because it was an extra expense we couldn't afford. Marlo Thomas played Ann Marie, an aspiring actress who moved to the big city to get famous. Her dazzling white smile showed off a perfect set of teeth.

I stood with one foot on the other and flicked my tongue back and forth like a lizard between the gap in my front teeth. Maybe I'd go to sleep one night and wake up with a smile like That Girl and a full head of chestnut hair that flipped on the ends.

Clover nudged me aside to get a better look. "It says, 'Plus—*a classic underground novel*.'" She turned and eyed Mama. "Is the magazine talking about *your novel*, Mama? *The Awakening?*"

Mama twirled her book in the air and smiled, a smile she shared when talking about her favorite books. "The one and only. Kate Chopin's classic."

About then, Ruthie's mom walked in, smelling like bakery cake and Christmas. "Clover, Marigold, and Tansy, did you girls enjoy the donut holes your daddy bought for you this morning?"

"Donut holes?" We all turned and frowned. What was she talking about? The only time Daddy treated us to donut holes was Christmas and Easter. I mouthed off and called Daddy cheap and Mama told me to hush my sassy mouth.

I glanced sideways long enough to see Melody's face break out in a rash that went all the way down her neck. Her eyes got big before she slunk away and sucked the end of one pigtail, avoiding my gaze as she pretended to look everywhere but in our direction.

Was I the only one who noticed she'd left?

I hurried over, leaving Mama still talking with Mrs. Romero. "What's wrong, did you get your period?" Had Melody's sudden mood swing been brought on by a surprise visit from Aunt Flo? I couldn't help but think of our talk back in September when we were discussing *Are You There God? It's Me, Margaret*.

She squeezed her eyes shut and shook her head fast. "No-ah, you'll be the first to know. Remember, we promised."

I glanced back at Mama and Mrs. Romero. *Why would Daddy buy donut holes from the bakery and not share them with us? Mrs. Romero wouldn't make something like that up.*

I leaned closer to Melody. "Then what's wrong? Are you sick? You're all blotchy, even your neck."

She yanked off her poncho and blew out a lungful of air. "I'm hot, that's all."

Later, after we cut across Main Street and filed into the bakery, Melody took one donut hole while the rest of us took three. She waited until we started chomping and licking glaze from our fingers before she took her first bite. Her eyes watered up like she was biting into a chili pepper, not a fried ball of dough.

Something wasn't right.

In all the years Melody and I had been best friends, this was the first time I sensed she was keeping something from me.

17 SNOOPING

NOVEMBER 27, 1972

THE TYPEWRITTEN PAGE LAY face down in the shallow drawer of Mama's Make-Do. At twelve and thirteen, Clover and I agreed this was a silent invitation to turn the page over and see what it said.

It was Monday afternoon. Mama was still at work. Melody had just gone home, and Tansy and Ruthie were next door playing with Hobo and helping Mrs. Sanchez around the house. Clover and I were supposed to be doing our homework and starting a load of laundry.

But the temptation was too great.

As we bent over to read Mama's words, the late western sun glowed through the naked limbs of a cottonwood tree, its golden leaves having blown across the alley into our yard, filling our fountain and hiding the holes left abandoned inside Daddy's rectangle of wooden stakes and twine. Mama said most cottonwoods require a lot of water, but this old tree had learned to adapt.

One glance at the opening line and we realized for the first time

Mama had no intention of mailing this letter or any of the letters she'd written to famous authors. Were we shocked? A little, but not as shocked as we were about the stuff Mama wrote.

Hunched over her letter, I shivered at the thought of two ghostly figures peeking over our shoulders. One was the old-timey doctor, pointing a gnarled finger at us for snooping; the other was Kate Chopin, an author who'd been dead for over sixty years.

Dear Mrs. Chopin,

I've finished reading The Awakening *for the third time. How did you do it? After losing your husband, how did you wrangle with six children and find the time—or the energy—to write short stories and your novel? I admire your dedication.*

Miss Mavis and I had a heyday discussing it after she let me check it out for the third time in a row. Miss Mavis is the head librarian at our public library here in Sandhill, New Mexico, and I'm a receptionist in a doctor's office. We both agree Edna Pontellier was a lady of leisure, whereas we're both working women. And unlike Edna, who had the whole Gulf of Mexico at her disposal when she lived on Grand Isle during the summer, Miss Mavis and I are hundreds of miles away from any large body of water.

Yet even with waves lapping against the shore and servants tending to her every need, poor Edna Pontellier must have felt like she was drowning in the oppressive heat, humidity, layers of clothing, and expectations of high society and her husband, Leonce. Until your book came along, it was so easy for someone like me to dismiss a wealthy woman like Edna. To imagine her promenading up and down a boardwalk or beach, a parasol overhead protecting her delicate complexion. But your book forced me to peek under the parasol and see the signs of unhappiness that caused Edna to do what she did.

Like Edna, I've thought about leaving, but I don't have the sea to escape to unless I close my eyes and imagine myself strolling along the seashore. Flinging my clothes off one piece at a time, until I'm free as a newborn, I walk into the sea, letting the foamy waves buoy me up to my shoulders in brine until I'm cleansed of all care or worry. Like Edna, I start swimming, gliding through the currents until I'm so far out no one can catch me. As liquid arms encircle and caress me, I dive below the surface, my hair growing longer, fuller, flowing behind me in fluid movement with my tail, as I move through the water, bare-breasted and proud.

Flicking away all responsibility and demands on my body, no one tells me to put meat on my bones or to buy the cheap peanut butter that tastes oily and gritty at the same time. Down below the surface, I swim farther and farther away from the house on Vista Boulevard where my marriage bed is becoming lonelier and lonelier the more Dorian stays away.

Then a sound pierces my heart. A sound that sends me torpedoing to the surface of my daydreams, a sound causing me to glance over my shoulder to the stairwell where sound travels upward from below. "Mama, Mama. Are you up there?" one of my girls calls. And I'm back at my Make-Do, typing faster and faster in my place of make-believe at the top of the stairs, trying to get my thoughts down before I scan my work and roll it out of the typewriter to place in my drawer for safekeeping. Dorian would never think to look here, to read anything I've written. Why should he? He barely looks at me anymore.

Unlike your Edna, who seeks romantic love outside of marriage, I've never been unfaithful, but it's not like I haven't thought about it. But if I left Dorian, who would want a single mother with three girls to raise?

Miss Mavis says you never wrote another novel after you were devastated by the reception you received when The Awakening *published. Oh, Mrs. Chopin, I wish you could've lived to see that people are reading your novel again. My goodness, the glossy magazine* Redbook *published your entire novel in this month's issue. It's all my friend Linda could talk about when the girls and I stopped by the bank last Friday to deposit my paycheck. I was about to show Linda the little orange book in my hand, when she whipped out a copy of* Redbook *and thumbed through the pages.*

About then my neighbor, Carmen Romero, came into the bank to deposit her check. She's such a pretty woman, even in her white baker's apron splattered in frosting and a hairnet barely visible over her dark beehive. Her daughter, Ruthie, and my youngest, Tansy, are best friends.

When Carmen asked my girls if they enjoyed the donut holes their daddy bought them that morning, they looked at me in confusion.

"What donut holes?" Tansy asked before I could find my tongue, which I had nearly swallowed.

Marigold crossed her arms and frowned. "Daddy didn't bring us any donut holes. He's too cheap."

"Hush your sassy mouth." I couldn't help it. I snapped at her, embarrassed.

Clover, my oldest daughter, elbowed her sister and scowled at me as if I was keeping something from them. I wasn't keeping anything from them. This was the first I'd heard about Dorian buying donut holes.

Carmen pursed her plum lips and gazed around the lobby, her dark eyes flitting everywhere but on me. After a second, she glanced past me toward the teller window where Linda rubbed the tip of her nose, slipped the magazine in a shelf below her counter, and motioned for Carmen to step forward with her check. Linda must've overheard everything.

"Sorry, Letty, I guess I misunderstood." Carmen scratched at something on her temple. "I didn't wait on Mr. Hubbard. I only heard him tell Polly as she rang him up on the cash register. I thought he said he was buying donut holes for his girls."

Mrs. Chopin, I squeezed your book so hard to keep the rest of me from shaking.

About then my tongue began to work. "Maybe he meant the office girls at the insurance agency," I said, trying to smooth things over for Carmen, but even I wasn't buying my own words. Opening my pocketbook, I placed the deposit receipt inside the pages of your novel, dropped it in my purse, and turned to leave.

"Letty, wait up," Carmen called over her shoulder as she slid her paycheck toward Linda. "I might be able to rustle up some donut holes for the girls if you'd like to follow me back to the bakery. They're not as fresh as they were this morning, but they'll do."

Ruthie had left Tansy's side and was leaning into her mama, her arm wrapped around Carmen's slender waist as she gazed up at her then back at us. My heart squeezed again to see this child's big brown eyes and wide grin brimming with pride that her mother, Carmen Romero, a single working mother holding down two jobs, was going to treat us to donut holes left over from that morning.

After a moment, I turned, realizing I didn't see our spunky Melody anywhere in sight. Melody was my responsibility, and I panicked.

Scanning the lobby, my heart calmed when I spotted her sucking on one end of her pigtail in the corner by The Princess of Time where Tansy and Ruthie had parked the wagonload of books. Marigold was with her.

One time, when the public was invited to the statue's dedication, Dorian had the nerve to let out a wolf whistle during the ceremony. I wanted to clobber him. I don't suspect Mr. Chopin ever did anything like that, embarrassed you in public. My Lord, Dorian carried on like a teenage boy. All because we could see the statue's breasts and nipples under a gauzy slip. She reminds me of a Greek goddess I've seen in a book, all regal, holding a clock in one hand while two birds perch at her feet.

Back to the donut holes. When I asked Dorian that night if he'd stopped by the bakery, he hemmed and hawed and said he'd purchased a small bag of donut holes for some new policy holders on his route.

The presidential election was last week. Miss Mavis and I are disappointed that Nixon beat McGovern, but she's glad I voted. Miss Mavis has been needling me for years to register to vote. Weeks ago, she gently reminded me that even a famous author like you didn't have the right to vote back when you were alive.

While I've never seen Miss Mavis outside of the library, not even at the grocery store, I consider her a friend. She takes me seriously and doesn't treat me like I'm some uneducated woman because I haven't been to college. Not yet anyway.

Once I return my little orange copy of The Awakening, *I'm going to thank Miss Mavis for recommending your novel. Honestly, Mrs. Chopin, I can't stop thinking about Edna. Your ending was so bittersweet. I'd like to pretend Edna's seated on the beach with her sketchbook in hand, drawing pictures of seagulls. Her young sons are nearby, playing in the waves with their nanny. From the corner of her eye, Edna sees a young woman strolling alone on the beach. Without realizing it, Edna has stopped drawing birds and is sketching the woman walking nude into the sea.*

Your new fan,
Letty Hubbard

"Clover, did Kate Chopin's character turn into a mermaid like Mama did in her letter?"

Clover hesitated before answering and placed the letter face down in the drawer. "No, I think she drowned herself."

"Oh . . . Are you going to read the novel when you're old enough?"

She glanced sideways at me and nodded. "Yeah."

"Me, too," I murmured and followed her down the stairs. At the washing machine, I said, "Clover, why did Mama say I have a sassy mouth?" I felt Mama's words sting me all over again.

"Because you tell it like it is," she said without looking at me as she stuffed dirty clothes into the washer.

Bending over the hamper, I let my sister's words sink in. Maybe what she meant to say is I tell people what they don't want to hear.

18 SOMEONE PLEASE HELP ME!!♫

OCTOBER 2017

I HAND DADDY MY cell phone opened to Melody's cryptic message.

My heart hurts as I watch him cup the phone in his trembling hands like he's scooped up water and is trying to keep it from slipping through the cracks. Stooped over in his chair, he squints at the image. His milkshake and half-eaten croissant with ham and cheese sit on the TV tray. Fritz curls around Daddy's ankles, purring into the silence of the room. The AC unit is off as it's cooled down since yesterday.

A few seconds pass before Daddy raises his head, his cracked lips and marble blue eyes open in a silent "Oh?" He is at once a little boy and an old man in thick black glasses, caught in a jam as he tries to convey innocence. I search his eyes for a hint of deception that might peek out behind his crow's feet spread out like sunbursts around each eye. The eyes that convinced Mama to marry him, the earnest eyes of a salesman making his sales pitch. The blue eyes I trusted too much as a child.

Finally, he says, "Who wrote this?" His voice is all air and gravel. He swallows so loudly I can hear the muscles in his throat constrict.

"Melody, Daddy. I stopped by the old church at Rosemont on my way into town the other day. I found this message by the entry."

"Well, what does it mean?" He continues to stare at the image.

"It was a plea for help. She must've written these words right before she drove to the Blue Hole. I found them in the same spot where you forbade her to write her name on the wall when we were kids. Don't you remember?"

Drool slips from his lips. I can hear his throat constrict again as if he is trying to swallow memories too painful to comprehend.

It would be so much easier if he was forty years younger, and we could box it out. I'd pull him out of that chair and say, "Daddy, put up your dukes. I get the first punch." But he's fragile, and I'm terrified my confrontation will undo him in my need for the truth. I shift on the sofa as my gaze darts around the room, grazing past the photo of Daddy, Edie, and Melody at the beach to another one of Daddy and Edie standing by an ancient volcanic rock full of petroglyphs. *Petroglyphs!* Writings and drawings by people hundreds of years ago. People like Melody who simply wanted to leave her mark, to write her name on the wall of an old church her grandmother attended as a child.

Pushing up from the sofa, I dash the few feet across the room and snatch up the photo. Turning, I thrust it in Daddy's hands in exchange for my cell phone, where I glance down once again to see Melody's message.

I pace in front of the coffee table, staring at her message because I'm afraid to look at him. "So, it was okay for ancient people to write on rocks, but it wasn't okay for a little girl to write her name on a wall in an old church even God forgot? My God, Daddy, what was that all about?"

He tries to clear his throat, conveniently coughing instead of answering me. After a moment, he holds out the photo for me to take back. "I don't remember."

Reaching over, I relieve him of the photo and place it back on a shelf. "Well, I've never forgotten it. And obviously, neither did Melody."

With jerky movements, he picks up his milkshake and takes a few sips, his mouth opening and closing around the candy-striped straw, sometimes baring his yellow teeth like a horse.

"Melody was my best friend, Daddy!" I say, as if I need to remind him. I sit back down, aware Fritz has jumped up on Daddy's lap and is curled up, staring at me. Clutching my phone, I continue, "You have never apologized or taken any responsibility for what happened. We all suffered when you left Mama for Edie."

He says nothing. His silence enrages me more, and I assault him with words that rip into him like the rapid-fire of a machine gun. "Mama died of stomach cancer, Daddy. You wanna know my theory? She got *cancer* because she'd had a *bellyful* of your shenanigans."

Daddy slams back against the recliner like he's been shot. Seconds later he hunches over, patting his shirt pocket and trousers out of habit. With antsy fingers, he pats Fritz instead. "That was a long time ago," he grumbles. "I paid for my mistakes."

"How did you pay?" I glance around the tiny living room that always felt welcoming when Grandma Dot and Melody were alive, back when Edie wasn't at home. "By letting Edie rack up thousands of dollars in credit card debt without your knowledge, then making excuses for her when the debt collectors called?"

Daddy starts to cry.

"We all got hurt, Daddy. But Melody paid for it with her life."

"I loved that girl like she was one of my own."

Melody's message yanks at my gut: *I knew right then this wasn't how most moms and dads acted in our hometown . . .*

I stall, searching the tops of my clogs as if they will cough up the answers. At last, I blurt out, "Melody considered you her surrogate dad. Did something happen between you two the day she went missing? Besides the obvious . . . that you left Mama for Edie?"

He swings his head up like an angry bull, his eyes almost glowering, his lips puckered up in a knot. "You mean something *perverted*?" He spits the word out like it's a cyanide pill.

His comment stings me to the core. I look away, sickened by my need to poke and prod him, to hurt him the way he hurt Mama. The way he hurt all of us. But despite Daddy's wolf whistles at other women and even at us girls as we grew into young women, he never once touched us inappropriately nor did anything that smacked of abuse. But to be honest, the second I saw Melody's message the thought had crossed my mind.

Then a memory from decades ago paddles up and reminds me of the time I barged in on Daddy standing at the commode, shaking his thing off after he'd peed. It was poking out of the slit in his cotton boxer shorts. The second he saw me he turned away, shielding himself with his hands. "Knock next time, will you?" he yelled as I scrambled down the stairs and ran outside into the sunlight where I was momentarily blinded.

Later I heard him telling Mama, "Letty, you need to teach those girls how to knock," and Mama shot back, "Well, nitwit, next time lock the dadgum door."

The word *perverted* lingers in the tiny living room on Mesa Lane like tear gas. Both of us are brushing away tears as Daddy begins to hack up more phlegm and starts to choke. I'm killing him with my words. If someone walked in on us, they'd accuse me of elder abuse. For a second, I take a sick pleasure in watching him suffer. The next second, I'm horrified and jump up to slap him on the back. "Daddy, Daddy, are you okay? Can you breathe?"

After he recovers from this latest coughing jag, he pushes me away with one gnarled hand and motions for me to sit back down. "Edie and Melody had a huge fight that day."

I back up to the sofa, plop down, and cross my arms, glaring at him. "About *you*, most likely," I huff, feeling my blood pressure rising.

He fixes his piercing blue eyes on me, a defiance dancing against decades of regret. "What happened was a horrible accident. I had nothing to do with it."

"How do you know it was an accident? Did you see it happen? Were you there?"

He stares at me like I'm a stranger. "What are you accusing me of, Marigold?"

That maybe you had something to do with Melody's death. But I don't have the guts to come right out and say it.

Anger and grief move in and out of us, each clashing heads in this small space. Fritz meows loudly and jumps from Daddy's lap, dashing past me as he disappears under the sofa. I don't blame him.

Daddy starts to say something, then stops and clamps his mouth shut like he's changed his mind. Seconds pass, then his cell phone rings, a welcome sound against the weight of silence erupting between us. He grapples for his phone and peers at the screen.

"It's Dr. Hubbard," he announces proudly, adjusting his glasses as he lifts the phone to his ear. "Well, hello, Tansy. Yes, doing fine."

One phone call from his youngest daughter lifts his spirits.

Saved by the bell. I sigh, thinking Daddy was right on the verge of telling me something important.

"Nah, I'm sitting here visiting with your sister." He glances over at me, a boyish grin returning to his weathered face. "Marigold brought me lunch. Yup, your sisters are taking good care of me."

Tansy says something, and Daddy glances at me and says in exaggerated tones, "Fritz is doing fine. I found him curled up under the carport a few weeks ago." He nods at something she says then glances over at me. "Tansy says for you to take a picture of me and Fritz and send it to her." He holds the phone away from his ear, glancing toward that spot where the cat darted under the sofa. "Fritz, come here, boy," he sputters, spittle spraying from his lips.

The cat slinks past me, rubbing against my ankles before he trots over and jumps back up on Daddy's lap. I swear that cat thinks he's a dog.

I press the camera app on my phone. "Okay, Daddy, you and Fritz say meow."

"Meow," Daddy says, grinning playfully as that boyish side of him peeks out. I snap the photo then send it to my two sisters.

It's that grin that makes it impossible to hate him.

Daddy passes me his phone. "Tans wants to talk to you." He's all innocence as he burrows into his recliner, closes his eyes, his hands resting protectively around Fritz.

"Hey," I say, turning away and lowering my voice. "What's up? You on lunch break?"

"For fuck's sake!" she says. "Why didn't you tell me about that creepy message last night when we FaceTimed?"

"It was late, sis. You'd had a long day."

"Hang on a sec. I just got your text." Tansy pauses to open the message. "Oh, that's a good photo of Daddy with his cat. But man, he sure has aged in the last year. I'll send it to Ruthie. She likes to keep up."

"Tell her hi for me. We need to catch up."

Tansy sighs. "Keep an eye on Daddy, okay? I'm worried about him. Let me know if you think I need to come. I can get another vet to cover for me." She pauses. "And Mari?"

"Yeah?" I gaze out the living room window at the fountain still brimming with water.

"I've been thinking about Melody's message all morning. Mind if I share it with Ruthie?"

"Please do. I hate that she got dragged into everything."

After we hang up, I take out Daddy's trash and leave him and Fritz snoozing in his chair. Heading back to the Sands Motel, I take a backroad that passes by a field of pumpkins, mostly picked over. I remember another field of pumpkins, and my mind searches for a slender young mother wearing a headscarf and castoff cape over a cotton dress. In her secondhand nursing shoes polished brown, she walks up and down rows of bright orange globes tangled in thick scraggly vines, calling to five little girls, "Look for the ones with their sides bashed in. The imperfect ones that'll be left to rot. The farmer will sell 'em to us cheap, and that'll make the *tightwad* happy."

"And we took those ugly pumpkins home, didn't we, Mama?" I say, turning my gaze back to the road as my words whoosh out of me like an angry wind blowing over the curve of the steering wheel. "We scooped out the seeds for roasting and carved out faces. We kept them long after Halloween, even when their faces began to cave in."

Taking a deep breath, I squint in the rearview mirror, hoping to catch a glimpse of Mama gazing back at me. But it's Daddy I see, the firm Hubbard jawline, the mouth clamped shut in determination and silence.

And then the flute player with ginger-colored hair growing frizzy and wild swims into view. "I stopped by your old house today." I glance sideways as if she's riding shotgun. "I'm going to get to the bottom of this. I promise."

I crack my window for fresh air; the wind whistles in, whispering, "Share, don't be stingy. Don't be mean. Stick together. Don't cheat."

"Sorry, Mel, but those rules were for little girls too naïve for our own good. Little girls who grew up too fast when the world caved in."

19 A CONVENIENT OMISSION

OCTOBER 2017

THE NEXT MORNING AS I leave the motel to head to the bookshop, Tansy calls. "Daddy hasn't been forthcoming about Fritz's history. He never took Fritz to the vet."

Irked, I peel out of the parking lot, spraying gravel. "Daddy hasn't been forthcoming about a lot of things." A freight train on the opposite side of the four-lane heads east toward the New Mexico–Texas state line five miles away. I watch my speed and stay in my lane as a white farm pickup splattered with dry mud passes me on my left.

"Didn't you notice Fritz wasn't wearing a collar or tags?" Tansy's tone isn't accusatory, just rushed. She's calling between patients.

"Sorry, sis. Guess I was overcome being back in Melody's old house."

Tansy sighs. "I can imagine. Listen, I need a favor. Can you take Daddy and Fritz to the vet this morning? Get Fritz checked out. See if he has a chip."

I hesitate and clinch the steering wheel in resistance. I'm not in the mood to see Daddy this early, not until I get my first dose of caffeine. But I sense urgency in Tansy's voice and give in. "Sure, sis. What time?"

"Ten a.m. Don't worry about the bill. It's taken care of. One of my assistants has already made the arrangements."

"When did you get his confession about the cat?"

"Last night when I called to check on him before bed."

"Let me guess—he had a boatload of excuses."

Tansy sighs again. "Daddy's afraid if Fritz has a chip, someone will claim him, and Daddy doesn't want to lose Fritz. He's gotten quite attached."

"How come Clover never mentioned anything to me?"

Tansy chuckles. "You know our sister. She's not exactly a cat person. Besides, it's all she can do to get *Daddy* to the doctor these days."

Right before we hang up, Tansy rattles off the vet info along with a list of supplies I need to pick up at the pet store if Daddy gets to keep the cat.

After I make a quick pass by Clover's bookshop for coffee—she's in her office on the phone, so I don't stop to chat—I chomp on a toasted bagel between slurps of coffee and head to "the little house of fountains" on Mesa Lane. Sarcasm is my shield when dealing with Daddy.

Ten minutes and one indignant cat later, I load Daddy and Fritz up and we head out.

A block from the vet's office, Daddy points his gnarled finger straight ahead. "Up there, past the hardware store." His gravelly voice competes with the direction lady on my GPS.

Fritz meows inside an old pet carrier perched on Daddy's lap. The cat is pissed, confined in a small space that probably still smells like dog from all the small dogs Edie and Dot owned over the years.

We pass the hardware store and turn into the parking lot. Daddy leans forward, gazing up at the nondescript building where white lettering on an industrial glass door announces, "Sandhill Animal Hospital."

He turns toward me, and I see a frail old man following orders from his youngest daughter, *the animal expert*, who I suspect is Daddy's favorite. I turn the heater down. This morning Daddy smells like old carrot peels, not the Aqua Velva Man of long ago. The lenses of his eyeglasses are still grimy.

"Daddy, let me clean your eyeglasses later. And I don't want to hurt your feelings, but you need to take a shower and put on some clean clothes. I'll help you if you'd like." I unbuckle my seatbelt, trying to shake off my revulsion.

He mumbles something then bends his head to peek down at Fritz inside the carrier. "It's okay, boy." His speech is slow, as if his mind is scrambling to form each word. "Don't be scared." Daddy's gnarled hands rest protectively on both ends of the carrier.

I pat his bony shoulder, treating him like a child. "If Fritz belongs to someone else . . ." I stop, afraid to say more, startled by the sight of whiskers sprouting from Daddy's ears.

He nods, biting down on his bottom lip too late to catch a strand of drool. I grab a tissue, swipe the drool, and get out of the car. Opening the passenger door, I take the carrier from Daddy, lift it by the handle, and set it on the cold ground. Fritz caterwauls, cursing me in cat.

Daddy grips his cane between his knees and stares straight ahead. "You read the note yet?" His voice is gruff but even.

"What note?" I glance around, impatient. It's chilly out, and I want to get us inside where it's warm. What if he refuses to get out of the car?

"The note in Mel-o-dy's flute case." He draws out each syllable as if he's pronouncing a foreign name. "It's hidden inside the body. The long joint, if you recall your flute parts."

"I haven't opened the case yet," I admit, my voice shaky. "Why is it hidden?"

He slowly twists around in the passenger seat, wincing as I lift him from the car. "Because Edie was going to burn it after the funeral. I stashed it in a place she'd never think to look."

Once he's on his feet, he leans on his cane and waits for me to shut the door and pick up the cat carrier. Gripping my left arm, Daddy and I hobble toward the building, his cane one step ahead of us.

Halfway there, he pauses and fumbles in his back pocket and pulls out a hanky. After he hacks up a loogie, he stuffs the soiled hanky back in his pocket and we proceed. *At least he didn't spit on the sidewalk.*

As we shuffle along, Daddy says, "Edie found it on Melody's pillow after she went missing. Edie never showed it to the police."

I squeeze the carrier handle harder, hoping the poor cat doesn't pick up on my anxiety. "Why not?" By the time I open the door and usher Daddy into the lobby, I'm on edge.

Daddy looks at me and blinks his watery eyes. "She figured Mel-o-dy was high when she wrote it."

"What did the note say, Daddy?" I don't even try to hide the irritation in my voice.

"Something about going to look for the rail swimmer or some such nonsense."

My heart skids to a halt along with my feet. I freeze in place and stare at him, dumbfounded by his revelation. "What did you say?" My voice is hoarse, barely above a whisper.

"Who do we have here?" A friendly young vet tech with cropped hair and a nose ring approaches us from across the lobby. Daddy greets her with a grizzled grin. "Say hell-loh to my boy, Fritz."

The young woman reaches for the carrier. I sputter something about checking for a chip. She tells us to take a seat; she'll be right back after they run a scan.

Daddy sits in silence in the warm lobby, resting his chin on the crook of his cane. The voices around me fade, muted as if I'm underwater.

The past glides up to me, and Mama's voice sings out across the plains . . . "Girls, do you see her?"

20 THE RAIL SWIMMER

SUMMER 1973

"DID YOU TELL DADDY where we're going?" The landscape flashed by outside my window as we careened down the two-lane blacktop in Mama's station wagon. We passed a clapboard farmhouse set back off the highway. It leaned sideways like it was fixing to keel over. Red cattle with white splotchy faces grazed on both sides of the road, fenced off by barbed wire and wooden posts.

"I told him we're going to look for the Golden Carp and the Mermaid." Mama leaned forward and turned the air conditioner down a notch then settled back against the driver's seat, both hands on the wheel.

With a sly grin, Clover twisted in her seat and glanced back at the rest of us. "That's funny, considering they're not real." She held up Mama's library book, *Bless Me, Ultima*.

"They're as real as you want them to be," Mama countered, not taking her focus off the road. "According to a story I read in *Sandhill Times*, Rudolfo Anaya says Ultima came to him late one night while he was writing. She appeared out of thin air and told him to put her in his novel."

I got goosebumps. *Was she an angel or a ghost?*

Melody looked up from her pink notebook where she'd been doodling. "Who's Ultima?"

Mama wore big white sunglasses and a turquoise headscarf. I thought she looked like a movie star as I gazed at her reflection in the rearview mirror. "She's a wise old woman, a *curandera*, in Mr. Anaya's novel. She watches over a little boy named Antonio. The author grew up in Santa Rosa, where the story is set. Except he changed the name of the town."

"What's a curandera?" Tansy asked over my right shoulder.

"A healer." Clover flipped open the novel and continued reading where she'd left off. After a moment, she said, "I'm still trying to figure out if the owl in the story and Ultima are one and the same."

"Ooh, that sounds good," Melody said, tickling the back of Clover's neck. "I wanna read it next."

Clover swatted Melody's hand away and continued. "I overheard Miss Mavis say some schools around the country are trying to get the book banned from their libraries and reading lists."

I looked at my sister. "Why?" I envied the way she could carry on intelligent conversations about books in a way I never could.

Clover adjusted her cat-eye glasses. "Because it talks about things some people are afraid of."

"What kinds of things?" Tansy blurted in my right ear.

Ruthie sat next to her, quiet until now. "Witches and healers," she cut in. "And white male priests who try to tell everybody else how to live."

I gazed at the two youngest sitting behind me.

Tansy narrowed her eyes. "How do you know all that?"

Ruthie shrugged. "Mommy read about it in *The Albuquerque Journal*. She says Rudolfo Anaya is Chicano, like us."

Tansy frowned. "You're *Chicano*? I thought you were Spanish, like Mrs. Sanchez."

Ruthie blew her bangs off her forehead and threw her hands in the air. "Honestly, I think it's the same thing."

Tansy tilted her head, looking thoughtful. "What am I?"

Melody spun around and laughed. "You're a mermaid, silly, like the rest of us."

"But today we're *Indian* mermaids," Ruthie reminded her. We'd all worn our hair in pigtails tied on the ends with rubber bands and matching buckskin moccasins with fancy beadwork Mama claimed came from a *genuine* Indian reservation. Later Clover told me Mama bought them cheap at Payless.

I slid my arm over the back of my seat and tickled Tansy's bare shoulder. "You're still my little water bear," I whispered.

Tansy giggled, then pushed my hand away. A gentle reminder she was no longer a baby.

I fidgeted with the frayed hem of my cutoffs. My stomach growled although we'd just eaten pimento cheese sandwiches on wheat bread marked half off from the day-old bread store. "How much longer, Mama?"

"We're about an hour out, Marigold."

About then the abandoned church in Rosemont came into view on our right.

Melody cranked down her window as a blast of hot air rushed in. "Can we stop by the old church? I wanna write on the wall."

Mama yelled over the sound of the wind. "We'll stop by on our way back. Look, there's already somebody there."

We gawked at a fire engine red Pontiac GTO parked in front of the church. It looked like a car we'd seen in a parade Daddy took us to. He carried on that day like he was watching a beauty pageant. If he'd been with us today, he'd have whistled like the car was Miss America. Her shiny red paint stood out against the gray church. A dark-haired woman in a cowgirl hat emerged from around the side of the building, a large camera slung around her neck.

Melody swiveled in her seat and stared out the window until the church and car went out of sight as the road curved to the left.

I reached over and patted her on the shoulder. "Don't worry, Mel. You'll get a chance."

She nodded and smeared cherry-flavored ChapStick over her cracked lips.

It was Saturday afternoon. Mama didn't work on weekends, but lately Daddy had started working more and more, sometimes seven days a week.

Right after lunch, as Daddy was backing the Edsel down the driveway, Mama stormed in the house, tore off her apron, and announced, "Girls, get your things. We're headed to the Blue Hole." As she stomped up the staircase to change clothes, we all heard her mumble, "Damn you, Dorian. Someday you'll pay for your broken promises."

As we scrambled into our swimsuits and grabbed old bath towels, I peeked out the bathroom window that overlooked our backyard. The fountain brimmed with water where Tansy and Ruthie had filled it the day before, but the stakes and twine from Daddy's big production a year ago now resembled a relic from another time. The ocean still waited for us hundreds of miles away.

But today, as Melody rolled up her window and Mama cranked the air conditioner on high, we could feel the excitement building: we were going swimming.

Clover read. Tansy and Ruthie jibber-jabbered quietly between themselves. Melody and I leaned against our respective windows, lost in our thoughts.

Mama's voice interrupted the quiet hum of the road and the cool air blowing from the vents. "Girls, do you see her?"

I bolted up, squinting out the windshield as we headed west.

Clover glanced up from her book and over at Mama. "See *who*?"

Mama's gap-toothed grin and her sunglasses greeted us in the rearview mirror. "The Rail Swimmer." She sounded giddy as all get-out as she flicked her head in the direction of the approaching freight train, weaving serpentine down the tracks that followed the slope of the terrain, dotted in sagebrush.

We all glanced out the windshield and then to the left side of the car to see what Mama was talking about.

As she rolled down her window, keeping her right hand on the wheel, I ran my tongue over my own set of tracks that ran along the top row of my teeth where a pink plate pushed against the roof of my mouth. Mama gave up a portion of her paycheck each week to pay for my new retainer. It smelled nasty if I didn't brush my teeth after I ate, and I had to remove it to practice the flute. I'd gladly wear the retainer the rest of my life if Daddy would let me quit band.

Clover looked skeptical sitting next to Mama. "All I see is an ol' freight train."

Mama hollered over the whoosh of wind. "Girls, close your eyes then open them again. Sometimes you have to start over to see what's really there."

Melody scooted next to me and placed a hand on Mama's right shoulder. "Mrs. Hubbard?" She practically shouted in Mama's ear. "What's 'The Rail Swimmer'?"

"A giant mermaid," Mama chanted at the top of her lungs. "See her, girls, she's gliding along, six feet above the glistening tracks, her long tail swishing from side to side. She's pink and purple and turquoise, the color of a New Mexico sunset." Mama flung her left arm out the window as if she were flagging her down. The wind whipped our hair around something fierce; even the back of Mama's scarf fluttered behind her.

"I'm still looking," Melody roared. "Is she real?"

"She's as real as you want her to be." Mama rolled up her window. With her left hand on the steering wheel, she reached over her shoulder and gave Melody a reassuring pat. "All you have to do is believe."

Melody crossed her eyes and fingers and shoved up against me, her cherry-laced breath brushing my cheek. "I see her, I see her," she squealed. "She's as long as a train."

Of course Melody saw her. She wanted to please Mama. *My* mama, the woman who'd first heard mermaids. Now she'd seen one. I wanted to see one too.

Behind me, Ruthie and Tansy had worked themselves into a frenzy as they pressed their faces to the side window, screaming "Where? Where?" into the solid pane.

Finally, I crossed my eyes and fingers, imitating Melody. Then I made a wish: "If you're there, God, please let me see the mermaid." Squeezing my eyes shut, I wanted to believe, as the rhythm of Mama's voice painted watercolors in my head.

"Legend has it she swims through the air, gazing back and forth in search of water, her head in sync with her tail." Mama paused to catch her breath. "Any water will do: a cow tank, a pond, an irrigation ditch, a dry creek bed or arroyo after it rains. Anything that looks wet. Tonight, after it gets dark, she'll jump the tracks and swim off in the direction of the water. She only needs enough to dip her scales in. Even a few drops are better than nothing, and they give her the energy to keep going."

Melody kept playing along. "Is she the only giant mermaid that exists?"

"No, there are others throughout the Southwest," Mama answered as my eyes popped open. In one brilliant flash, I saw the mermaid swimming down the tracks. Then poof, she was gone, along with the train.

I was a believer.

Mama's voice continued to swirl around me. "But she's the only giant mermaid in these parts. The only place you can see her in the daytime is when you're coming around the bend. Legend says hobos call her 'Our Lady of Hope.'"

Tansy had rested the side of her face on the back of my head. "Why do they call her that?" Tans asked. I could tell she was listening with her whole self. We all were.

"Because sometimes she takes pity on them," Mama said. "Once they climb on board, she takes them to the next town where they might be able to find food and shelter."

We were all quiet for a moment. Then Tansy leaned back in her seat and said, "I think 'Our Lady of Hope' sent us Hobo so Mrs. Sanchez wouldn't be so lonely."

Melody laughed. "That little rascal. He likes to hide her slippers."

I scooted to the edge of my seat and nudged Mama on the shoulder. "You should type up your story and send it to *Reader's Digest*. I bet they would publish it."

Mama tapped the steering wheel a couple of times, as if her fingers needed to dance. "That's sweet of you, Marigold." She paused a moment, sitting up straighter. "Maybe I could include the part where she calls out to all the other mermaids, along with all those lonely women who feel lost and hopeless."

Before us, the highway straightened like a long gray ribbon. Off in the distance, I could see a herd of antelope grazing and a lone coyote loping across the flats.

I glanced over at Melody, back on her side of the car. I could tell she was thinking hard about something.

Leaning back against my seat, I caught a glimpse of Mama smiling at me in the rearview mirror. I decided that in her white sunglasses and turquoise scarf Mama looked more like a famous writer than a movie star. At almost thirteen, I knew today was one of those times when Mama made do with whatever was on hand.

When that train came around the bend, Mama saw opportunity.

21 BLESS US, BLUE HOLE

SUMMER 1973

BY THE TIME WE chugged into the caliche parking lot, it was already three o'clock in the afternoon. The station wagon's tires kicked up dust as steam hissed from under the hood.

"What's that smell?" I wrinkled my nose as Mama shoved the gearshift into park and cut the motor.

"Not sure. Maybe the engine overheated." Mama let out a heavy sigh and sat there a moment. Once the air conditioner stopped running, it didn't take long for the inside of the car to heat up, too. Despite the rising temperature and our excitement about going swimming, nobody moved. "Well, we'll just have to let it cool." Mama pulled the keys from the ignition and opened her door.

"Too bad Daddy's not here to fix it. He'd know what to do." No sooner had Tansy spoken than a grubby-looking man with dark curly hair and baggy pants came toward us across the parking lot. He had a sketchpad tucked under one arm, his chest pocket stuffed with pens and pencils.

"You folks need some help?"

Mama hesitated, then got out of the car, slinging her tote bag with her wallet hidden inside over her right shoulder. "Looks like my engine overheated."

We all blinked at the man with a puffy tanned face, realizing at once he wasn't a man at all, but a woman in men's clothing. "I'd be happy to take a look."

Mama glanced at the stranger then back at us. "Girls, stay in the car."

"The name's Dewey, ma'am. I'm a local artist. I come by here a few times a week to cool off and draw."

"So, you live around here?" Mama sounded cautious, scanning the parking lot like any second she might need to scream for help.

"Sure do. Been coming here for inspiration for years." Dewey gestured in the direction of the Blue Hole, hidden from our view where we sat in the parking lot.

"May I see one of your drawings, please?" Mama tugged her tote bag closer. She wanted proof before she would trust this stranger.

Taken by surprise, Dewey fumbled with the sketchbook a second before she flipped it open and held it up. I rolled down my window to get a better look and to keep from roasting to death. "Here's what I've been working on today."

We gazed at the drawing. It showed a pile of large flat boulders at one end of a circular pool where a splash of water broke the surface.

Mama's face softened. "That's really good. I always wanted to take art, even though I can't draw a decent stick figure."

Dewey tapped the sketch, the tips of her stubby fingers stained with something. "I'm calling this one *Señora del Agua*. The Water Lady."

"The Water Lady?" Mama tilted her head as she studied the drawing. "Is she invisible?"

I got goosebumps.

Dewey cracked a grin, exposing a mouthful of broken teeth. "The locals say she's been around since the time of the conquistadors.

They say she swims through the channels in the underground caves running under the llano. If you're a nice person and she likes you, she might make an appearance. But keep in mind, all you might see is a splash."

Mama glanced quickly back at us over her shoulder. "You hear that, girls?"

Dewey leaned down and smiled at us through the window. "Howdy, girls. I'm Dewey."

"Howdy," we waved in unison before the whispering began, breaking two of our commandments: Don't stare at people who are different and don't talk behind someone's back.

"She's missing a bunch of teeth," Tansy hissed in my ear.

I held my palm to my mouth, checking my breath, grateful for the smelly retainer that would eventually close my gap.

Clover muttered out the side of her mouth, "I bet her gums hurt. Maybe she can't afford to go to the dentist."

Melody slid next to me. "You guys. Look at her eyes. I've never seen eyes *that blue* except on a dog."

Tansy tumbled over the seat and landed between me and Melody. "You mean that Siberian husky we saw at the park that time? Yup, her eyes are the same color."

Ruthie nudged Melody in the back. "Can we get out? I'm burning up back here."

Mama shut her door and motioned for us to get out of the car. After Dewey set her sketchpad on the roof, she grabbed a rag from her back pocket and pried open the hood. More steam poured out.

I pushed open my door, keeping a wary eye on her. I was both fascinated and scared of her at the same time.

We all huddled around Mama as Dewey poked around under the hood, reminding me of Daddy tinkering on his Edsel.

"How do you know how to work on cars?" Melody stuffed her towel under her arm, inching closer.

Dewey shrugged. "Dunno, just do, I guess. I can fix about anything if I have the right tools."

Crossing her arms, Ruthie walked up to Dewey. "I didn't know ladies can work on cars. I wanna fly airplanes when I grow up."

Glancing over her shoulder, Dewey's eyes crinkled in a grin. "How old are you?"

Ruthie bared her teeth like she was saying *cheese*. "I'm nine."

"Her mom, Carmen, is working two jobs to save up for Ruthie's flight lessons," Mama interrupted with pride in her voice.

I gazed at Mama in her sleeveless cotton shift she wore as a swimsuit coverup. It showed off her slender legs right above the knees. One time when I told Mama she had pretty legs, she knuckled me on the chin and said, "That's sweet of you, Marigold, but books will take me farther than these legs ever will."

Dewey poked around under the hood a few more minutes. Finally, she wiped her forehead with the back of her hand. "Looks like you need a new fan belt. I can fix it if you'd like." She propped one foot on the front bumper, one elbow resting on her knee.

"How much do you charge?" Mama looked around, like she was weighing her options. Trust this stranger to fix her car or attempt to drive home with a broken fan belt, resulting in a burned-up motor, stranding us in the middle of nowhere?

Before Mama could say anything, Clover stepped in with her two cents. "We can try and get to a pay phone and track Daddy down, but the problem is we have no idea how to find him on his route, especially on Saturday since the office is closed. And even if we could find him, it would take him at least two hours to get here before he could even start working on the car. By then it might be dark."

I envied my sister. In some ways Clover acted like Mama's equal, even at fourteen.

"There's no charge, ma'am." Dewey removed her foot from the bumper and stood rubbing the heels of her hands together. "I know a fella who runs a garage. He owes me some favors. Why don't you gals go cool off, and I'll see about getting your car fixed. You picked a good day to come. There's hardly anyone here."

Still, Mama hesitated.

"Once I track down a new fan belt, I'll come get you so you can witness my work. How does that sound?"

At that moment, I began to trust Dewey. Apparently so did Mama.

"That's so very kind of you," she said. "By the way, my name is Letty."

"Nice to meet you, Letty." Dewey shut the hood of our station wagon and grabbed her sketchbook. "Is this your first time here?"

We all nodded, then Mama said, "Funny thing is, we only live two hours away, but gas costs money and you know how it is."

"That I do. Lots of locals never stop by here. You can be surrounded by magic and not even notice. One second the water can look turquoise, the next cobalt blue. The Blue Hole is a desert oasis in a land more brown than green. You gals know the Blue Hole is a natural artesian spring? It's sixty-one degrees year-round."

"Brrrrr." Mama feigned a shiver.

We watched Dewey walk toward a beat-up chalky white Corvair before we headed across the parking lot, all of us glistening with sweat as the sun glared down on top of us. "Stick together. Mind your manners," Mama said, bringing up the rear.

Right before we rounded the bend where a wooden sign said BLUE HOLE, eighty-one feet deep, Dewey's voice echoed across the parking lot. "Girls, don't let the concrete steps leading into the spring fool you. They're slippery as all get-out. Make sure you hold on to the center handrail. There's no lifeguard on duty. Be careful and have fun. See y'all in a bit."

"Thanks for the warning," Mama said.

Melody grabbed my elbow and pulled me forward. "Watch out for the Water Lady," she teased, knowing I was squeamish about such things.

Tansy and Ruthie scurried past us, each of them taking turns carrying the blue water jug.

Mama chuckled behind us. "Clover, honey, you might want to

put that book away until later. You're liable to walk straight into the water if you're not paying attention."

As we approached the shimmering pool, Mama said, "Wait up, girls, let's set our things down on that picnic table right over there." She pointed to a spot next to a tall cottonwood.

Two older Hispanic women treaded water near the steps while two little boys dashed past us, squealing with their teeth chattering as their mother wrapped them each in a towel and led them toward the parking lot.

We practically had the place to ourselves, which was fine by me since I was still self-conscious about my body, even though I'd lost most of my baby fat. As we shrugged out of our clothes, all five of us already in our bikinis, I realized I would never be long and lean like Melody. Even covered in freckles, she had the kind of body boys noticed, especially now that God had granted her part of her wish: she was growing boobies. I was too, but mine were Brussels sprouts compared to her heads of cabbage. We'd both started our periods a couple of months earlier, Melody first by a few days even though I was a week older.

While Mama gathered our things and stuffed them into her tote bag, we took turns rubbing each other with suntan lotion that smelled like Coppertone but cost less. Mama was the last one to undress. She unzipped her cotton shift and stepped out of it, then folded it neatly and placed it in the tote bag. Being modest, she still wore a one-piece although we'd tried to convince her to get a two-piece.

"Marigold"—Mama handed me my retainer case—"There's no way I'm diving eighty-one feet to retrieve your retainer if you lose it while you're swimming."

Turning away, I removed it and placed it in the case and handed it back to Mama.

"Okay," she said. "Let's form a circle and hold hands. There's something I want to say first." I reached for Melody on my right and Clover on my left, expecting Mama to rattle off a full list of rules about safety.

"Bless us, Blue Hole," Mama began. "We're the Llano County

Mermaid Club." We all glanced at each other, shocked by her prayer. This was the first time she'd included herself in our club, and she was praying to a body of water, not God or Jesus. "We've come from Sandhill," she continued, "to pay homage to a great writer named Rudolfo Anaya. And while some might argue his story is fiction, we ask that his beloved Ultima watch over us while we cool off in this crystal-clear gem in the desert."

Clover elbowed me and giggled. But my eyes were on the water, waiting for Señora del Agua to surface.

We scrambled for the steps. "Remember what Dewey said," Mama hollered.

The concrete steps were six feet wide and divided by a center handrail, its yellow paint chipped in places. The top two steps stuck out of the water, the gray concrete contrasting in tone with the other steps, about eight of them, fully immersed and covered in yellowish green algae.

Ruthie rushed forward, fearless as ever. She grabbed hold of the center handrail and started down. "They're slimy," she squealed, right before she slipped on her butt about halfway down. Pulling herself up, she plunged into the water, laughing and splashing. "Come on, guys. It's freezing."

The rest of us grabbed hold of the rail and clambered down the slick steps, laughing and screeching as we took turns plunging into what felt like a giant bucket of ice water. Our teeth chattered until we began moving about, using our arms and legs to propel us forward and backward. After a while we forgot about the cold as the sun beat down on top of our heads and we glided through the water effortlessly, like we'd been born here.

Mama waded in the shallow section on the second to last step, one eye on all of us, the other on her tote bag nearby on the picnic table. Melody was the first one to hoist herself out of the pool and trudge up the winding path that led to the boulders.

"Hang on," Mama yelled. "Nobody jumps or dives unless you have at least two spotters in the water."

For the rest of the afternoon, we worked on perfecting our cannonballs. Even Mama agreed nobody could do a cannonball like Dorian Hubbard.

"If he were here," Tansy laughed, "I bet his bottom would touch the bottom."

Eighty-one feet was a long way down, especially if you couldn't find your way back up. I tried not to think about how deep it was.

"You see the Water Lady yet?" Melody joked as we scrambled up the path for the umpteenth time.

I shook my head, catching my breath. The bottoms of my feet fried as I walked out onto the scorching boulder next to Melody. Ruthie joined us.

"Look, there she is," Ruthie yelled, right before Melody plunged into the water where Clover and Tansy waited as spotters. Ruthie held herself, giggling. The second Melody's head popped up, Ruthie wrapped her arms around her right knee and leapt off, making a big splash.

I stood at the edge of the flat boulder, peering down into the sparkling water that glittered like diamonds in the sunlight. I glanced over at Mama. She'd finally let her hair down and braved her way into the cold water. As she floated on her back near the edge by the steps, her hair fanned out like seagrass.

If Daddy could see you now, I thought, taking a deep breath. Then I yelped like Tarzan and flew into the air, hitting the water, and going down, down, down . . .

By the time Dewey got back, it was already six o'clock. She apologized profusely, saying she had to hunt down the ol' boy who owned the garage since he'd closed his shop early to attend a funeral. Then on her way back, she stopped to help a farmer whose goats got out.

After all that time waiting for her to return, it took her less than thirty minutes to make repairs. She brought a gallon of water and poured some into the radiator. It was nearly dusk by the time we said our goodbyes and left.

At a convenience store at the edge of town, Mama made a beeline for the pay phone hanging on the outside wall. We huddled around her, everyone sunburnt but Ruthie. Mama fed a dime into the coin slot and dialed our number. It rang and rang. Mama breathed through her nose and tried to pretend she wasn't peeved because Daddy didn't pick up.

I fiddled with the ends of Mama's hair, hanging damp and stringy down the middle of her back. From behind, she looked like a teenager.

Next, she called Melody's house. When Grandma Dot picked up, Mama said, "It's Letty. Yes, Melody's fine. Hope you and Edie aren't worried sick. Oh, Edie's not home either? Well, neither is Dorian, dadgummit. I tried calling my house and it rang and rang. Listen, we had a little car trouble earlier, but everything's fine." Mama paused to catch her breath. "Will you call Carmen and let her know we're on our way home?" Mama rattled off Ruthie's phone number. "We're grabbing some cold drinks and a snack, and we'll be on our way. See you in a couple of hours."

After she hung up, she smiled a little too brightly as we filed into the store, breathing in the aroma of hot dogs and burritos as our empty stomachs growled with hunger. We took turns using the restroom, soaping our hands in the foamy pink suds from the dispenser.

At the counter Mama fumbled in her wallet and pulled out a ten-dollar bill. "Girls, how 'bout we treat ourselves to ICEEs and burritos?"

We all cheered, happy and grateful Mama had enough money to pay the bill. As we stood outside, wolfing down our burritos, the heat from the day surrendered to the cooler air of a desert night. Somewhere in a nearby tree, an owl hooted. Mama looked up from her burrito. "Some people believe it's a bad omen when an owl hoots. Not me. Not after reading *Bless Me, Ultima*. I believe that's Ultima, and she's giving us her blessing for our drive home."

No one argued with Mama that Ultima was a made-up character

in a novel. For all we knew, she was as real as the feathery night air that blew across our faces.

As we headed down the road to Fort Sumner, then onto Sandhill, darkness was setting in. Soon it would be pitch-black except for the stars and a half-moon shining overhead. Stopping by the abandoned church was no longer an option. If Melody was disappointed, she didn't let on.

Mama stashed her ICEE between her knees. "Look at the western sky, girls. It's ablaze in pink and purple and turquoise."

"Like the giant mermaid," Melody slurped, her mouth full of cherry-flavored slush.

Dewey's drawing rested on the seat between us. After she'd fixed the car, she tore the drawing from her sketchpad and gave it to Mama, saying, "I'm nobody famous, but I wanted y'all to have a sample of my art."

Later, after we'd thanked Dewey and she'd left, Mama said, "I've got more girls than I've got drawings. Pick a number between one and twenty, and the closest to the number I'm thinking gets the drawing."

Melody picked sixteen and won the prize.

In the darkness of the car, with tiny pin lights on the dashboard and the headlights illuminating the road in front of us, Mama's voice rang out into the night. "Girls, Dewey didn't have to help us, you know. She could've looked the other way and walked right on by. It's just a hunch, but something tells me she's another landlocked mermaid."

Everybody jabbered at once.

"Why do you say that?" Clover asked.

"She doesn't *look* like a mermaid," Tansy countered.

"Maybe she's a mermaid in disguise," Ruthie offered.

Even in the dark, I could see Melody twist around in her seat. "That's right, Ruthie. Like the Rail Swimmer. One second we saw a freight train, and the next, well . . ."

“What if Dewey’s the Water Lady?” Mama added. “Think about it. Her eyes were the same color as the Blue Hole.”

My scalp tingled. I shuddered and gazed out the window into the darkness, reminding myself that I was too old to believe in fairytales. And yet . . . somewhere out there across the rolling plains, I pictured the Rail Swimmer jumping the tracks and gliding through the night air, in search of water.

22 CAT BUSINESS

OCTOBER 2017

WHEELING INTO A PARKING slot at the corner of Fourth and Main, I reach for the flute case and slip it inside my tote bag. After dealing with the cat all morning and making sure Daddy got a shower and put on clean clothes, I don't want to be alone when I open the case for the first time.

Breathing deeply, I get out of the car and head toward the bookshop. The temperature has dropped since I left Daddy's place and stopped by the motel. Even in the short distance from my car to the door, I feel the cold nip at my nose.

Clover is chatting with a customer at one of the display tables. She sees me and excuses herself. "Well, fill me in. You look like something the cat dragged in."

Ignoring her lame joke, I brush hair out of my face and swipe a tissue across my runny nose before I proceed. "Why didn't you tell me Daddy's been making do with an old metal paint tray and shredded newspaper in lieu of a litterbox?"

She jerks back, one manicured hand on her bosom. "Ooh."

Wrinkling her nose as if I've carried the stench with me into her shop, she says, "I had no idea."

I want to believe her, but honestly . . .

"How could you miss it? It's right there between the toilet and the bathtub in the only bathroom that exists in that house." I realize the second the words fly out of my mouth that I sound like Tansy earlier: *Didn't you notice Fritz wasn't wearing a collar or tags?*

Her chest rises and falls as she closes her eyes before she fixes me with a haughty look. "It's not like I ever use the restroom there. Like I said before, I get in, and I get out quick."

Tossing my used tissue in the trash bin by the counter, I squirt hand sanitizer into my palm and work it in as I start to laugh, finding the absurdity in our conversation.

"What's so funny?" She tilts her head, a hint of annoyance in her expression.

"You realize if Mama were here, she'd have taken one look at Daddy's makeshift litterbox and said, 'Well, look at you, Dorian. Aren't you clever making do with whatever's at hand?'"

Clover chuckles as tears spring instantly to her eyes. Using her middle finger, she lifts the lenses of her glasses with a polished nail and dabs at the corners of each eye to keep her makeup from smearing. "If Mama were here, do you honestly think she'd step foot in that house?"

I shrug, shifting the tote bag on my shoulder. It's heavier today, the flute adding extra weight. "Daddy lucked out. He and Fritz get to stay together."

Clover glances around, checking to make sure everything is running smoothly in her shop. "Did the cat have a chip?"

I nod, glancing toward the bakery as the smells of freshly brewed coffee and spiced tea intermingle, teasing my senses. "Turns out Fritz was named Fred before Daddy found him curled up under his carport. He belonged to an old woman who died. The cat disappeared sometime during the funeral. Her son lives up north and didn't have time to deal with a missing cat before he had to get back. According to the vet tech, the son was relieved Daddy found the cat."

Clover nods and gestures toward the bakery. "You have lunch yet? Maybe some hot soup? You look chilled."

"I'm good, just tired from getting Daddy in and out of the car all morning. We swung through McDonald's. Daddy wanted a fish sandwich and a milkshake. I suspect both are easy to swallow. I had a wrap."

She nods. "So, is the cat all caught up on its shots?"

"Yup. Thanks to Tans, who made all the arrangements. Daddy and I stopped by the pet store. I bought a new litterbox and a month's supply of cat food. Then I made sure he got a shower and started his laundry."

"Let me give you some money," she offers, clicking her nails.

I hold up my hand. "Nope. You've done enough for Daddy. It's my turn." I start to head toward the back of the shop. "Oh, I swung by the motel on my way here and grabbed Melody's flute case." I pat the side of my tote bag. "Daddy says there's a note inside."

Her head swivels around, her eyes searching mine. "A note?"

"From Melody," I say as a blast of cold air gushes into the shop.

A tall gentleman in a navy overcoat and dress slacks shuffles in the door, a wool scarf draped around his neck. Despite his stooped shoulders and thinning hair, he still resembles the boy at the pool who called me Little Lotta. The boy who had made fun of Norman's spastic movements and called Ruthie a dirty Mexican.

Thornton Hinkle, president of the Sandhill Chamber of Commerce.

Hands in his coat pockets, Thornton gazes around as if he's forgotten why he's come inside the bookshop. We'd spoken briefly at Sawyer's last book signing over a year ago, when Thornton accompanied his mother to the standing-room-only event. He was cordial and friendly that night, hardly the bully from long ago. If anything, he was overly polite. Perhaps it had something to do with his standing in the community.

When he spots us, Thornton's gray eyes twinkle in recognition.

He removes a hand from his pocket, and I detect a slight tremor as he lifts it in greeting. "Marigold Hubbard," he says, reaching for the back of the nearest chair by the door. "I wondered if you were in town. Thought I saw you walking down the sidewalk the other day. You looked like you were on a mission."

"Good to see you again, Thornton." I'm not about to tell him I was chasing down memories and Sawyer led the way.

Clover signals one of her employees to take over for a few minutes so she can continue to chat. "Sis, Thornton lost his mother a few months ago. Bless her heart. Geneva was one of my best customers."

Geneva. Yes, of course, Clover was on a first-name basis with the woman who called Daddy *that awful man*. Clover is a savvy businesswoman. She knows how to play the game.

"I'm sorry to hear that," I say, picturing the fancy lady getting drenched when Daddy jumped off the high dive. I prefer that image over the last time I saw her here in the bookshop over a year ago, when she fingered a string of pearls at her sagging neck and looked like every other white-haired old lady enamored as Sawyer signed her book.

Thornton starts to unravel his neck scarf. There's that tremor again, ever so slight in his hands. "Thank you so much, I . . ." He pauses for a moment as if collecting his thoughts. "I loved her, but . . ." He takes a deep breath, bats at his left ear, and gives us a sheepish grin. "Do you know how hard it was to be Mother's only child?" He glances up at the ceiling a moment and sighs. "Mother, God love you, but . . ."

Then he fixes his gaze on us. "Mother meant well, but she was the most critical person on earth. No one was ever good enough, especially me, her son." Clover and I stare at him, shocked by his admission. I catch my breath, grappling with how to respond.

But Thornton presses ahead. "The truth is, ladies, Mother's death has caused me to reflect on things."

"Death has a way of doing that," I toss out, surprised by my sudden empathy toward him.

"Look," he glances around, lowering his voice. "I've done a lot of stuff I'm not proud of. I know I was a little shit when we were kids." His apology seems genuine.

Clover studies a spot on the floor then inspects her nails. "You weren't that bad, Thornton. It was a long time ago."

"Stop making excuses for me." He places both hands on his knees, his long fingers splayed out as he grips each knee. He swings his face toward me. "When I saw you in town, I decided to take a chance and stop by to apologize to both of you. Will you relay it to the others? Well, to those of you who are still left?"

He didn't mention Melody. He didn't have to. Her absence hung over all of us.

"Yes, of course," I volunteer, my voice wavering as I hug my tote bag closer.

Thornton leans back in the chair and stuffs his hands in his coat pockets. "Remember that time you girls got escorted out of that revival?"

"Oh my God," Clover laughs, removing her eyeglasses. "I can't believe Melody and I stood up to that preacher."

Thornton chuckles, throwing his head back. "That old dragon. He deserved it. And if I'd had any guts, instead of heckling you girls, I'd have gotten up and followed you out the door. But my father was a church deacon, and he was running for mayor. And Mother, well, she was always threatening to pack me off to military school if I screwed up."

I walk over and plop down in the chair next to Thornton. Setting the tote bag on the floor, I elbow him, my turn to tease. "Remember what you called us?"

He winces apprehensively, lifting his shoulders and squeezing his eyes shut like a little kid. "Oh, Lord, am I in trouble."

No new customers have come in the door since Thornton arrived. Clover pulls up a chair and joins us. "Thornton, if I recall, we wore it as a badge of honor."

We all laugh as the decades slip away and we are teenagers once again . . .

23 STILL CAUSING TROUBLE

1974

MAMA DROPPED US OFF in front of Central Baptist Church down on Grand Avenue. The church grounds and parking lot took up an entire city block. Mama told us she'd be back in two hours. A revival had come to town, and all the kids at school were going, whether you went to church on a regular basis or not. As we filed through the heavy wooden doors on a Sunday afternoon in early October, clean-cut men in suits and ties handed us paperback copies of the New Testament.

"We get a door prize for showing up," Clover joked as she led the way down the center aisle and slipped into a pew near the altar. The rest of us squeezed in, no wiggle room between us.

The sanctuary filled up quickly with teenagers and young adults in bell-bottoms and tie-dyed T-shirts. Kids waved their arms in the air and crooned "Hallelujah" and "Praise Jesus." Five minutes after we arrived, an all-guy band with long hair and platform shoes performed the contemporary campfire hymn, "Pass It On." We joined in, familiar with the lyrics.

When the band finished playing, a hush fell over the sanctuary as a portly white preacher in glasses and a black robe approached the massive pulpit. He reminded me of a judge I'd seen somewhere on TV. After he introduced himself, he instructed us to bow our heads. I could've sworn he said "Repent" at least three times in his opening prayer as he prayed for "all the lost sheep of the world, the unsaved sinners who don't know Gee-zus!"

Then he began to preach.

The louder he preached, the more I flinched every time he thundered the Lord's name. It's like he was speaking directly to me: "Marigold Hubbard, repent from your evil ways or you're going straight to hell. God Almighty will toss you into a lake of fire." After about five minutes of this, I felt a stirring within me. It wasn't fear anymore but anger. Anger at being judged a sinner.

At first, I thought it was just me until I noticed Clover out of the corner of my right eye. Her feet wiggled as she tossed loose change back and forth between her palms. She rolled her eyes and huffed out the side of her mouth, "He's an old windbag." Any second I thought she might throw her hands in the air and send pennies and dimes raining down on all of us as we waited for the preacher to stop yakking so they could pass the offering plate and everybody could feel good about themselves.

To my immediate left, Melody drummed her fingers on her new Bible and let out a theatrical sigh. "I sure wish Jesus would show up. He'd shut that preacher up right quick."

I burst out giggling, picturing Jesus walking up the center aisle in a dove-white robe, waiting for the preacher to step aside so Jesus could talk. The more I tried to stop giggling, the worse it got. Then Melody and Clover got the giggles, along with Tansy and Ruthie.

We held our stomachs, trying to suppress our giggles. Then Tansy got the hiccups, which made things worse. Our heads snapped up when we realized the preacher had stopped talking. His jowls jiggled with indignation; his hammy mouth hung open like a black hole; his round pasty face grew more crimson by the second. From behind his glasses, his beady eyes glared at us for what seemed like eternity.

"Young ladies . . ." He cleared his throat and leaned into the microphone. "Perhaps you'd like to share your joke with the rest of the congregation. Obviously, it's far more entertaining than my sermon."

A collective gasp was heard throughout the sanctuary.

Mortified, I slid down in the pew, wishing I could disappear. Not Clover or Melody. They both jumped to their feet as if the preacher had extended an invitation.

I heard Clover swallow before she squared her shoulders, thrust her chin out, and began, "We didn't mean to laugh, sir. It's just that after sitting here listening to you tell us what bad people we are, we had to laugh to keep from quaking in fear. Your words make a person feel guilty for being alive. You talk more about the devil and hell than you do about love and forgiveness."

Melody joined in, "That's right, Pastor Reed. When you preach, you make me afraid to come to church. I never feel that way when I go to the public library. There I feel accepted for who I am. The librarian might tell us to keep our voices down, but she never tells us we're bad people."

The preacher gripped the sides of the pulpit. "Young lady," he fired back, "this is a House of God, not the public library." He gestured with a fleshy hand. "Around here, that New Testament you received today is the only book that matters."

Ruthie clinched her fists and glared up at the preacher. "He's not the Pope," she mumbled to Tansy.

The preacher looked stricken, as if he'd overheard Ruthie. After a moment, he leaned forward, clamping his gaping maw shut before he hissed through clenched teeth into the microphone, "You two! Sit down!"

My mouth dry, I tugged on Clover's and Melody's arms for them to abide by his command. They brushed me aside and didn't budge.

Still red-faced, the preacher gestured toward the back of the sanctuary. "Ushers," he boomed into the microphone, "will you escort these young ladies out? Some fresh air will do them some good."

A familiar male voice yelled from the back of the sanctuary, "Y'all are going to hell."

About then, Clover signaled for the rest of us to stand up. Since Ruthie sat nearest the aisle, she filed out first, leading the way. With our heads held high, we marched down the center aisle toward the back of the church.

We passed stunned teenagers, some scowling, some smirking, toward the grim-faced ushers in suits waiting in the narthex to usher us out the doors.

At the second to last pew, I recognized the bully from the pool, Thornton Hinkle, sitting on the end. It had been years since I'd seen him.

We'd been at the library when Melody spotted him sitting alone at a table looking through a View-Master. Thornton saw us and waved us over. We hesitated at first, not sure if it was a trick or if he was going to be nice for a change. The moment he went to let us take turns looking at the pictures in his View-Master, his mother walked up and led him away by the ear. As they went out the door, he glanced back at us, his face beet red.

He was older now, in his late teens, his shoulders broader, his cleft chin and cheeks spotted with acne. Despite a few pimples, he was still cute. As we strode past, he lowered his chin and coughed into his fist, "It's the *odd squad,* still causing trouble."

Without missing a step, Melody reached over and pinched his ear.

"Ouch," he yelped, grabbing the side of his head, taken by surprise as Clover and I followed Melody and the two youngest into the narthex. The men in suits swung open the doors and ushered us out into the crisp autumn air.

After we scrambled down the steps and stopped long enough for a group hug, we linked arms and did the monkey walk down the sidewalk. "Keep your eyes peeled for a pay phone," Clover said.

"You got Thornton Hinkle good," I told Melody. "You should've seen him blush."

Melody laughed. "Yup, I grabbed him by the ear like his mother used to."

About twenty minutes later, Mama pulled up in front of the Greyhound bus station a block from the church. We held our breath as she left the engine running and stepped out of the car long enough to eye us over the top of the station wagon. "So, I guess you won't be attending the revival anymore this week? Glad we don't attend church there."

"Are you mad at us, Mama? We broke some of our own commandments," I confessed, mentally checking them off in my mind.

"Sometimes you have to put a bully in his place," Melody cut in, giving me a reassuring look.

Clover pushed a strand of hair behind her ear and jingled the offering money in her hand. "You mean the preacher or Thornton Hinkle?"

Mama looked on, amused. "I see you girls at least got free Bibles out of the deal." She climbed back in the car, and a few minutes later we hooked a right on Main and headed north.

Clutching our copies of the New Testament, we sailed through a green light at the intersection of Fourth and Main. "The preacher said the Bible is the only book that matters," Clover said. "But I think he's wrong. Books are magic. Without books, we'd still be living in the dark ages. One day when I grow up, I'm gonna open a bookstore and carry all those titles that offend people."

"You do that, honey." Mama nodded and hung a left at the intersection of Sixth and Main. As we cruised past the public library on our way home, she reminded us, "Girls, remember what I told each of you the day you got your first library cards. I said you are card-carrying members of an institution where knowledge is power. I wasn't there today to witness what happened, but I trust your judgment. And I suspect when you walked out of that revival today, you weren't walking out on God but on one man's *assumption* of who God is."

Melody burst into tears, covering her face with her Bible.

Mama dug through her pocketbook and passed Melody a tissue and a Midol. Somehow Mama knew Melody was *on the rag*, so she took her dramatic outburst in stride. "Am I dropping you off at your house?"

Before Melody could answer, I leaned forward, touching Mama's right shoulder. "Melody left her flute at our house." I glanced sideways at Melody, knowing she probably didn't want to go home to a lonely house. Grandma Dot was out of town, and Melody's mom was rarely home these days. And because Melody didn't carry a purse, Grandma Dot and I were the only ones who knew Melody sometimes stashed her housekey in her case (her secret hiding place), along with a couple of tampons when she was on her period.

"Okay," Mama said, "but don't forget it's a school night. You can walk her halfway home later."

Dabbing her eyes, Melody nodded, then sniffled and started to laugh. "I bet that preacher would hate *Are You There God? It's Me, Margaret*."

"Yeah," Clover chimed in, "he'd probably want to burn it."

As Mama turned onto Vista Boulevard, I kept hearing Thornton Hinkle's voice in my head. But instead of feeling shame, I felt pride.

Reaching over, I poked Melody playfully on the arm. She poked me back. Glancing over my shoulder at Ruthie and Tansy, then up at Clover, I began to snap my fingers and shimmy my shoulders. "Hey, mermaids," I caroled, "we're the *odd squad*, still causing trouble."

"Depends on how you define trouble," Mama chimed in. "Sometimes causing trouble can bring about change for the better."

24 THORNTON

OCTOBER 2017

INSIDE CLOVER'S BOOKSTORE, OUR former nemesis hoists himself out of the chair and turns to leave, his gait stiff from sitting too long. As he reaches for the door, his hand tremors again. Does he have palsy or the beginning stages of Parkinson's? I shudder, remembering the way he made fun of Norman decades ago at the pool: the spastic jerks, the cruel words. Surely all that meanness hasn't caught up with him. You know what they say about karma though.

"Well, ladies. It's been nice chatting, but I better get back to the office before my secretary sends out a Silver Alert." He pauses, smiles at his own joke, and then presses a shaky knuckle to his lips. "There's something else, and it's been bothering me for years." His voice wavers. "Melody came to me for help, right before she died. By then, I was already in my first semester at college."

The sound of Melody's name pierces the air like a gong.

Clover huffs herself up from the chair. "I didn't know y'all were on friendly terms."

I grab my tote bag and stand up, holding it against my chest. "Me neither," I stammer, trying to gather my wits. *How could we not know that Melody had become friends with the guy who used to pick on us?*

He shrugs. "I ran into her at the park that summer. She asked if I knew where she could buy pot. So, I hooked her up."

"Were you her supplier?" There's no judgment in Clover's voice.

"Yeah," he nods. "I know how it must look. Me being the mayor's son back then." He pauses a beat. "We smoked together a few times. Mostly we compared stories about our crazy mothers. I was shocked when she drove that beat-up Rambler all the way to campus a few months later to find me. I hated to turn her away."

Clover stiffens at the mention of that ratty ol' car. I can still see the trunk flap open whenever the rope came loose. After Melody died, I vowed I'd never ride in that car again, much less drive it.

Thornton continues, "That poor girl. By then everybody in Sandhill had heard the rumors about your dad and her mom. Melody said she needed a place to stay. I told her I couldn't possibly sneak her into my dorm room. I was already on a short leash with Mother." He rubs his neck, his face blotchy like he's had a sudden outbreak of acne. "When I heard the tragic news the next day, I felt sick. I didn't have the guts to attend her funeral. Rumor had it she committed suicide, but I didn't believe it."

"It *was* an *accident*," Clover blurts out. I detect my sister's need to defend her.

He nods. "I know. I feel bad though. When she told me she was in trouble, I assumed she was pregnant. Man, she lit into me and stormed out. Said she wasn't as stupid as her mother. I wasn't sure what she meant."

Clover clings to my arm, her nails digging into my long sleeves. *We knew what she meant, all right.* But Clover and I play dumb.

Thornton looks around as if he's checking for hidden gossips lurking among the bookshelves. "Funny, out of all the friends I had back then, Melody was the only one I trusted with my secret. Y'all know I'm gay, right?"

Clover and I nod, a little too quickly, caught off guard by his sudden candor.

"Melody said she knew before I did." He pauses, a faraway look in his eyes. "I stopped by the cemetery years ago on my way to Santa Fe for a meeting. I stood at her lonely grave and apologized for being a lousy friend."

You're not the only one, I want to say.

"Well, back to work I go." Halfway out the door, he throws his head back and chuckles, a dry deep chuckle full of rancor. "This town has its share of scandals. That's for sure. What town doesn't? Somebody ought to write a book about it."

Heat fires through me as cold air gushes in before the door closes behind him.

Clover releases her vice grip on my arm and pushes past me. "Guess you'll put all that in your book, eh?"

I ignore the snark and head toward the back of the shop, my mouth dry.

At the Make-Do, I take a deep breath and set Melody's flute case next to Mama's typewriter. I'm not ready to open the case yet. I'll wait until Clover drifts back this way later. I stare at the worn leather, at Melody's name on the nameplate. *How could I not know you and Thornton Hinkle had become friends? I thought you and I told each other everything.*

Don't be a doofus, her words hiss through my head. *You couldn't even handle the truth the day I told you everything on the ride home from Rosemont.*

The truth. Some of it was hidden in a letter Mama penned to the author of one of the most notorious novels ever written. It had been years since I read the letter and the novel.

I retrieve the velvety brown envelope from the narrow drawer and lift out the letter addressed to Grace Metalious, a writer who dared to uncover small-town secrets.

25 PEYTON PLACE

FEBRUARY 18, 1978

Dear Ms. Metalious,

On this day in 1964, my youngest daughter was born in the middle of a rare blizzard here in eastern New Mexico. Tansy's birth didn't make the headlines, but your death did seven days later, on February 25.

Even the title of your 1956 groundbreaking first novel became slang for any group of people who hide tawdry or racy secrets behind closed doors. Want to hear something funny? Rumor has it Geneva Hinkle, the snobby wife of our current mayor, snuck Peyton Place *out of the library in a brown paper bag.*

Not me. When I finally got around to checking it out a few years ago, I sashayed down those marble steps with your novel face out.

I read somewhere it's considered the first blockbuster in the United States, and yet it was banned in several places and even Canada. You were read by millions in secret and shunned in public by book critics and often those who never even read the novel. On top of that, you were criticized for your looks and lousy housekeeping skills by people who never set foot in your place. I love that photo of you in a flannel shirt and blue jeans at a manual typewriter, your round face free of makeup and hair pulled back in a ponytail. I guess you went against the June Cleaver image of what a respectable woman in the fifties was supposed to look like.

I think you were brave and courageous to write about things like rape, incest, suicide, abortion, and inequality at a time when women were expected to stay home and be good little housewives. If you had been a man, critics and the reading public might have raved about your book instead of raking you over the coals.

I'm glad you bucked the system.

I'm learning to buck the system, too, but it wasn't always that way. There was a time when I never stood up for myself, especially when it came to my husband, er, my ex-husband now! We've only been divorced a few weeks. I'm still putting up with people who refer to me as missus even though I'm considered a "divorcée." I'm starting to sign my name using the prefix Ms. when I'm writing checks or filling out forms. With help from Miss Mavis, I've been applying for grants and scholarships so I can go to college and make a better life for me and my three daughters. I'm hoping to take a couple of classes this summer at our local community college here in town. At thirty-eight, guess I'll be known as a nontraditional student.

Two days after Dorian left, I traded my old station wagon for a used 1976 four-door Volkswagen Rabbit with automatic transmission. The girls aren't keen on the alpine green paint job (Clover says it reminds her of Dorian's Edsel), but they like the saddle tan cloth interior and I like the gas mileage, thirty-nine miles per gallon on the highway and twenty-five in town. This will help when I start commuting to the university, twenty miles away.

I heard through the grapevine that shortly after I traded my old gas-guzzler for a late-model car with better fuel efficiency, Dorian parked his Edsel in Edie's backyard and bought a used two-door yellow Volkswagen Rabbit with a few dents in the side. Copycat! After Melody's funeral, Dorian handed Clover the keys to the Rambler. I get rid of one gas-guzzler only to get stuck with another. At least he's paying for liability insurance. The two oldest girls pay for gas with babysitting money, although Marigold still refuses to drive it.

Tonight, when I get off work, we'll celebrate Tansy's birthday. On Saturdays, I work at a dress shop (like the Thrifty Corner Apparel Shoppe in Peyton Place) to supplement my regular earnings as a receptionist at a doctor's office. Every little bit helps along with the meager child support. As part of my divorce decree, Dorian will help with the mortgage. After nearly nineteen years of marriage, he's not getting off scot-free. Considering he moved in with Edie and Dot, I say that's fair. I don't expect he'll stop by tonight, but knowing Tansy, she'll feel sorry for him and invite him at the last minute. But he better not bring Edie. She's not welcome in my home. I don't mean to sound coldhearted. It was hard enough seeing those two at Melody's funeral. I was cordial, because the way I see it, I had no choice.

Back to the day you died. I was still in the hospital propped up in my bed, giving Tansy a bottle, when a young nurse popped in, all aflutter after reading about you in the newspaper. She said you were only thirty-nine and left behind three kids. How sad, to be so famous but die so young.

Another nurse bebopped in to check on us. While she cooed and fussed over the baby, she sang the lyrics to Lesley Gore's hit song, "You Don't Own Me." At one point, both nurses hooked arms and did a dance step like the June Taylor Dancers from the Jackie Gleason Show. I cuddled Tansy and swayed along, admiring the nurses' crisp white uniforms and confidence.

I didn't grow up surrounded by books. I was mostly raised by a spinster aunt in a tiny farming community north of Sandhill. My folks were sharecroppers. They were killed when my pop swerved into an oncoming car on the way back from some honkytonk over on the state line. My aunt was a tightlipped old biddy, a teetotaler who only read the Bible and implied my pop was either three sheets to the wind or my mama was so unhappy with her life, she jerked the steering wheel into an oncoming car.

When I turned eighteen, I came to town one day with a girlfriend and saw this handsome young fella strolling along Main Street. We struck up a conversation. He told us he was a professional musician from Indiana. In between gigs he made his living as a traveling salesman. He convinced me to buy into his grandiose dreams. I was too dumb and ignorant to know what I was getting myself into, and the next thing I knew, I was pregnant and married. I was nineteen when I had Clover.

Looking back, I'm glad I kept her and didn't go to some back-alley butcher.

Despite our hardships, I tried to be a good wife. I overlooked Dorian's roving eye and tried to make the best of things. But I could no longer overlook his and Edie Calloway's affair. Lord knows how long those two had been coupling! I'll refrain from using crass language, although I don't think you'd be offended by the word I'm really thinking of!

Those two scamps would've fit right into your novel. Although neither classify on the same level as, say, the evil molester, Lucas Cross, they aren't exactly upstanding citizens when it comes to morality. While the good Dr. Swain in Peyton Place was performing an "emergency appendectomy," on Lucas's stepdaughter, Selena Cross—because abortion was illegal when your story took place, and it didn't matter that Lucas had raped her—you could have thrown in an extra scene where a married man (Dorian) drove a pregnant, unmarried woman (Edie) to some backwoods practitioner for her own "emergency" procedure. To up the stakes, you could have killed off Edie's character by having her die from a botched abortion.

In reality, Edie didn't have to go to such extremes thanks to the landmark 1973 Supreme Court decision Roe v. Wade. Unlike when you were alive and writing your novel, women today have a choice. As much as I detest those two and the horrible chain of events that led to Melody's tragic death, at least Edie had a choice. And call me callous, but I'm glad my girls and I won't have to bump into their love child. For all I know it could have been born with a set of hooves and horns.

Like Peyton Place, Sandhill has our own Norman, but he in no way resembles your Norman Page in the novel. Our Norman is an older man who suffers from the aftereffects of polio as a child. I can't imagine his mother giving him enemas as a treatment for all that ailed him when he was a young boy.

After I read Peyton Place, *I penned this poem about you. Miss Mavis framed it and hung it in her office at the library:*

MY ODE TO GRACE METALIOUS

By Letty Hubbard

You sit there in blue jeans and a flannel shirt
Tapping your daydreams
Into the keys of your typewriter
In a filthy kitchen in New England
Surrounded by small-town gossips
Who assume they can read your thoughts
Even before you've put them on paper
Rumors invade
Like a town crier
Dispensing news of the day
As the hillsides of Indian summer
Light up in flames
And the locals wag their tongues
And wait for you
A housewife and mother of three
To finish your story
The story they think is all about them.
Your fingers keep pecking away
While your thoughts try to douse out the fires
They are trying to start
Even before they've read one single word
Of your unfinished manuscript

Miss Mavis once told me her favorite library will always be a little plain-brown-wrapper of a building behind the courthouse in her dusty hometown of Spoke, New Mexico. She said it was her introduction to the magic of pulling out those narrow wooden card catalogs and rifling through the cards for the perfect title. And now she's passed the magic onto me as a reader and searcher for truth. After all, it was at the public library where I found myself "awakening" to a better life.

Even though it's tough scraping by now that I'm divorced, I think back to the morning fourteen years ago when that nurse came in singing, "You

Don't Own Me." In some ways that's my new mantra whenever I must deal with my ex-husband or with men in general who want to tell me what to do and what to say.

Lesley Gore's song came out a few months before you died. It's probably wishful thinking, but part of me hopes you sang "You Don't Own Me" at the top of your lungs and let those words sink in when it came to the public's perception of you and your body of work.

Single and surviving in Sandhill,
Ms. Letty Hubbard

PS: After Dorian left and Melody died, Marigold dropped out of band at the end of the semester. Can't say as I blame her. The girl is tone-deaf. We hocked her flute and my wedding band to pay for Clover's senior class ring. Marigold is a staff writer on the high school newspaper, but she mopes around the house on weekends. I'm trying to encourage her to apply for a summer internship at the Sandhill Times. Melody's death hangs like a dark cloud over all of us.

Deep inside, I blame myself for not taking that poor girl in the day she stopped by the house. It was bitter cold, a hard rain coming down. I'm ashamed to admit I allowed my hatred for her mother to cloud my judgment. But I also had to protect my own daughters as well as Ruthie. Carmen shared my concern that Edie might show up at the house and cause trouble, so I couldn't possibly give that woman any reason to come near us. Plus, I didn't want to cause issues for Dot. She's a good woman, a hard worker. When I reached to hug her at Melody's funeral, Dot whispered in my ear, "I'm sorry for everything. Some people are born lost. My daughter is one of them."

26 THE JOINT

2017

CLOVER'S VOICE STARTLES ME. "Are you going to stare at that thing the rest of the day or open it?"

I blink up at her as if she's an apparition. "How long have you been standing there?"

"Long enough to see you haven't opened the case yet."

"Sorry, I got carried away reading Mama's letter to Grace Metalious."

"I was wondering when you would get around to reading it."

"I'm going to include it in the memoir."

Clover studies her nails a second. "I figured as much. Mama stopped writing to authors after that."

I glance one last time at the letter then slide it in the envelope. "She was too busy working, taking care of us, and going to school. She went from typing letters she never mailed to writing papers for college."

Clover glances around, impatient. "Open the case, Marigold. I need to get back up front."

My fingers tremble as I fiddle with the brass latches and pop open the lid. A musty odor floats up from the interior then dissipates. The once shiny instrument appears tarnished and dull against the blue velvet lining, worn in places.

"So, where's the note?" Clover leans in, her chiffon duster brushing against me.

Lifting the long tube, I peer through one end. "Daddy said it's hidden in this section."

"Did Melody put it there?"

I shake my head. "No, it was Daddy, sometime after the funeral." Inserting my finger in one end, I feel for the paper rolled up in a tight scroll. "Daddy said Edie threatened to burn it. She didn't want Dot or the police to see it."

As I coax out the paper, Clover moves the case over so we can unroll the note and anchor it at both ends. It's Melody's handwriting, her perfect penmanship in blue ink still intact after forty years.

Clover nudges my shoulder. "What does it say?"

Handing Clover the flute's midsection, I began to read the note out loud:

"Mom,

Why do you hate me so much? Would you rather I'd never been born?

You're kicking me out for smoking pot? All because you found weed hidden on my side of the room. You're such a hypocrite. What about all the times you've driven drunk with me in the car? You could've killed both of us. You've been looking for an excuse to get rid of me since you started messing around with Marigold's dad. This house isn't big enough for the four of us. You're good at getting rid of things that get in your way. Like a baby for instance. Was that before or after we went to Galveston?

Do you know how hard it's been on me to keep silent? I've been forced to act like everything's hunky-dory, but my world is falling apart!! My best friends have turned on me. It's all yours and Mr. Hubbard's fault. You two are the most selfish people I know.

When Grandma Dot gets back from her trip, she'll kick you both out! Then I'll finally have a room of my own! Grandma Dot knows all about the weed. Like she told me, 'Just be careful, honey, we all have our vices.'

Not that you give a crap, but if anyone asks about me, tell them I've gone to stay with a friend until Grandma Dot gets back. If Plan A doesn't work out, I'll switch to Plan B and go look for the Rail Swimmer. If I don't see her, I'll look for Dewey. Or maybe Señora del Agua will make an appearance, because I'm a good person despite what you say."

♫

I shiver at Melody's last words and gaze up at Clover. "Plan A must have been going to ask Thornton for help."

Clover dabs the corners of her eyes and nods. "Don't think I'm crazy, sis. But I hope the Water Lady surfaced right before Melody slipped and hit her head."

I catch my breath at the image of Melody flinging off her windbreaker and running toward the water. With her body pumped full of alcohol, she wouldn't have felt the cold. "Maybe Señora del Agua was there to greet her, and Melody didn't die alone."

I stare at the note, guilt-ridden after my confrontation with Daddy. *What happened was a horrible accident. I had nothing to do with it.* "Sis, I'm ashamed to admit it, but after I found Melody's plea for help on the church wall, I've harbored thoughts that Daddy might've done something inappropriate that caused Melody to run away."

"I was thinking more along the lines that Melody had caught Daddy and Edie in the act. You know, like when I walked in on Harold . . ."

After a moment Clover picks up the flute's foot joint to insert it in the body. Something falls out one end and lands on the note. "What the hell? Is that what I think it is?"

We stare at what appears to be a mummified joint. One end looks like it might have been lit for a quick toke, then snubbed out.

My eyes mist up as I start to pick it up, but it crumbles in my fingers. "What if this was Melody's last joint?"

Clover holds the disassembled flute. "If homewrecker Edie hadn't blown a gasket over a little marijuana, Melody might still be alive."

I gaze at the dried flakes, brownish in color. "I hate that I was so judgy back then. I said some awful things to Melody on the drive back from Rosemont. The day she told me everything."

27 RAMBLIN' ALONG

NOVEMBER 1977

THELMA HOUSTON'S DEEP SOULFUL voice belted out in a moaning plea, "Don't Leave Me This Way," over the car radio. I rode shotgun and lip-synced, grooving to my favorite disco hit. I glanced over at Melody, who knew how to carry a tune. "Come on, Mel, how come you're not singing? You love this song."

She shrugged and kept both hands on the wheel, a cigarette scissored in her right hand. A few seconds later she took a puff, inhaled, then cracked the window and blew smoke out the side of her mouth, like I'd seen Daddy do a thousand times over the years.

I could tell something was wrong. Any other time Thelma Houston's number one hit came on the radio, we either sang along or broke out dancing if we weren't in the car. I reached over and turned off the radio. "Are you mad at me for calling you a pothead back at the church?"

"Don't be a doofus." She took an extra-long drag on her cigarette, held the smoke in her lungs, then released it like she'd been practicing this move her whole life. "I need to tell you something."

I leaned against the passenger door and waited. "What's wrong. You've barely said a word since we left Rosemont."

With her fingers still holding the burning cigarette, she scratched the tip of her nose and stared straight ahead. "They're getting married. As soon as Dorian divorces your mom."

Dorian? Divorcing my mom? I squinted at her, her frizzy halo blowing in the wind. My brain scrambled to comprehend. "What did you just say?"

"Don't play dumb, Marigold. Surely, you've seen it coming for years."

"Seen what?" What was she talking about?

Melody rolled her eyes. "Edie and Dorian. They're like the couple in that sexy song, 'Me and Mrs. Jones.' They got a thing going on."

I covered my ears. "Mel, I think pot has warped your brain."

She pressed on as if she didn't hear me. "I'm not sure where I'm supposed to sleep. Grandma Dot says I can sleep with her, but she snores and passes gas all night. Maybe I can stay with y'all, at least until we graduate."

"Melody, stop, okay? I think you're still stoned." We were about thirty miles outside of Sandhill. The pumpkin pie I'd nibbled back at Rosemont churned in my gut and sprang up my gullet like liquid fire. A slimy mix of snot and grief began to pour out of me as her jabber closed in on me like a chokehold.

"Look on the bright side." Her voice reeked with sarcasm and a new smokiness I'd never detected before. She sounded a lot like Edie and Grandma Dot. "We'll be stepsisters. We can share the car."

"*Stepsisters!*" My head was pounding.

She took another puff then blew smoke through those puckered lips that moments ago had played Bob Dylan and chastised me for whining about band. "I know it's a lot to take in. They sprang it on me back in October when they made me go to Galveston with them."

I shook my head, pretending this wasn't happening. "*Galveston?* It's by the ocean."

"Technically, the Gulf of Mexico, but yeah. Just so you know, the whole weekend sucked. When we got back, Dorian gave me the keys to this piece of junk. Guess he was trying to make it up to me. At least the radio works."

I squeezed my eyes shut. I was still trying to drown out the image of Melody at a beach without the rest of us. When I opened my eyes, it all began to sink in. "Wait, who gave you this car?"

She chewed her bottom lip. "Dorian, your dad." Her voice was barely above a whisper. "I'm so sorry, Mari. I didn't know how to tell you. It's been eating me up inside."

A new kind of jealousy invaded my body. Hot lava fired through my veins. I gritted my teeth. "Clover and I have been asking Daddy for a car since we got our learner's permits. Clover even told Daddy it didn't matter if it came from a junkyard."

"Probably where this heap came from," Melody muttered. "It was parked in front of the house a couple of days after we got back from Galveston."

The news strained my ears, punctured my lungs, cut off my air supply. I couldn't breathe. All the words I wanted to scream were trapped inside my skull. My jaw moved up and down like a guppy out of water, but no sound came out.

Melody kept yapping, "And you wanna hear something gross, my mom either had a miscarriage or an abortion. Even Grandma Dot doesn't know what to believe."

"Grandma Dot knows?" I felt dizzy. I couldn't take it anymore. I made a fist, punched the air. "Melody, stop talking. I swear, you're still high."

She took a final puff on her cigarette and tossed the butt out the window. "The weed wore off a long time ago, Marigold. You're in denial, that's all."

We rode the rest of the way back in silence except for the tires rubbing the road and the engine humming under the hood. I stared out my window as the weight of betrayal began to sink in. He screwed around on Mama. No surprise there, but Edie?! Melody's mom?

A new kind of rage boiled inside of me. "Mel, why did you cover up for them for so long?"

"I didn't know what else to do. Put yourself in my place."

God help me, I knew it was petty in the big scheme of things, but when you're a girl from the Southwest . . . "He took *you* to the ocean, Mel. Not me, not my sisters or Ruthie. Just you. Why?"

"I don't know." Her voice sounded meek, unfamiliar. "Maybe he thought he could bribe me into going along with everything."

I felt numb.

Seconds later, Daddy's Edsel came toward us on the opposite side of the street. He stared straight ahead, like he was in a daze, a cigarette clamped between his lips.

"Prick," I screamed, snot flying from my nose. I flipped him off and glared at him through the windshield as he drove past, my eyes blurry with tears.

As my house came into view, I could see some of his clothes strewn around the yard, along with his galoshes that normally sat by the front door when he wasn't wearing them. Mama stood on the front porch, wringing her apron, still clad in the buttercream pantsuit she wore to work on Saturdays at her part-time job at the dress shop. Upstairs in the corner bedroom, Clover, Tansy, and Ruthie peeked out the window, all three looking lost and forlorn.

Seeing Mama standing there hurt me to my core. Unraked leaves scuttled by as I climbed out of the car. "What's this gonna do to Mama?" The moan that came out of me sounded like some wounded animal. I grabbed my camera and tossed the photos at Melody.

She hugged the steering wheel, her body heaving with sobs. Nobody came to her rescue. Nobody bent down to look in the car window to ask if she was okay.

I stood numb, my back to Mama and the others, and waited for Melody to leave. Part of me wanted to invite her in, pretend everything was okay. But I was too heartsick. And nothing would ever be the same again.

Finally, Melody sat up straight, wiped her face with the heel of her hands, then jammed the gearshift into drive and pulled away from the curb. As I watched her drive away, Thelma Houston's song looped through my mind, "Don't Leave Me This Way," along with the blurry image of Melody in pigtails as she poked my finger with a needle in first grade.

She hadn't gone far when the rope came loose, and the trunk popped open. As the lid flapped up and down, I turned to see Mama's face glistening with tears. Her mouth worked, but no sound came out.

28 BANNED

NOVEMBER 1977

DADDY STOPPED BY THE next day to retrieve his briefcase and a few other things. While he and Mama battled it out upstairs in their bedroom and then down in the kitchen, Clover, Tansy, Ruthie, and I hid in the parlor. We didn't want to look at him, talk to him, have anything to do with him.

After he left, Mama stormed upstairs and told everyone to leave her alone—she was "making a plan." About thirty minutes later, Melody showed up, her tentative knock barely audible between the claps of thunder and Mama banging away on her typewriter.

Clover opened the door, letting in the clean scent of rain. She didn't invite Melody in. "What do you want?"

Melody stood hunched in her windbreaker, the ends of her bell-bottoms soaking wet where she'd walked from the Rambler parked at the curb to our front door. Water dripped off the eaves of the awning overhead but mostly kept the front porch dry until the wind started blowing. "Can I come in?" She sounded hoarse.

Clover thrust one hand on her hip and jutted her jaw. "What for? We're not exactly in the mood for company."

Melody spotted me perched on the landing, a hardback book in my lap. She took a step forward then stopped when I didn't get up as usual and go bounding down the stairs toward her. "Guess y'all didn't go to church this morning?"

"Hardly," Clover said as rain pelted the roof. She nodded toward the street, her mouth tightening. "Must be nice having your own set of wheels."

Shrugging, Melody glanced over her shoulder at the car. "I didn't ask for it. I tried to tell Marigold that yesterday." She flashed me a look then faced Clover. "It's ugly, huh?"

Clover clenched her teeth. "It drives, doesn't it? Who cares what it looks like?"

I sat with the dictionary Melody had given me still opened to the *b* words. I'd been looking up *bastard* after Mama hurled the insult at Daddy earlier. After hearing the word all my life, I'd finally decided to look up the definition.

Gazing at Melody's bloodshot eyes, the secret she'd revealed to me when we were eight years old teased and awoke every mean bone in my body. *Grandma Dot said my daddy took off before I was born. Never bothered to marry my mom.*

Mama's shrill name-calling at Daddy earlier egged me on. Repeating Mama word for word, the same obscenity exploded out of my mouth like vomit as I hurled the dictionary straight at Melody: "Get out. Get out, you *bastard!* I never want to speak to you again."

The sickening thud of a heavy book hitting the floor added to the insult. Melody took a step back and bent to stare at the book that landed inches from her feet. She glared up at me, a new defiance in her voice. "I haven't done anything to deserve that. Quit acting like a brat, Marigold."

From the corner of my eye, I saw Ruthie scurry from the parlor and pick up the broken dictionary. Cradling it against her flat chest, her brown eyes brimmed with tears as she blinked up at me. "Yeah, don't be mean."

I caught my breath at Ruthie's audacity to recite one of our mermaid commandments. It meant nothing to me after what Daddy and Edie had done to our families. To my friendship with Melody. I forgave Ruthie; she was still young.

Tansy ran up behind Ruthie and reached around her to touch the damaged book. "It's falling apart, like us."

Melody shivered out on the porch.

The wind picked up, blowing the rain sideways in sheets. A golden leaf from a cottonwood tree swirled in the door past Melody; it didn't need an invitation to come in. Clover let go of the door handle long enough to bend over, pick up the leaf, and examine it before tossing it back out on the porch.

Any other time, Tansy would have bolted out the door and started spinning in the rain. Instead, she let go of the book and kept repeating "I hate this," over and over as she twirled her tawny hair round and round her fingers, before letting go and grabbing another section.

My insides coiled with a mixture of shame and rage. But I didn't apologize to Melody. I rose from my self-righteous throne on the landing, crossed my arms in a smug stance, and glared at her again. "You heard me. Get out."

Melody's lips trembled as the wind lifted her hair in a tangled mass, covering part of her face. She didn't brush hair out of her eyes, she didn't turn to leave. Ignoring my hateful remarks, she rocked back and forth on the soles and heels of her Dr. Scholl's, her wet toes exposed to the cold. Her teeth chattered when she spoke again. "C'mon, Old Mother Hubbard. Let's go for a ride." She shook her car keys in the air, looking pathetic and yet hopeful, like I would give in to her because she was the prettier one, the smarter one, first chair to my last chair in flute.

"Don't ever call me that stupid nickname again," I lashed out. "I hate it."

Melody's face crumpled. She averted her eyes from me and turned to the others, pleading for acceptance.

But Clover, Tansy, and Ruthie looked everywhere but at Melody, their silence sending a signal that we'd banned her from our lives.

Mama's gentle voice came floating down the stairwell past me. "That's enough, Marigold." She touched me lightly on the shoulder and lifted her quivering chin toward the door. "Get on home, Melody. Your grandmother will be worried sick. You'll catch your death of cold standing out there in the rain."

Melody turned and disappeared into the downpour.

29 MESA LANE

MARCH 1976

"BREAK ONE NINE, THIS is Goldilocks, how 'bout it, Little Red Riding Hood. Got your ears on?"

C. W. McCall's hit trucker song "Convoy" blared over Melody's transistor radio. In better days when the mermaids were still united, Melody and I would hang out in her room and practice like we were cruising around town ratchet jawing on a CB radio. We'd come up with our own CB handles not long after the song hit the airwaves.

"Ten four, good buddy. But it's breaker one nine, not break one nine." Melody made a silly face and turned the volume down. "Come on, Goldilocks, you don't want to sound stupid when we finally get to talk on the real thing."

I hopped off the twin bed on Melody's side of the room. "Ten four, Little Red Riding Hood. Got it. Now, may I use your restroom?"

"Sure." Melody glanced up from flipping through a copy of *Seventeen Magazine*. "Don't forget Grandma Dot's number one rule."

I rolled my eyes. "I know. If you get pee on the seat, wipe it off."

It felt weird not having Pugnacious around. Normally, he'd follow me everywhere, even into the restroom. But he'd had surgery the day before on a hind leg and was recuperating at the vet over the weekend.

As I went to close the bathroom door, Melody hollered from her bedroom, "Try and ignore the unmentionables." There was a hint of sarcasm in her tone.

An array of sexy bras and panties were draped over the curtain rod of the bathtub, along with several pairs of pantyhose. None of the lingerie belonged to Dot or Melody. Because like Mama, Dot and Melody hung their laundry, including underthings, on the clothesline out back.

Unzipping my jeans to sit down, I noticed a *Frederick's of Hollywood* catalog on top of the hamper. The catalog was addressed to Edie Calloway. While I peed, I glanced up at a pair of red crotchless panties dangling above my head. Closing one eye, I could peep through the slit.

As I washed my hands, I studied the countertop lined with tubes and jars of makeup and creams and a brand-new pair of false eyelashes still in the case. Some of the makeup belonged to Dot and Melody, but most of it was Edie's.

"You'd think your mom was an exotic dancer, not a bookkeeper," I joked as I came out of the bathroom and entered the bedroom.

Melody made a face and continued to flip through the magazine. "I know. She's so annoying."

I sat down on the edge of the bed. "How can you stand to share a room with her?"

Cocking her head, Melody shot me a look. "C'mon, Marigold. Like I have a choice?"

"I know, sorry. That was a cheap shot. I should've kept my mouth shut."

"It's okay. You're stating the truth. You know I never bring anyone home except you. And you're the only friend who's ever been allowed in my room."

"You let Clover, Tansy, and Ruthie see it one time."

"But that's different. Y'all are like sisters."

I picked up *My Darling, My Hamburger*, a book Melody checked out from the Sandhill High School library. "Any good? Clover's probably read it."

"I dunno," she shrugged. "I haven't started it yet. I think it's about two friends and what happens when one of them gets pressured to have sex with a guy she's been seeing."

I swallowed and set the book down. I wasn't sure if this situation applied to me, but I felt a heaviness return to my chest. It all started a few days ago when a boy from school who I barely knew asked me to go steady. Tim had shoulder-length blond hair, dropped out of football to play golf, and told me I was cute.

Now as I fidgeted with the chunky ID bracelet I wore on my left wrist, I glanced around the room, working up the courage to ask Melody what to do.

Her side of the room was neat and tidy. Trophies for music competitions lined a double shelf bracketed to the wall above her headboard. Her flute and schoolbooks sat on top of a small bookcase near the foot of her bed. Her black music stand—not the flimsy metal version I owned—stood in the corner next to a sliding closet door.

But instead of saying what was on my mind, I asked, "How come you and your mom don't get your own place?"

She pushed the magazine aside and slouched against the wall. "Grandma Dot says she likes having us here, especially *me*. But honestly, I think my mom doesn't want to spend the money."

"I'm thinking of breaking up with Tim," I blurted, feeling a sense of relief for finally admitting it.

She chewed the side of her mouth. "But you've only been going steady a week. What changed?"

I twisted around on the bed and faced her. "Oh my God, for starters, his breath smells like bologna sandwiches. And sometimes he tries to jab his tongue down my throat."

Melody burst out laughing. "Break up with him, doofus." She grabbed a pillow and tossed it at me.

I caught the pillow and hugged it. "Mel, he grabs my butt between classes and does this nasty thing with his tongue. Like he wants to lick me."

Melody sat up straight and grabbed my hand. "Listen to me, Hubbard. The guy is an inconsiderate ass."

"I know," I nodded. "You're right. I'm going to break up with him."

"He sounds like a Rodger-Dodger type. You know, the creep who slips his hand up a girl's skirt on the first date, the second he gets them into a dark theater."

"I never should have agreed to go steady with him."

Melody's face softened. "Why did you?"

I glanced away, embarrassed. "Because he's the first guy who's asked. I've never had a boyfriend. You know that."

Melody closed her eyes for a second; she was thinking hard. Finally, she leaned toward me, getting in my face. "Here's the deal. Just because other girls are putting out or going steady or wearing promise rings doesn't mean we have to."

"What if we're the last virgins on earth?" I joked, poking fun of my own insecurities.

Melody threw her hands in the air. "Who cares? We decide when and with who. We don't let anyone pressure us to do something we don't want to do."

I tossed the pillow back at Melody. "I wish I had your confidence."

"Give me your wrist," she ordered, motioning with her hand.

I held out my arm. She unhooked the bracelet and dropped it in my palm. "You don't need my permission to break up with him, but this is a start."

I breathed easier. "Now I have to figure out when and how."

Melody studied my face a long time. "Girls like us from the wrong side of town, we're expected to fail. People assume we'll get knocked up, drop out of school, or get married right after graduation." She jutted her chin toward her mom's side of the room. "I'm not going to end up like her. Sponging off others and dependent on men for approval."

A smoker's cough came from the hallway outside Melody's room. Grandma Dot stuck her head in the door. "You girls want to help me unload groceries?"

She reminded me of an older version of Edie, but rounder, with cropped faded hair and a housedress that hid her middle-aged girth. And when Dot smiled, it was genuine.

We hopped off the bed and followed her out to the carport.

"You think she heard us?" Melody whispered as she reached into the trunk of Dot's Ford Falcon and lifted a brown paper bag and placed it in my arms.

"I hope not," I whispered back, my arms full as we headed back inside.

In the kitchen, we set the bags on the counter and put away groceries.

Dot rummaged through her pots and pans in a cabinet next to the range. "I'm going to roast a chicken. Melody, why don't you whip up one of your famous chocolate cakes?"

As I stashed the milk in the fridge, I turned to Grandma Dot. "You're on your feet all week working in the hospital kitchen. How can you stand to cook every night at home?"

Her smoky laugh filled the room. "Have you ever tasted hospital food?"

We all chuckled and continued to put groceries away.

Dot tied an apron around her expanding waistline and lit a cigarette. After she took a puff, she dangled it over the edge of the sink and plopped a whole chicken into a roasting pan. "Marigold, you wanna stay for supper?"

"I'd love to, but—" I glanced at the kitchen clock. It was already four-thirty. "I'm babysitting for the Millers tonight at six."

"A raincheck, then." Dot patted me on the cheek and smiled.

Melody was measuring cocoa into a large mixing bowl. "I'm babysitting tonight, too, but Mrs. Washington isn't picking me up until seven."

"Lucky you." I set out a carton of eggs and handed one to Melody. "The Washingtons live in a fancy house on the eastside and have a trampoline in the backyard."

Melody cracked the egg on the side of the bowl and tossed the shell in the sink. "Yup, and their little boys are sweet. They pay top dollar, too."

She waited for me to pass her another egg.

Dot sprinkled poultry seasoning over the chicken, took another puff from her cigarette, then balanced it over the sink. "Doctor Washington makes a nice salary. Sandhill was lucky to get a cardiologist of his caliber."

As Melody cracked open another egg, I slipped the carton back in the fridge. "Grandma Dot, I'm going to break up with this guy who asked me to go steady. I never liked him to begin with, but . . . Melody convinced me it was the right move."

Dot shoved the roasting pan in the oven and set the timer. "Best not to string a fella along if you don't have feelings for him."

"The thing is, I'm too chicken to tell him to his face," I admitted.

Melody poured the cake batter into a long metal pan and slid the cake next to the roasting pan. "The guy's kinda creepy, Grandma."

Dot wiped her hands on her apron. "I have a solution. Write him a note."

Melody giggled, arching her eyebrows. "Like a Dear John note then."

"Only in my case, it'll be a Dear Tim." I covered my mouth to hide my grin, feeling kind of guilty at the same time.

Melody scratched her temple and looked at me. "Okay, I have a plan. Stick the bracelet in an envelope with a note and drop it in his mailbox. He'll have spring break to recover."

"Do you know where this boy lives?" Grandma Dot asked.

Pressing my hands together, I flashed Melody a hopeful look. "Two doors down from Doctor Washington's house," I squeaked.

Melody crossed her arms, eyeing me with a half-grin. "You want me to deliver the news?"

Jumping up and down, I acted like she'd already said yes. "So, you'll do it, then?"

Melody rolled her eyes and sighed. "You owe me, Hubbard." She thrust one hip out and bumped me hard. I bumped her back.

We laughed and danced around Grandma Dot before she shooed us away and took a final drag on her smoke. Dousing it under the faucet, she tossed the soggy butt in the trash, and removed an ice tray from the freezer.

"Cocktail time," she announced, dropping a few cubes into a gold-rimmed glass. Stooping, she pulled out a bottle of bourbon from a bottom cupboard and untwisted the cap. She poured a healthy dose over ice, followed by a splash of lemon-lime soda.

Turning, she lifted the glass in a toast. "To Marigold, for having the courage to break up with a fella who turns out to be a creep." She took a healthy swig. "And to Melody, who will assist in the breakup."

Drink in hand, she padded into the living room. "House sure is quiet without Pugnacious here. He'll be so glad to get home on Monday. Poor thing probably thinks I've abandoned him."

Melody and I followed Dot into the living room. She thrust a notepad and pen at me. "Start writing."

I took the pen and notepad. "What should I say?"

"Oh, Lord, Marigold. You're the writer. Do I need to dictate, too?"

Grandma Dot chuckled and sipped on her bourbon and seven.

As I racked my brain about what to write, I gazed at a black-and-white photo framed on the wall behind Dot's chair. A young Dot in a frilly dress and bonnet stood on the stoop of the old church in Rosemont, holding an Easter basket in her gloved hands. She was smiling, like she'd found the golden egg.

I pointed to the photo as Dot reached for a paperback on a TV tray next to her chair. "How old were you in that picture taken at the church?"

"About five. I can still remember that day. We always had a big Easter egg hunt every year. Sometimes we'd find colored eggs hidden among the tombstones across the road." She opened her book and chuckled. "Whoever played the Easter Bunny sure had a wicked sense of humor."

Melody poked me and motioned for me to follow. "Come on, let's get this over with."

Back in her bedroom, I plopped down on her bed, pen poised to write, while she paced up and down, thinking out loud. "Okay, here's the deal. You need to come across as firm but kind. Let him know you're serious without sounding mean. From here on out, we shall refer to your little missive as the *breakup-gram*."

I giggled. "You should be a writer."

Mel shot me a look. "I'll stick to the flute. You ready?"

"Ten four, good buddy," I grinned.

Melody began to dictate, pronouncing each word slowly, giving me sufficient time to form each letter in my uneven scrawl.

When she was done, she scooted next to me on the bed and double-checked my spelling. "Perfect." She patted me on the back and handed me an envelope. "We did good."

"I don't know what I'd do without you, Mel." I gave her a hug and glanced at the note one more time:

Dear Tim,

I regret to inform you, but I must break up with you. Please consider this your official notice. I'm returning your ID bracelet in good faith, with zero new scratches. Thank you for the opportunity to go steady, but I have other plans moving forward.

Good luck finding a new girlfriend. There are plenty of girls around who I'm sure will enjoy your company. I'm sorry I couldn't be one of them. No hard feelings, okay?

See ya around,
Marigold

Satisfied, I folded the note, stuffed it in the envelope, along with the bracelet, and licked the sticky flap to seal it.

Muffled voices came from the living room. Sound carried in this tiny house.

Melody jerked her head up. "Ugh, my mom's home. Sounds like they're bickering again."

I jumped up. "I better go. Your mom probably won't like me being back here."

"Stay. This is my room, too."

We waited, barely breathing, listening to the heated exchange in the other room.

"Your daughter will be grown and gone before you know it. You can't even stay home for a few hours on your days off? You think you've got all the time in the world, but you don't."

"Get off my back, Ma."

Grandma Dot sniffed. "And that getup you're gallivanting around in. You look like you came from some discotheque in Lubbock."

"Blah, blah, blah," Edie muttered under her breath as we heard her approach.

"I hate how she treats you and Grandma Dot," I said.

"She's probably been drinking," Melody warned. "Ignore her."

I froze, knowing that was impossible. Like it or not, Edie Calloway was hard to ignore.

"My mom is a mom in title only," Melody admitted, not making excuses for her. “She’s never attended any of my musical performances or award ceremonies. Besides, I’d rather have Grandma there. She gives a crap. My mom didn’t even have a name picked out when I was born. It was Grandma Dot who named me. She said my tiny cry sounded like music to her ears.”

The moment Edie appeared in the doorway, she let her presence be known. In a slinky purple jumpsuit with a plunging neckline, she leaned suggestively against the doorframe and slipped off her rhinestone platform shoes. Leaning over to scoop up her shoes, she paused long enough that we could see all the way down the front of her jumpsuit.

Cleavage, I saw lots of cleavage. I tried not to stare.

Melody glared at her mom, not bothering to mask her irritation. “We helped Grandma unload groceries. Are you sticking around for supper, or are you just stopping by between *changings*?”

Batting her thick lashes in our direction, Edie ignored Melody’s comment and sashayed into the room. As she proceeded to sit down on the other twin bed, she curled her ruby lips in an icky smirk. “So, sweetie, how’s your mom? Is she still working at the dress shop on Saturdays?” Her sultry voice reminded me of a lounge singer I’d seen in the movies.

I squirmed under her questioning. Something about it felt as false as her eyelashes. “Yes, ma’am. Every bit helps.”

A sly look came over her face as she slowly began to unzip the front of her jumpsuit, exposing more cleavage with each inch. “And how’s your father these days?” Her sensuous green eyes, accentuated in black eyeliner, pinned me in place.

Tongue-tied, I couldn’t look her in the eye, but I couldn’t look away either as she slowly revealed creamy mounds of flesh spilling over each cup of her lacy black demi bra. “He’s fine,” I stammered, glancing away the second Melody elbowed me in the side. “He’s working today, too.”

“Mom, do you mind holding off on the striptease until we leave the room?”

My face grew hotter by the second. I glanced at the alarm clock next to Melody's bed. "Whoops! Gotta go."

Edie wriggled out of the rest of her jumpsuit. "Oh, I was hoping we could visit some more." Tossing it aside, she stretched out on her bed like a feline, showing off her trim but curvy figure and wearing nothing but her scanty bra and matching panties.

"Sorry, Miss Calloway. I'd love to stay and chat, but I'm babysitting for the Millers tonight." This was one time when our commandant to "mind your manners" came in handy. If nothing else, be polite.

Melody hooked her arm through mine. "Come on, I'll walk you out."

Edie yawned. "Tell your parents hello." Her sleepy gaze followed us as we crossed the room.

"Exhibitionist," Melody hissed over her shoulder, loud enough for her mom to hear.

I expected Edie to snarl back, but Melody's remark was met with silence.

As we filed past Grandma Dot dozing in her chair, the aroma of roasted chicken and chocolate cake followed us out the door. As much as I wanted to stay and have supper with Melody and her grandma, I was glad to escape Edie's presence. There was something sinister and secretive about her.

I looked at the envelope still clutched in my hand. "Oh, I forgot to write Tim's name on the outside."

Melody took the envelope. "I'll print it in big block letters. That way he can't miss it. And don't worry, I'll call you tomorrow after you get home from church."

"Thanks, Mel. Oh, he lives in the big split-level house with a circular driveway and desert landscaping."

"I know the one. Don't worry, I'll take care of it. I'll wait till it's dark and the boys are asleep. It'll only take a jiffy to dash there and back."

"You're the best, Mel." After I climbed on my bike and rode away, my left wrist felt lighter, and the heaviness in my chest was gone.

Turning right onto Vista Boulevard, I pedaled faster and faster to work my thigh muscles. By the time summer rolled around, I wanted my legs to look as toned as Melody's did in shorts. Right before I cruised into the driveway, I saw Daddy's Edsel coming up the street.

As I hopped off my bike and leaned it against the side of the house, I thought about how Melody had called her mom an "exhibitionist." On one level, I knew the word meant "attention seeker." But did it mean something else when it came to Edie Calloway? She remained both a mystery and a stranger to me. Before I left the house again to babysit, I planned to look up the word in the dictionary Melody gave me in sixth grade.

A week after school started back up after spring break, I saw Tim in the hallway between classes. He strutted past in designer hip-huggers and platform shoes, his chest puffed out in a paisley dress shirt opened at the collar, acting the epitome of cool. He gave me a chin nod and kept going. About three months later, rumors started flying that he got some freshman pregnant. Supposedly his rich daddy took care of it.

If Melody hadn't dictated the breakup-gram and placed it in his mailbox, I could've been the girl everyone was talking about.

30 THE CAT DID IT

OCTOBER 2017

THE DAY AFTER CLOVER and I found Melody's note stuffed in her flute, I get a text from Tansy: Can you go check on Daddy? He said it's not an emergency, but he needs you to come quick.

I read her message twice.

Irritated, I text back: Why didn't he ask me himself instead of having you be the go-between? Any idea what it's about? I was just by there at lunchtime. He's probably still pissed at me because I confronted him as to why he waited so long to tell me about the note. You know what he said? It made Edie look bad. So he waited until she was dead.

O, Jeez, what a lame excuse. I told Ruthie about the note. Like Ruthie said, Dot was more of a mother to Melody than that nasty twit Edie.

Shutting my laptop, I stash it in my tote bag and scurry past the front counter where Clover is ringing up a customer. "Daddy needs me for something."

"Sorry you have to be the gopher while you're in town," she calls as I'm halfway out the door.

When I pull up to Daddy's place, he and Fritz are waiting for me on the porch. He has the storm door propped wide open like it's a spring day.

"You and Fritz heatin' up the whole front porch? Your furnace is gonna give out."

Setting Fritz down, Daddy points with his cane toward the hallway and growls like a grizzly bear, "The bathroom."

Sniffing the air, I try to detect what kind of problem awaits me. But all I smell at this point is mildew and dust, combined with a whiff of fake evergreen from a waxy air freshener dispenser on the coffee table. "Did the toilet overflow or something?"

"Nah." He watches silently as I set down my bag and amble toward the hallway. "It's okay, boy," he croons to the cat as I round the corner.

At the entrance to the outdated bathroom, I find the toilet seat down, lid up. Bowl needs cleaning, but no surprises.

Don't forget Grandma Dot's number one rule.

I know. If you get pee on the seat, wipe it off.

A hand towel hangs haphazardly from a ring next to the medicine cabinet. The countertop is cluttered with various toiletries, including a tube of toothpaste missing a cap. Daddy's toothbrush and gunky black comb jut out from a cracked coffee mug next to a half-empty bottle of Pepto Bismol.

Gone are the lacy underthings and pantyhose draped over the curtain rod.

A foul odor permeates the air. An odor I've chosen to ignore until I see the evidence. Fritz has done his business in the new litterbox hidden in the corner between the toilet and bathtub. No big deal.

"Daddy," I start to laugh, "did you bring me all the way back here just to change Fritz's litterbox?"

Leaning on his cane, Daddy hovers in the doorway but doesn't say anything. The room gets deadly quiet. Then I hear Fritz mewing and realize he has slinked into the room and is sitting at Daddy's feet.

I glance back at the litterbox. It takes me a moment to process what I'm seeing: the kitty litter isn't the biodegradable pellets I purchased the other day, but instead grainy sand. Grainy sand that once filled the inside of a small white cardboard box. The box sits empty on top of the toilet tank.

My heart pumps wildly as I read the silver label on the side of the box: Edie Calloway, Sandhill Funeral Home and Crematorium.

My gaze shifts between the empty white box on the tank and the contents on the floor.

A noise emits from somewhere inside of me. *What the holy hell?*

"Is this a good enough apology for you, Mar-i-gold?" Daddy's croaky voice fills the tiny room, boxing me in. His words come out broken. I can hear spittle forming on his lips as he drags out my name.

I whirl, sickened and sad all at the same time as Fritz scampers from the room. Daddy begins to cry. I gather him in my arms, and his bony body crumples into mine. We make our way back into the living room where I get him situated in his recliner. Fritz dashes across the room and curls up on Daddy's lap. He meows contentedly as I back up, dodging the coffee table, and plop down on the sofa.

Clenching my hands, I stare at the floor a second. "I don't get it. Why did you protect Edie, even after she divorced you? I wish you would have shown me the note years ago. And an apology for dumping Mama for Edie could have gone a long way in helping all of us heal. Did you have to go to such extremes?" I reach for my cell phone.

His head snaps up. One gnarled hand continues to stroke Fritz's back. His watery blue eyes are accusatory. "Are you calling the police? They'll arrest me for desecrating human remains."

I gaze at him and sigh. "No, Daddy. I'm calling Clover and Tansy to fill them in on what's happened." *And to tell them I think you've officially lost it.*

Daddy glares at me and snarls, "Tell 'em the cat did it." A hint of determination and fire has returned to his once robust voice.

I stare at him across the tiny living room. He stares back, his lips puckered in a pout. I start to laugh at the absurdity of it all. At the black-and-white glamour shot of a bare-shouldered Edie her senior year in high school reeling with the images of her ashes back in the bathroom.

My laughter melts into tears as my eyes fix on the photo of Melody huddled in her blue windbreaker on a lonely beach. She must've been thinking, "I wish I was anywhere but here."

An hour later, Daddy and I hurtle down the two-lane blacktop at seventy miles an hour. He sulks next to me as he holds the white box containing Edie's ashes, or what was left after I salvaged what I could from the litterbox.

I'm miffed that he stiffed me with the cleanup.

His solution an hour ago as I was phoning my sisters: "Dump it all in the trash."

"She was a human being," I countered, finding myself defending what was left of her on the floor of the tiny bathroom on Mesa Lane. "She was Dot's daughter and Melody's mother. And as much as I despised her, I cannot fathom dumping the remainder of her ashes in the trash."

A wooden sign looms in the distance for the one exit in and out of the remote park.

"Actions have consequences," I harp on, as if I'm the parent and he's the child. "Forty years later, we are still cleaning up your messes."

His blue eyes burn into me as we turn onto a gravel road that winds around a smattering of picnic tables and trees that have already shed their leaves. We come to a stop near a shimmering pond and a sign that says: Fishing Only. No Swimming.

There's no one around except a herd of cattle grazing on dry grassland on the gentle slope of a nearby hill. "There," he points. "That small cluster of junipers."

"This is where you and Edie had your first fling?" My voice is reedy with disbelief. "Hiding behind some trees like a couple of horny teenagers?"

Clamping his jaw, he stares straight ahead through the bug-splattered windshield. At last, he mumbles, "We came here a few times."

I picture the two lovers sprawled out on a picnic blanket, their bodies writhing around while the rest of us were back in Sandhill, clueless of their affair. "Didn't you worry you'd get caught?"

He shrugs and seems lost in thought, incapable of answering me.

I want to scream, "Was she that good in the sack?" But even I have my boundaries. Where Mama was wholesome, Edie was trashy. But what's repulsive to one person is compulsive to another. It's the only way I could come to terms with Daddy's attraction to Edie. Maybe Daddy was born lost, too, and he and Edie felt at home in each other.

I get out of the car and walk around to help him out. The wind has picked up and it's freezing out. He burrows inside his coat and refuses to look at me. "You do it," he says. "Please, Mar-i-gold." His plea is pitiful.

"Me?" I flinch and take a step back, appalled that he's brought me all the way out here to do his bidding. "Daddy, it's bad enough what I had to face back at the house, but I'll be damned if I let you get away with this. This is your responsibility. Get out of the car. I will help you walk."

"Goddammit," he grouses, thrusting the box toward me. He grabs his cane, and I help him out of the car. We hobble on uneven terrain toward the junipers.

"Please tell me you never took her to the sand dunes or to Rosemont. Those were our special places when we were kids."

He pauses, glaring at me, but doesn't answer.

I realize it will be impossible for Daddy to bend over enough to spread the ashes. The deed will be left up to me. "You wanna say anything special?" I stoop and open the carton, trying not to inhale as I tilt the box low to the ground to keep the ashes from blowing up in my face.

"I'll see you in hell," he grumbles, his voice wrought with emotion.

"You're not going to hell," I say as Edie's ashes blend into the grainy soil of the high plains. The smell of juniper is strong. It reminds me of a cross between cat urine and the air freshener back at Daddy's.

He grips my forearm as I straighten, as if I'm the one who needs support. "Do you hate me, Mar-i-gold?"

I choke back a sore throat coming on as the sound of Melody's flute echoes through my mind. *Don't hold grudges . . .* "No, Daddy. I hate things you've done, but I don't hate you."

Once I get him tucked back in his seat, I toss the white box in a trash barrel, and squirt a pearl of hand sanitizer into each of his outstretched hands. "Here," I say, taking his hands in mine as I work the gel in and out of our fingers and palms.

He watches me, and his eyes fill with tears. "I remember when you were baptized. The preacher sprinkled your tiny head with holy water."

I stare into his watery eyes, and lean to kiss his whiskered cheek, letting the salt from his tears linger on my lips. "Let's grab some hot cocoa in town then get you home to Fritz."

The western sky is ablaze in pinks and purples and a note of ginger as we approach the outskirts of Sandhill.

As I ease my foot up on the gas pedal, I am overcome with the need to tell Daddy about Mama's last day and how we celebrated her life, since she didn't want any kind of formal service.

"You know how we said goodbye to Mama? We did it while she

was still with us. We thought we were gathering for her birthday. We thought we had more time. At least several more weeks. She was a good woman, Daddy. And we gave her the kind of sendoff she deserved."

He turns slightly in his seat and grips his cane, a captive audience for what I am about to say.

31 WOMEN IN TRANSITION

SPRING 2001

A HOSPICE NURSE HOVERED NEARBY. She'd given Mama something to keep her comfortable. Mama hadn't talked much or eaten anything in two days, and I could tell it took every ounce of energy for her to keep her eyes open when we walked in the room.

Mama rested against a cloud of pillows in the double bed in Clover's spare bedroom. My twelve-year-old daughter, Libby, and I stood at the end of the bed. Libby twirled her hair, hesitant to come closer. She reminded me of Tansy when she was younger, the way Tansy twirled her fingers round and round through her tawny mane whenever she was anxious.

"Mama, you turned sixty-one yesterday. Do you remember?" Mama's hazel eyes followed Clover's voice where she sat hunched in a chair next to the bed. Clover clutched a scrapbook and leaned forward. "You were a little out of it yesterday."

Tansy snuggled up in the bed next to Mama, stroking her hair and face. "Sorry I missed your birthday, Mama. My flight got canceled and I had to wait several hours for the next one out."

Mama turned her head and gazed up at Tansy. She blinked her tired eyes as if to convey, "That's okay."

"Hi, Grams." Libby's voice wavered somewhere between bravery and fear. "Mom took me out of class so I could ride over with her. Dad wanted to come, but he had to be in court." She paused to glance up at me, her hazel eyes the same color as Mama's. "Right, Mom?"

"That's right, Libs." I nudged her gently and we scooted around and sat on the edge of the bed, near Clover. "Good to see you, Mama. Sawyer sends his love and birthday wishes."

Mama's eyes followed us. "Libby," she whispered, as if the sight of her granddaughter was the elixir she needed.

Libby let go of her hair and patted the comforter around Mama's legs. "You talked, Grams. Mom and I got here yesterday, but you were sleeping. We saved your birthday cake until later when you feel like eating."

Mama licked her chapped lips, and the hint of a smile escaped. "Read any good books lately?" Her raspy voice reverberated around the room, filling us all with joy.

"That's the most you've said in two days." Clover looked over at the nurse then back at Mama.

Libby scooched closer. "Too many good books to name right now, Grams. Listen, Aunt Clover put together a special scrapbook for your birthday. It's full of photographs and special mementos. I hope you're up to looking at it?"

Mama's eyes widened. "Oh"—she motioned toward a hospital bed tray shoved against the wall.

Tansy reached for a plastic cup with a lid and straw. Mama took a few sips of water before Tansy set the cup back on the tray next to a small bouquet of fresh flowers. Their sweet scent helped mask a sour odor in the room.

Clover held up the scrapbook and tapped her finger on a faded colored photograph displayed on the cover. "Remember this, Mama? You were always good about writing names and dates on the back of pictures. This one was taken the day Ruthie and Tansy got their own library cards. Sometime in 1969."

Mama studied the photo then turned her head toward Tansy. "You'd both just turned five."

In the image, all five of us were lined up in front of the library at the top of the steps. Like bookends, Mama stood on one end and Miss Mavis on the other. Tansy and Ruthie stood in the middle holding up their library cards and grinning from ear to ear like they'd each just won a prize.

"Look at Melody," I chuckled. "She's holding up rabbit ears above my head, and as usual, I'm clueless."

Libby twisted around on the bed. "She's your friend who died. Right, Mom?"

"Yes, honey." I gave her a pat and glanced up at Mama, catching her eye.

"That was a hard time, Libby girl." Mama didn't elaborate, and I was grateful.

"We're all wearing pants, so it's gotta be fall," Tansy said. "By the way, Mama, I spoke with Ruthie the other day in one of our marathon phone chats. She said to tell you happy birthday. She always thought of you like a second mother."

Mama closed her eyes a moment as if remembering something. When they fluttered open, she stared at something off in the distance. "My mama was taken from me when I was just a girl. When I became a mama, I tried to fill in all those gaps that were missing from my own childhood."

Clover eased onto the bed next to Mama and opened the scrapbook. A familiar headline in black bold font from an old newspaper clipping jumped out at me. *Women in Transition* was pasted at the top of the first page. Clover had even included some of the sub headers: *Junior High Students Volunteer at Animal Shelter and Airfield*; *Senior Student Works Part-time to Help Family Budget*; *Single Mother Juggles Job & College*.

"Oh my gosh," I yelped. "My first photo feature in the *Sandhill*

Times." I swallowed and mouthed a silent "Thank you" at Clover. "Back then I did everything from take pictures to write short articles and get coffee for all the bona fide reporters."

We all scooted closer to get a better look.

Mama rallied and glanced over at me. "That was your first real job before you started college."

"It sure was, Mama, and you're the one who convinced me to apply for an internship."

Mama began to pore over the photos, a mixture of black and white with a few colored prints here and there.

"You took all these pictures, Mom?" Libby looked at me wide-eyed.

"Sure did, Libs. Or at least most of the black and whites. I was nineteen. Took them with a thirty-five-millimeter camera that belonged to the newspaper. My editor, Willy, let me drive around town taking pictures of anything I found interesting."

"So, you took pictures of your friends and family," Clover snorted with a chuckle.

"Did you have your own car?" Libby asked.

"No, but Aunt Clover did." I waited for my sister's snide remark, and sure enough—

"If you could call that *rolling junkyard* a car," Clover sniped right on cue.

Clover and I exchanged glances before I continued. "Mama occasionally let me borrow her Volkswagen Rabbit on days when I needed a car to take photos or go interview people."

"I remember this one," Mama said with a hint of pleasure and pride in her raggedy voice. "I was walking out of class on my first day of community college. I'd enrolled in summer school. I was thirty-eight years old, the oldest person in class. You'd think I was the teacher. How did you know which classroom I was in?"

"I can't remember, Mama. I guess I just got lucky."

"Here's the one you took of me at the animal shelter," Tansy said. "I was fourteen. I look like a dork."

Libby pointed to another photo. "Aunt Tansy, is that your friend, Ruthie? The one that became a pilot. That looks like a small airplane in the background."

"Yup, that's Ruthie, alright. She hung out at the airfield during the summers and on weekends. She did odd jobs in exchange for flying lessons."

I pointed to another one. "And here's your Aunt Clover . . . standing in front of a display case full of magazines and books."

Clover chuckled. "Lordy, I was a gangly nerd back then. Ha-ha. I worked at Town Crier up on Hilltop Plaza across from TG&Y. We sold records, magazines, and paperback books."

Tansy cut in. "Here's Ruthie's mom, Carmen, posing in front of a three-tiered wedding cake." She read the cutline out loud. "Single Mom Juggles Two Jobs to Pay for Daughter's Flying Lessons."

"Marigold, did you know the editor was going to publish these photos when you took them?" asked Clover.

"Sorta," I shrugged. "At least I was hoping he would. I wanted to show him pictures that didn't include boys or men, so I focused on girls and women. Because, let's face it, guys always got way too much coverage in the newspaper back then, at least in the sports section. And most of the time, women and girls were relegated to the social pages. Like all women did was attend weddings and teas."

We all laughed. Even Mama's lopsided grin returned for a fleeting second.

"Here's my favorite photo of you, Mama. The one your principal took." I pointed to a picture of Mama seated on a barstool at the head of her classroom. She was wearing white dress slacks and a smart green blazer, her hair twisted in an updo, and she was reading *A Wrinkle in Time* to her fourth graders. Mama was one of those women whose true beauty blossomed at midlife. Before she got cancer and it ravaged her body, leaving her gaunt and with sunken cheeks, I thought she resembled the fashion model Lauren Hutton, with her trademark gap between her front teeth.

"You'd just been honored *Teacher of the Year*," Tansy bragged.

"Grams, you were *Teacher of the Year*? How cool is that."

Mama studied the photo, then looked at my daughter with love in her eyes. "Libby, honey, always remember it's not about earning lofty titles that matters. It's about what we do with what we learn that's important. Getting that award was nice, but it only made me try harder to be there for my students."

Libby nodded. "I'll remember that, Grams."

"Mama, here you are with one of your former students. Looks like you're at a restaurant." Clover tapped her finger on the photo. "Was she your server?"

"Now that was a hardship case if I ever saw one. Poor girl." Mama's voice trembled with empathy. "Her mama ran off when she was a junior in high school. Her daddy worked south of here in the oilfields. Rarely came home. She was juggling school and work and helping raise two younger siblings."

The room grew quiet until I broke the silence. "Mama, how did you do it?" I asked, still amazed even though we all lived through those hard times.

Mama's face twitched. "Crockpot dinners and you girls pitching in around the house. Remember, it was a team effort."

"No kidding," Clover replied. "Not to mention academic scholarships, grants, and work-study that helped pay for our tuition."

"Grams, here you are in a cap and gown. So, you graduated from college in 1986? That was three years before I was born."

"Took me eight years," Mama yawned as her voice began to falter. "Earned my bachelor's degree in elementary ed along with my teaching certi . . ." Mama yawned again, and her voice trailed off. Her eyes grew heavy, and she nodded off to sleep.

"She didn't get to look at all the photos," Libby whispered, looking sad.

"She can look at the rest of them later after she takes a nap." Tansy gently removed the scrapbook from Mama's lap and handed it to Libby. "We can look at the rest of the photos out in the sunroom."

The nurse signaled that it was time for us to leave. Our visit had worn Mama out.

As we went to walk out of the room, I leaned over, kissed Mama's cheek, and said softly, "Mama, when the time comes and you get to wherever you're going, look for the girl in the patchwork jeans. She'll be playing her flute and guiding you home."

Mama died shortly after midnight. The nurse told Clover that Mama never woke up after our visit. The next morning, we gathered back at Clover's house. Libby served everyone a piece of birthday cake for breakfast.

While we ate cake, Tansy called Daddy and told him the news. I don't know if he cried, but Tansy reported that Daddy's voice got all funny. And right before she went to hang up, she said it sounded like he whipped out his hanky and blew his nose.

32 GATHERING OF MERMAIDS

NOVEMBER 2017

ABOUT A WEEK AFTER Daddy blamed the cat for his misdeed, Clover stopped by his place one morning on her way to work. After she knocked on the door and he didn't answer, she used a spare key and let herself in.

She found him in the recliner, still in his clothes from the day before. Fritz was wailing something fierce in front of his empty food dish by the carport door. Clover said it scared the bejesus out of her when she first walked in. She thought Daddy was dead in his chair and a newborn was crying in the kitchen.

After she woke him and helped him to the bathroom, she felt sorry for Fritz and cleaned his dish and set out fresh kibble. Once she made Daddy coffee and toast, he asked her to call Tansy. "See if she can come home. Tell her I have something I want to say to you girls, especially before Marigold leaves."

Clover said hearing Daddy say the word *home* caught her by surprise.

Two days later, Tansy's on a flight to Albuquerque. That morning I pack up my stuff and check out of the Sands and drop my things off at Clover's house on Fairway Terrace, a one-story stucco built in the seventies, complete with a wrap-around porch with wide arches and ornamental wrought-iron window bars that are more for show than security. I take the spare bedroom with the single bed overlooking the golf course and leave Tansy the room with a queen-size mattress. I avoid the room with the double bed, the room Clover moved Mama into in her final days.

The interior of the house is dated, with lots of amber light fixtures and dark wood paneling in the den and study, but it's spacious and there's plenty of room to spread out. Clover says why spend money on updates when she spends most of her time at the bookshop. Photos of her two stocky sons adorn the walls throughout the house. Ever since they left for college, they rarely visit Sandhill. Can't say I blame them.

I make myself a sandwich and mosey into the sunroom. There's plenty of cushioned garden chairs and side tables. I pick a spot where I can look out onto the fairway and see golfers zipping around in their carts. Sawyer and I were never country club people. He knew enough golf to get by. Before Clover's divorce, my now ex-brother-in-law, Harold, drove Daddy around the neighborhood in his own personal golf cart. Harold kept calling Daddy *big guy* and Daddy ate it up.

I pull out a pad and mechanical pencil and scribble a few notes for warm-up before I open my computer and get to work. A noise somewhere in the house startles me. *Mama?* Gripping my pencil, I get up and walk down the hallway and peek in the room where she died, halfway hoping to see her sitting in a chair in the corner and looking like she did in that photograph Clover included in the scrapbook. The one Mama's principal took of her when she won *Teacher of the Year*.

"Mama, I can't believe you've been gone sixteen years. Was that you stopping by to say hi? Or a poor little bird who's now dazed with a headache outside the window?"

Heading back up the hallway, two voices swirl around me: Mama's and Melody's.

Girls, can you see her . . . ? She's gliding along, six feet above the glistening tracks, her long tail swishing from side to side. She's pink and purple and turquoise, the color of a New Mexico sunset.

Is she real?

She's as real as you want her to be.

Back in the sunroom, I get readjusted and try to lose myself in my work.

But seconds later, I look up and say, "Mama, if I'd had my way, instead of donating your body to science per your wishes, I'd have had you cremated, and your ashes scattered over the marble steps of the old library and along the railroad tracks at the bend in the road."

Tansy's rental car is already in front of Daddy's place when I pull up late in the afternoon. Clover is pacing in front of the picture window. She sees me and waves as I get out of the car. She opens the storm door and whispers as I pass, "He's asking for Ruthie, too. I wonder what's up?"

Tansy is sprawled out on the floor, playing with Fritz. The room is warm, and she's removed her jacket, her bare athletic arms toned, her skin still supple for a woman her age, especially one who loves the great outdoors. She's brought Fritz a cat toy, a mouse on a string. Out of all of us, Tansy is the only one who can still get down on the floor like a kid.

I set down my bag and go to hug her. "It's so good to see you, Tans. Glad you were able to get another vet to cover for you on short notice."

She reaches up to hug me back. "Van is great. We cover for each other all the time." Van is short for Vanessa, another female veterinarian caring for critters along the Emerald Coast.

"I saved you the room with the queen bed." I straighten, knowing Tans will appreciate my subtle message that neither one of us will have to sleep in the same bed Mama died in.

Turning, I walk over and greet Daddy with a wispy kiss. His whiskers scratch my nose. "Well, you've summoned us all here."

"Not quite," he growls, but there's no malice in his tone. "Tans, can you get Ruthie on the phone? You think she's up there in the clouds?"

Tansy dangles the mouse in front of Fritz one last time then tosses it a few feet. Fritz pounces on it like he's a kitten. Tansy hops up off the floor in one springlike move. "Let me send her a message. I know she's on a trip, but I forget where she's off to. Japan. Maybe China or Kuwait."

A few minutes later, a middle-aged woman in a dark silky bob and with fine lines feathering out from the side of her mouth, appears on Tansy's iPad screen.

Fritz scampers across the living room and jumps up on Daddy's lap.

Clover, Tansy, and I gather around the recliner. Tansy holds the iPad at arm's length so we can all see the screen.

The brown-eyed girl from decades ago gives herself away when she flashes her sparkly white grin and chuckles, "Hello, Hubbard family." Along with her airline uniform, the deep crow's feet around her eyes from flying into the sun at thirty thousand feet only enhances her successful image.

Daddy clears phlegm from his throat. "Ruthie? You sure are looking sharp these days."

"How ya doing, Mr. Hubbard? I've changed a bit since the last time you saw me."

"I'll say," Daddy rallies with a goofy grin, a vigor returning to his voice long enough to give the impression he's doing better than he is. "You still a first officer?"

"No, sir, I'm a captain." She holds up one arm and shows us the four stripes on the end of her uniform jacket sleeve.

Daddy whistles through his teeth. "Carmen must've been so proud of you."

"Mom lived long enough to see me make captain. That woman

sacrificed so much for me." Ruthie looks down for a second, her forefinger rubbing the tip of her nose.

Daddy glances at Fritz then back at the screen. "You flown any more elephants around?"

Ruthie chuckles. "Only had the pleasure of that experience once. I'm glad I did it, but I'd rather haul boxes. They make good passengers. They're quiet, and they don't generally smell."

We all laugh and wait for Daddy's grand announcement.

Finally, he glances tentatively at all of us then directly into the screen. "Girls . . ." He starts to choke up. He fishes his hanky from his back pocket and blows his nose. After a few swipes he continues, his voice all garbled, "I'm sorry I never took all five of you girls to the ocean. I know I promised, but . . ."

I catch my breath. Tears blur my vision as Ruthie's image wavers on the screen. I can hear the others sniffle. I glance at Daddy. His head is bent as he gazes at Fritz and strokes his back.

A framed eight-by-ten on the opposite wall catches my attention. It's faded with time, a church directory photo we all posed for a lifetime ago. Daddy is so young and handsome in a navy-blue suit and tie. Mama is seated next to him in a belted blue dress with white piping. All three of us girls are wearing Easter dresses and white gloves.

How long has it been hanging there? Was it there all this time and I just now noticed it? Did he wait until Edie died to hang it?

Ruthie breaks the awkward silence in the room. "Aw, it's okay, Mr. Hubbard. We know you meant well."

Clover massages the back of Daddy's wrinkled neck. "It's okay, Daddy. We all got to the ocean sooner or later."

Daddy nods, swiping his hanky over his mouth and grizzly beard. With a shaky hand, he removes his glasses and dabs his eyes.

"Let me go clean your eyeglasses," I volunteer, saying farewell to Ruthie before I leave the room. At the stained porcelain sink where Grandma Dot, Edie, and Melody once stood, I notice Daddy's few dishes are washed and stacked in an old-fashioned rack on the counter. Daddy is a contradiction: parts of his life are messy; others are neat and tidy.

Over my shoulder I hear Ruthie signing off FaceTime. Seconds later, Daddy is saying, "Tans, let's sing the sailing song. Here's the words, in case you've forgotten them."

Before I round the corner, I peek into Melody's old room. The twin beds are gone, replaced by a double mattress and an oak headboard I don't recognize. Daddy has attempted to make the bed, haphazardly spreading the coverlet up over his pillow. A matching nightstand and battered dresser are cluttered with stuff I don't allow myself to linger over. Any signs that Melody once slept here are gone.

Back in the living room, Daddy is handing Tansy a piece of paper with the words he's painstakingly written down in his familiar crooked scrawl.

Daddy and Tansy begin to sing, "Tansy's ship's a-sailing . . ."

Later at Clover's, Tansy pours red wine into three goblets and proposes a toast: "To Dorian and Letty. If those two hadn't gotten together, the three of us wouldn't be here."

"To Mama, the storyteller," I say, "for teaching us to find magic in everyday things."

"To Mama," Clover joins in. "She gave us backbone and taught us to make do."

Two weeks later, the three of us pile into Clover's SUV and head to the oasis south of town. We haven't been there in decades. I ride shotgun while Tansy sits behind me, holding the box containing Daddy's ashes. He'd gone to sleep in his chair a few nights ago but never woke up. Clover found him when she went to drop off an egg and sausage biscuit.

As the sun sinks lower in the west, we trudge up the side of a dune, Tansy in the lead. Clover and I bring up the rear, her leopard print cape with a faux fur collar furling about her. Both of us are panting, our knees reminding us we aren't young anymore. Somewhere beyond us, we hear the chatter of children. Our minds fill with the images of five little girls laughing and rolling downhill, before pulling themselves up and going back for more.

At the crest of a tall dune, weeds sprout up from the sand. We stop to catch our breath, inhaling the cold November air. Craning our necks, the three of us gaze at a few wispy clouds riding across the brilliant blue sky growing darker by the second.

Then Tansy licks the tip of her finger to test the direction of the wind. As she lifts the lid from the box and clears her throat, she releases his ashes and begins to sing:

"Daddy's ship's a-sailing,
Sailing across the sea.
Daddy's ship's a-sailing,
Sailing away from me . . .
Sail, Daddy, sail, way out upon the blue . . ."

Clover and I join in, lifting our voices with this new version as we sing it two more times. A *V* of geese fly overhead, honking and joining in the requiem to a man who made his living sailing up and down the roadways of life.

33 BLOWIN' IN THE WIND

DECEMBER 1977

A BITTER COLD WIND blew across the plains a week after everything fell apart.

At the Rosemont cemetery, a girl with mousy brown hair named Theresa Hornbuckle played "Amazing Grace" on her flute. Clover said it was eerie seeing the girl's breath, it was so cold. "Guess she's first chair now," I snipped later when Clover told me about the funeral.

A few band kids were there along with the band director. Edie and Grandma Dot wore heavy black coats and were seated directly in front of the casket. Both wore dark sunglasses. Daddy stood nearby, his head bowed, his face mostly hidden behind the brim of his hat, his hands stuffed in the pockets of his overcoat.

Some rent-a-preacher in horn-rimmed glasses and an ill-fitting suit—those were Clover's words—expounded on how Melody was a talented young lady who loved Jesus, music, and family. What he left out, Clover said, was her fierce spirit, her love of books and magic, and her loyalty to her closest friends.

Mama and Carmen huddled near the back, enfolding Clover, Tansy, and Ruthie in their arms as if motherly love could protect them from the hostile cold and the reality of what was happening. It was Mama and Carmen who broke the news to each of us after we were called out of class and told to report to the front office. Having already shed their own tears, they stood side by side, clutching tissues, and delivered the bad news.

Mama did most of the talking, her voice raw as she whispered, "Melody slipped on those slick steps and died when she hit her head."

"But it's *December*," I kept saying, as if it couldn't be true. "Who in their right mind would want to go swimming in December?"

"Dewey tried to warn us," Clover stammered, her green eyes all red with disbelief. "Remember how Ruthie slipped the first time she went in?" Clover gripped the hide shoulder strap of her fringed purse. "Did Melody drown?"

"No, she fell and hit her head about halfway down. She never fully made it into the water," Mama continued. "The vultures were already circling though."

"Stupid vultures," Clover snarled.

Mama paused to rub her temple. "They didn't do it, honey. It wasn't their fault."

"Whose fault was it?" I cried out, needing to cast blame. To reassure myself I had nothing to do with it.

"It's all a horrible tragedy," Carmen reached to embrace me, the whiff of buttercream icing clinging to her white uniform. "It's okay to be sad and angry at the same time. Your mama and I will help you and Clover get your things so we can leave. We need to head to the junior high now and break the news to Ruthie and Tansy."

Clover said at the end of the graveside service they all lined up and walked by the family to offer their condolences. Mama wore a stiff upper lip, embraced Dot in a hug, offered Edie a cordial, "I'm sorry for your loss," before she turned and walked past Daddy, acknowledging him with a nod.

Then Mama and Carmen gathered everyone and headed back to their cars. Daddy took Clover aside and gave her the keys to the Rambler.

"Thanks for coming," he said. "Tell your mother I'll take care of the insurance." That's when he looked around and noticed I was missing. "Where's Marigold?"

Clover stared at the keys in her hand. "She's sick. She stayed home. I think she has a bug or something."

Daddy chewed the corner of his bottom lip. Then he stuffed his hands in his coat pockets and talked out the side of his mouth. "The tombstone won't be ready for a few weeks. Maybe you can bring her back out to see it once it's installed."

Clover glanced over at the Rambler parked in the weeds next to Daddy's yellow Rabbit. "Is that a new rope on the trunk?"

Daddy shook his head. "The secret is in how you tie the knot."

"Is there enough gas to get home?" Clover asked. She didn't put it past Daddy to give her the castoff car only to run out of gas on the way back to town.

"Full tank," Daddy reassured as he gave her a stiff hug then walked off.

While all this was happening, I walked the streets of Sandhill, bundled up in an old parka Daddy left behind, my anger and grief weighing me down like a ball and chain.

"You'll never have closure if you don't go to the funeral," Mama had warned.

How could I tell her that if I'd attended the funeral, I might have swung my ball and chain at Daddy and Edie and knocked them into the grave?

They're like the couple in that sexy song "Me and Mrs. Jones." They got a thing going on.

But they weren't the only ones guilty of wrongdoing.

Angry words I couldn't take back were blowing in the wind like a sandstorm, pricking at my conscience: *Get out. Get out, you bastard! I never want to speak to you again.*

It was better I stayed behind, plodding along, letting the cold sting my cheeks and numb my fingers until I couldn't feel them. Until I couldn't feel anything.

With each step, Thelma Houston's relentless plea pounded in my head, "Don't Leave Me This Way," as a lone tumbleweed blew across the sidewalk in front of me.

I kept going, putting one foot in front of the other until I found myself standing in front of the tiny house on Mesa Lane. I stared up at the picture window, but no one stared back. For they'd all gone to Rosemont.

I pictured Melody bolting from her casket and sprinting across the dirt road toward the church. "Who wants to race me?" she challenged, getting a head start as the patches on her bell-bottom jeans blossomed like wildflowers.

POSTSCRIPT LANDLOCKED IN LLANO COUNTY: A MEMOIR BY MARIGOLD HUBBARD

OCTOBER 2018

In memory of Letty Hubbard,
the sixth mermaid, 1940–2001

Dear Mel,

I finally penned the book that's been living inside of me for decades. Clover, Tansy, and Ruthie have read the final draft and have given it their stamp of approval. Not even a peep of pushback so far. Will be interesting to see what Thornton thinks. I'll probably have to change his name before the book comes out. I sent the manuscript to my agent this morning. Hopefully it finds a good publishing home.

Clover has offered to host the book launch at her shop in Sandhill. Mama's Make-Do will take center stage next to the podium at the front of the store along with a scrapbook Clover made for Mama right before she died. After Daddy passed, Clover adopted his cat, Fritz, a rescue who lives at the bookshop. Clover says Fritz likes to curl up by the front counter and greet customers as they come and go. She says having a cat as the shop's mascot is good for business.

Tansy and Ruthie will fly into Albuquerque, and we'll ride over together. Clover will meet us in Rosemont. Instead of writing our names on the wall, we're going to form a half-circle around your message and invoke the spirits of the mermaids, for who's to say they're not real? Like Mama once said, "All you have to do is believe."

Then we'll visit your grave so all five of us can be together again.

You must have felt so alone and betrayed by everyone when you stopped by the church on your way to the Blue Hole. I'm sorry it took me forty years to find your plea for help, and I'm even sorrier I was forty years too late.

I've learned a painful lesson on this journey to get to the truth. Until I read the note you left for your mom, it was easy to jump to conclusions and sling vile accusations at Daddy. Especially after I found your message on the church wall. It's the stories we tell ourselves when we don't know all the facts that can help us or harm others.

Mama told us stories to try and give us hope. After you died, I heard Mama crying one night as I was getting ready for bed. I found her alone in the parlor. She told me if she hadn't taken us to the Blue Hole, you might not have gone there as your last resort when you were seeking refuge. I reminded her how she helped us believe in magic and how her stories inspired us during times of struggle.

My hubby, Sawyer, crossed over a couple of years ago. One second he was revving his engine, the next he was flying free. Maybe he's regaling you and Mama with tall tales. He was a lawyer by day, a storyteller by heart. I used to be afraid of the spirit world, but you and Sawyer and Mama have taught me there's nothing to fear.

After Sawyer died, I sold our home in Moriarty and moved to Albuquerque. I'm seated here in my courtyard at the foothills of the Sandia Mountains, surrounded by chest-high adobe walls adorned with potted plants. A Kokopelli wind chime rings in the cool breeze, its trickster flute players clanging against tubular bells. ♫

With the sale of Grandma Dot's house, we've set up a music scholarship in your name. Before your mom died, she bequeathed the house to "her three stepdaughters." No one was more shocked than Clover, Tansy, and I. We've also commissioned a small sculpture in the shape of musical notes to be displayed in the band hall at the high school. The artist will incorporate your flute into the piece.

I've been offered a position as an editor at an online news site. I'm contemplating whether to accept it or not.

Tonight's Halloween. Before the kiddies show up for treats, I'm going to FaceTime with my granddaughter, Letty Bleau, and read her a storybook. Starting her early, you know. Books and a kind librarian helped Mama swim to the surface when she was drowning in despair. In the end, I know books couldn't save her, or you for that matter, but I like to believe books gave us years of magic despite the hardships.

A package arrived yesterday postmarked Los Angeles. It was from Ruthie. I burst into tears when I opened it and saw the dictionary you gave me decades ago. Turns out Ruthie salvaged it from the wreckage and kept it all these years. After she read my manuscript, she took it to a man who repairs old books. He fixed the broken spine. Ruthie says she hopes it's a reminder that none of us are broken beyond repair. I've placed the dictionary next to the Polaroid I took of you that day playing your flute. I found it when we were cleaning out the house after Daddy died. It was well preserved in the pages of one of Grandma Dot's favorite novels, Gone with the Wind.

I think of you every day, especially when I gaze up at the sky and see the ocean. Sometimes I cross my eyes and fingers and make a wish . . .

Swish! Swish!

Old Mother Hubbard